UNTIL TOMORROW

KARI LEE HARMON

OLIVER
HEBER
BOOKS

Published by Oliver-Heber Books

0 9 8 7 6 5 4 3 2 1

To Christine Witthohn, agent extraordinaire and one of my very best friends. The last 15 years have been quite a ride that I wouldn't want to take with anyone else. Thanks for always believing in me and standing by my side through the ups and the downs, the laughter and the tears. It's always an adventure. Love you lots! This one's for you, Doll 😉

1

"**D**amn it," Emma Hendricks said out loud to herself.

It was the end of June in coastal Maine, with temperatures in the sixties, but a definite bite to the air still lingered as she walked the jagged, rocky shores of Beacon Bay. She tightened the pink silky scarf at her neck and tucked the ends more securely into her pale blue fleece coat as the ocean breeze blasted her in the face. Inhaling a deep breath, she tasted the salty brine in the air as it brought a welcome sting to her lungs. It was better than living with the constant sting at the back of her eyes and the humiliation that inevitably followed.

Beacon Bay was a small town along the middle of Maine's coast. Coastal Maine consisted of a rugged shoreline dotted with spectacular lighthouses, picture-perfect seaside villages, quiet coves, and peninsulas that jutted out like fingers reaching toward the sea in hopes of discovering lost treasures. There was nothing special about Beacon Bay in particular, which made it absolutely perfect for her. All she might have left was her work, yet her muse had deserted her. It had withered and dried out when she couldn't find any answers to all her questions.

Emma was a strong, independent, modern-day journalist

from Boston, known for her cutting-edge stories and knack for getting at the truth. But how could she get at the truth when all that she believed in was a lie? People didn't understand how she felt because they'd never seen her cry. She hadn't cried because she was still in denial, but that didn't mean she wasn't vulnerable like the rest of the human race. She'd been on top of the world, having achieved everything she'd ever wanted, and then, *Bam*!

Her fiancé had to go and lose his mind.

Her fiancé.

Technically he *was* still her fiancé. Nothing had been settled, and she didn't have any answers. She tucked the strands of her auburn bobbed hair behind her ears and stared out at the waves wildly crashing against the shore like King Triton's fist pounding out a warning for sailors to take heed and enter at their own risk. She should have listened to her gut. Maybe then she wouldn't have gotten blindsided. She felt like raging back at the sea over the injustice of it all.

"I hate you!" she shouted, giving in to the impulse.

Mark had created quite a scandal with what he had done. Yanking off her engagement ring, she threw it at the sea, and a lump the size of a boulder formed in her throat. As if words or actions would do any good.

King Triton wasn't Mark, and she had no clue if Mark would even care at all. She had no clue about anything, especially after what he'd done to her. She felt so helpless, which was the worst punishment imaginable for a person like her who had to be in control.

Mark had been acting like a different person for months. She'd tried to talk to him to no avail, so she'd brushed off her instinctual feeling that there was something serious going on that he didn't want her to know about. Nothing made sense. She clenched her jaw, fighting back a new wave of pain, but anger and bitterness had finally started to win the battle raging inside of her. One way or another she would get to the bottom of what had happened.

She could be tough—a no-nonsense kind of woman—but she'd had to be in her line of work. No matter how smart she was or how many degrees or connections she had, she was still a woman fighting to make it to the top in a man's world. Deep down inside of her beat the heart of a sensitive woman with real feelings.

Why did women have to start hiding their feelings to be taken seriously?

She'd thought Mark had seen the *real* woman inside of her, and not just the firecracker reporter who got the job done at any cost. He'd hurt her more than she would ever admit to her well-meaning, stifling family. She came from money and so did he, but she was beginning to wonder if that was all they'd had in common.

How the hell had she let this happen?

Emma started walking again as she reflected on the mess her life had become. She had always been too focused on work to worry about finding someone to share her life with, but at nearly thirty, she wasn't getting any younger. Her mother feared she would wait beyond childbearing years and leave her without grandchildren, heaven forbid, even though she already had some from Emma's sister. Frankly, Emma wasn't even certain she wanted children of her own. But when her parents had introduced her to Mark, he'd seemed perfect for her. It was a win-win for both of them—he'd even said so himself.

When had that changed?

Emma spent the past six months trying to figure that out, and her work had suffered because of it. She read self-help books and had even spoken to a therapist, but nothing had helped. Needing to get away and hoping for inspiration, she'd taken a leave of absence, packed her bags, and headed to coastal Maine for the summer. Her favorite local Boston poet, Katy Ford, wrote the most moving poetry set in Maine, so Emma figured that was as good a place as any to escape. Neither her family, nor her fiancé's, would be caught dead in such a small town like Beacon Bay because it wasn't one of the "it" places to *summer*—as if summer were a verb.

Emma couldn't face them right now, couldn't face anyone, because no matter what Mark had done, it was somehow her fault. No one came right out and said so, but she could see it in their eyes. When had he become the victim and not her? She wasn't angry at him; she was angry at them all. Being alone was her only option. Kicking a pebble with the toe of her hiking boot, Emma kept moving forward one step at a time, hoping she would be able to do the same thing to her life.

Emma was the go-to girl. People came to her for answers to their unsolved mysteries, but this particular mystery was too much even for her. So, she had stopped trying to figure it out and decided to move on with her life, though she knew a part of her never would give up until she had closure. She was searching for anything that might fuel her with inspiration because if she didn't start to write again, she might not have a job to go back to in the fall. And then she would have nothing and end up lost and alone, which had secretly been her biggest fear of all.

Not to mention if she kept dwelling on all the possible answers to her problems, she might start to believe she wasn't good enough, which was something she'd struggled with her entire life. She lived in a world where the people had impossible standards no mere mortal could live up to, and frankly she was tired. Tired of not being good enough for her family, not being good enough for the job, not being good enough for a man.

Just plain not being good enough.

An obsession like she'd never known took root in her gut. She'd survive this and prove them all wrong. Making her way further down the shoreline, Emma stumbled across a particularly treacherous section of the beach that looked as if it hadn't been walked on since explorers first stepped foot upon the stony bottom, if ever. It was low tide and the water was way out, but not for long, judging by the sun in the sky. A strong whiff of fish and seaweed wafted past her nose. She was about to turn back when she spotted a glimmer. She held up her hand to shade her eyes and squinted to see more clearly. It looked as if the sun was reflecting off a shiny object. The object appeared to be way off, and it wouldn't be long before the tide swept back in to dole out its punishment for those foolish enough to venture onto sacred ground.

Chewing her bottom lip, Emma debated what she was going to do, but really there was no choice. She needed this. A force she couldn't explain propelled her forward and made her investigate. She walked toward the shiny object as quickly as she could, given the perilous conditions. The last thing she needed was a broken ankle this summer, or worse.

When she finally reached her destination, she spotted an antique glass bottle that had apparently withstood the test of time wedged between two rocks in a watery grave. Emma glanced up at the high cliff, thinking someone had probably tossed it out to sea decades ago. The water level had already risen to her knees, quickly bringing her attention back to the task at hand. Common sense said to leave immediately. She was too far out. This wasn't smart. Yet her feet remained frozen to the ground and getting colder by the second as icy fingers seeped in and clawed at her tender skin.

She couldn't leave. She'd spotted something inside the bottle —maybe some ancient piece of wisdom or the secret to life or the cure for cancer. It could be trash for all she knew, but one thing was certain—she had to free her treasure. Some crazy, irrational force kept her pulling at the bottle in an attempt to free it. But no matter how hard she pulled, the bottle remained in the same nesting place it had been for decades. Emma glanced out at the rolling waves furiously charging toward her. If she didn't do something quick, King Triton would win and she would become fish bait. It was silly and stupid and basically insane, but deep inside her mind she knew she couldn't let King Triton win because that would be like letting Mark win.

With one final tug, the bottle broke in half and Emma winced as she cut her hand. The salt water stung her wound, but she'd freed her treasure and that was the important thing. Ignoring the pain, she held up the piece of paper in victory. The water was waist deep now, and she had to swim back to shore, which wasn't difficult at first since the waves kept slamming against her, propelling her forward in their angry fury over her stupidity. Salt water burned her eyes and coated her tongue as she gasped for air. She couldn't control her shivering, and her clothes felt like lead, weighing her down as if urging her to give up the fight and find peace.

Emma was a stronger person than that. Giving up wasn't in her nature, but she soon realized the task at hand was anything but easy. The roughest part was when the waves pushed her forward then sucked her back, having fun as they toyed with her. They let her get close to shore and then yanked her away at the last second. At one point she wasn't sure she would make it to safety, but finally King Triton released his hold and returned her to her earthly hell at long last.

For a brief second, Emma wasn't even sure she was thankful.

Shaking off that crazy thought, she pulled herself to her soaking wet feet and held up her prize, shouting, "I will not be defeated!" She blinked, wondering for a brief moment if she had gone crazy, because she could have sworn she heard a whisper

carried on the wind as it swirled about her in a voice as determined as her own...

"No *we* will not."

❧

MARCH 1942: *Beacon Bay, Maine*

"Mrs. Kathleen Connor," Kathleen said out loud, yet
somehow it still didn't feel real to her.

She'd been married for two weeks now. Most women she
knew married in their late teens, thrilled to have a man to take
care of them and babies to raise. Kathleen had been the only
one in her twenties—late twenties at that—and still single.
Frankly, she'd been fine with that. She enjoyed her job as a
teacher, loving everything about learning, having always longed
for something more in life. It was almost like she was born in the
wrong century. She often wondered what the future would be
like. Would women ever have a say or be taken seriously?

She had a voice, and she longed to be heard.

It was her parents who had insisted she stop dreaming, settle
down, and start a family. Be respectable. They'd told her she was
too smart for her own good, and one day it was sure to get her
into trouble. They meant well, but they didn't understand her.
Her mother was an artist, selling her paintings in town, and her
father and brother were fishermen who put food on their table.
Not wealthy by any means, just simple hard workers, yet they
still worried about how the townsfolk saw them. They never
wanted to make waves and had always looked at Kathleen as if
they couldn't understand why the good Lord had brought such
an outspoken, free spirit like her into their home.

Kathleen sighed as she checked her reflection in the beveled
mirror above the secretary desk by the front door of her new
house. She'd learned to conform and fit in, even though she

often felt she was born to stand out. Her house wasn't exactly *new*, as it was a twenty-year-old white Dutch Colonial with black shutters, but it was new to her. This life was all new to her, but it wasn't so bad. The house was charming, with its fireplace and living room embossed with box beams, oak built-ins, raised panels, and archways. Her husband wasn't wealthy either, but he had more than she'd ever had. Her parents felt he was quite the catch and they were happy.

At least that was something.

She smoothed her caramel brown, shoulder-length waves and studied the sea-green eyes staring back at her. She'd never cared much for flirting with men and had never been in love. It wasn't that she was unhappy. Her husband William was a decent, respectable man from a good family who ran the local store. He would take care of her, provide for her—or so her mother had said—even though Kathleen had been perfectly happy providing for herself.

What was so wrong with being independent and childless? Her parents were worried about how it might look to the citizens of Beacon Bay. Kathleen's happiness always came last. But now that the United States had joined the world war after Japan had attacked Pearl Harbor in December, what else was Kathleen to do but conform to society? Now was not the time to make waves, she reminded herself. It was time for people to band together and lend support. If her countrymen could make sacrifices, then so could she.

Kathleen stepped outside and walked down the street to The General Store. Their house was right in town on a side street a couple blocks away from her husband's store and the school where she worked. He owned an old Ford that he drove to work every day, but she preferred to walk along the streets lined with fluorescent and incandescent lights, flower boxes, and a few benches. It was spring, the temps still chilly, but the promise of new life hung heavy in the air. Maybe if she had a more positive attitude, she would feel better on the inside.

This was Kathleen's shot at a new life, and she decided right then and there she wasn't going to waste it. William was working late, and she was bringing him dinner. So far, he had treated her amicably. She knew he wanted children, and she was doing her best to accommodate him, even though he didn't stir her blood like she had imagined he would. She was realistic enough to know she wasn't the most beautiful woman in town, but that didn't stop her from wanting the fairy tale. She had always thought she would either remain alone or marry for love. Never did she imagine she would marry for convenience, stability, and appearances.

She blamed her desire for affection on her vivid imagination. It had always led her to believe there was more to love, more to marriage, more to life. Pulling her head from the clouds, she vowed to do better. William was older as well, with bright red hair and freckles. Not the most handsome man she'd ever seen, but he wasn't homely, either. He was a large man with big hands and was socially awkward. He didn't exactly fit in. She had thought that would make him her perfect match. She frowned. Maybe she hadn't given them enough time to bond.

While spring was upon them, winter had lingered, leaving an icy chill in its wake. Maine was like a wild animal—gorgeous, rugged, and untamed—but she loved everything about it and couldn't imagine calling any other place home. Kathleen pulled her ensemble of a matching gray coat and skirt closer together, trying not to shiver as she walked briskly down the street. To be honest, that's how Kathleen walked through life—briskly in search of an adventure, instead of strolling through the days, content with her lot like so many others. So far, that hadn't worked well in her favor. Maybe it was time she slowed down and enjoyed the possibilities right in front of her.

The war had caused the army to dole out restrictions on clothing in order to properly outfit the soldiers. The amount of new clothing a person could purchase was limited, as were the accessories they could buy. Hats and gloves were still in fashion, but nylon was restricted for military use, so women had to resort to wearing those dreaded cotton stockings. Kathleen didn't mind as cotton was practical, not unlike herself, but she knew a number of women in town who acted like wearing the plain material was the end of the world.

She had no tolerance for people like that, which was probably why she didn't have many friends. Soldiers dying in the war were the real tragedies. Silk was rationed as well as green and brown dyes, leaving women to opt for more red-dyed, simply-cut blouses, shirts, and knee-length skirts. In fact, a lot of the men's suits were remade into square-shouldered jackets to match the women's skirts. Sturdy and sensible made sense. How *pretty* she looked had always been an afterthought for her.

It only took fifteen minutes to arrive at The General Store. She came in through the back door and made her way to the front. The store had all sorts of goods, from food supplies to clothing to hardware goods to hunting paraphernalia. It had been a staple and success in Beacon Bay both before and now during the war. She heard her husband talking to a few older men up front. His vision wasn't the best, preventing him from joining the army or navy, but she gathered from his conversation he wasn't all that heartbroken over not being able to go fight for his country.

"We never should have joined the war in the first place, if you ask me," William said from behind the checkout counter, looking larger than life with his tall height and stature. "It was none of our business." The war had put restrictions on men's clothing as well. He wore more narrow black trousers and a simple white shirt with the cuffs turned up. His only accessory was a fedora he'd placed on the hook by the front door next to his short jacket. His clothes were suddenly forgotten as his negative words drew Kathleen to his side.

"Oh, you can't believe that, can you?" she said without hesitation, coming up behind him and setting his dinner on the counter. She pulled off her matching red hat and gloves as she talked. "Hitler's a monster, and the whole world recognizes that. I say it was about time the United States got involved. I don't know how anyone could stand idly by and not retaliate after a tragedy like Pearl Harbor."

"I agree, young lady," one of the old timers said, looking at her with surprise yet he seemed impressed.

"You sound like my son," another old man responded with a sad smile, shaking his head as if he didn't see the sense in any of it.

"Excuse me, gentlemen," William cut in with a pleasant smile of his own. "I'm sure you won't mind if I steal my wife away for a moment."

The men grinned wider with knowing eyes, responding with, *Not at all*, and, *Take your time*.

William wrapped his arm around Kathleen, resting his wide palm on her lower back possessively, and the first little thrill raced up her spine, giving her hope they might stand a chance after all. He grabbed her hat and gloves from the counter as he led her through the back room until they escaped into the bright sunshine and fresh air. Kathleen turned around in anticipation, wondering if this was going to be a turning point in their relationship.

A sharp pain exploded in her stomach, and she was sure she felt her rib crack. She doubled over in agony, struggling to catch her breath and fell to her knees. Her vision faded in and out as stars danced before her eyes. What had just happened? It took her several moments, but finally she was able to pick up her hat and gloves and stand up straight to look her husband in the eye. She sucked in a breath.

Big mistake.

He looked like a monster. She stumbled back a step. His thin, flat lips were curled into a snarl and his brown eyes were filled with fury. She didn't recognize him at all. "How dare you," he growled. His hand was still fisted.

"W-What did I do?" she managed to get out on a whisper-filled sob.

"Don't you ever contradict me in front of anyone again, do you hear me?" He thrust his finger in her face, and she flinched.

"I didn't contradict you. I know you can't join the war even if you want to because of your vision. I voiced my opinion on the war, not you, that's all." Fear like she'd never known seized her body, her muscles stiff and frozen, leaving her vulnerable.

She didn't know what to do. What to say. How could this be happening? She'd lived with him for two weeks and hadn't seen any signs that he could be capable of something like this. His father had been hard on him when he was a little boy, and from what she could tell, he still was even as a man. She'd seen that while growing up, but she'd never really known his father. No one had ever hinted that he'd abused his son, but if he hadn't, then William must have been born pure evil. The thought of being married to someone like that terrified her.

"You're a woman. You don't have an opinion," he hissed. "You made it sound like I am less than a man and a coward. No wonder you were still single at your age. I'm your husband. Doesn't that mean anything to you?"

"Yes," she managed to say. "I promise you it does." She looked him in the eyes and silently pleaded with him not to hurt her again.

Suddenly he changed, as if her look was one he knew well, reinforcing her fear that he hadn't been born a monster. He'd been *raised* into one. The rage left his face as quickly as it had appeared. He took a shaky breath, and then he wrapped his big arms around her, pulling her in for a tender hug. "I'm sorry. I'm so sorry. I didn't mean to do it. I didn't want to strike you, but you understand why I had to, right?"

His touch made her skin crawl, like tiny little bugs scurrying about beneath her skin. She fought back the impulse to vomit and pull away, though she would never forget his musky scent. It was ingrained on her brain, and she instinctively knew it would always bring back this haunting moment of his betrayal: the fear, the pain, the fury. "How dare you," he'd said. *How dare he*, she thought.

Clamping her jaw tight, she nodded once sharply, hoping it was enough.

"Thank you for dinner, by the way. It was sweet of you." He tipped up her face and pressed his wide, firm, dry lips against hers. "I love you."

"Me too," she ground out through her teeth and pressed her lips into a tight line. "I'll see you at home." She turned around and walked away as quickly as her shaky legs would carry her. As soon as she was out of his sight, she found the nearest bush and vomited as she crumbled beneath the weight of her tears. Her mother was wrong. He wasn't going to take care of her. He was going to ruin her if she let him. The problem was Emma wasn't sure if she was strong enough to do anything about it. Because if she did....

It would surely be the end of life as she knew it.

2

L ogan Mayfield poked his head out the door to the waiting room of Beacon Memorial Hospital's emergency room. It had been a slow night. Not that any night was particularly busy. They mostly saw boating or fishing accidents, broken bones, and cases of the flu or pneumonia. Occasionally they saw a heart attack or stroke victim, but that was about it. They didn't really have crime in Beacon Bay, so they never saw cases of stabbings or gunshot wounds other than unfortunate hunting accidents. All in all, they didn't have a lot of death in Beacon Bay. That's one of the main reasons he'd moved to Maine from New York City six years ago.

His wife Amanda had died four weeks after giving birth to their son Trevor from complications during childbirth, which led to her hemorrhaging weeks later. Logan had been on his own in raising the infant every day since then. Amanda was from Beacon Bay, and her parents still lived here. They were good Christians and would provide a stable family network for Trevor. That was the other reason Logan had left such a prestigious position at a high-profile hospital. If he couldn't give his son his mother, then he would give him the next best thing: his wife's family. He owed her that and so much more.

It was his fault she had died.

Logan had grown up an orphan with no family to speak of. He didn't want his son to go through what he did. And with no hope of future brothers or sisters, Amanda's parents were the only family Logan could give him. Besides, Logan wasn't too proud to admit he needed all the help he could get. He'd put himself through college and med school, vowing to make a name for himself at any cost. But then he'd met Amanda and realized some costs were too high. She'd been the angel in his life from the day he'd first met her at Columbia University. She was in the nursing program, and he was in medical school. They'd fallen in love, gotten married, and had a beautiful baby boy.

Then she died and left him empty.

Logan's heart ached, and his chest felt heavy. Just thinking of her pale blonde hair and blue eyes still tore him up inside and haunted his dreams every night. Trevor had his mother's hair and eye color but his father's curls and size, by far the biggest boy in his first-grade class. Logan had specialized in being a trauma surgeon, but then his wife died and he hadn't been able to do a damn thing to save her. He would always be there for his son, but he would never quit punishing himself or forgive himself for what he'd done.

Logan and Trevor moved to her hometown of Beacon Bay, Maine where he was the head ER doc. Beacon Bay was a small town, but they were fortunate enough to have their own hospital. The hospital wasn't big, but it served its purpose well. Living in Beacon Bay made it impossible not to know most of the residents, but Logan had managed to keep his wall up, refusing to get emotionally involved with anyone. He loved helping people and was good at his job. He was in his mid-thirties now. His work and his son would have to be enough for him because he didn't deserve anything more.

He was about to walk out of the waiting room and back to his office when the front door opened on a gust of wind. It was dusk already as the days hadn't yet grown longer. Most people were home for dinner by now, but the woman who entered wasn't most people. In fact, he didn't recognize her at all. She was a little thing—maybe five-foot-two—sharply dressed in designer jeans, boots and coat with a sophisticated-looking auburn bobbed hairstyle like something you would see in a trendy magazine. Definitely not local. Except her hair was all straggly waves from the rain now. Obviously, something had gone horribly wrong for her today. That aside, she reminded him of the high-profile women who came from money that he had known back in his New York City days.

Maybe she was a tourist passing through on her way to one of the bigger coastal towns. A lot of people toured the coast of Maine from spring through fall, but not many stopped in Beacon Bay. He frowned. Her hand was bleeding. Her eyes met his for a moment, and a strange sense of déjà vu swept over him. He felt this instant connection as if they had met somewhere before, which was crazy. He never forgot a face. His frown deepened, and she drew her eyebrows together, looking puzzled yet curious over why he was staring at her like that. He cleared his throat, donned a neutral expression, and then sent her a nod of hello before slipping back into the hallway and heading to his office to wait.

When the nurse was finished prepping the patient, she called him in. He walked into the room, wearing a stethoscope around his neck over his blue scrubs. He'd always hated white lab coats, feeling like they made a doctor look stuffy and unapproachable. He skimmed over the patient's chart and then turned to her with a pleasant expression meant to put her at ease. He'd always been complimented on his bedside manner, which he worked hard on.

He was a big man, at well over six feet, with thick, black, curly hair, an equally thick, black beard that remained heavily shadowed no matter how close he shaved, and eyes that were such a dark brown they looked like espresso coffee. That could be intimidating to the toughest of men, let alone women and children. Underneath it all, he was a giant teddy bear.

Holding out his large hand, he said with a pleasant, approachable tone, "Hello, Ms. Hendricks, I'm Doctor Mayfield. Welcome to Beacon Bay."

She shook his hand with her much smaller good one and met his eyes with strong, intelligent amber pools of skepticism. Looked like he wasn't the only one with walls up. "Thank you, though I'm not sure how welcoming your town has been to me." She held out her injured palm.

"I can see that." He took her hand, held it palm up, and inspected the damage. "That cut's pretty deep. You're going to need stitches. Lucky for you, I'm pretty good with a needle and thread." He tried to lighten the mood.

She arched a brow.

Tough crowd, he thought and bit back a chuckle. He instructed his nurse to bring him his supplies. "When's the last time you had a tetanus shot?"

"I'm a journalist. Never know where the job will take me, Doc. No worries. I'm up to date on all my shots."

"Good to know." He cleaned her hand, propped it up, gave her several shots until the entire area was numb, and then talked while he worked. "So tell me, Lois Lane. How did you get this nasty cut? And why in the world are your clothes damp? Did you hit your head, too? You do know it's not summer yet, don't you?" Even beyond the smell of seaweed and fish and salt water, she smelled good. He detected expensive cologne, hair products, and lotions. She came from class, and no matter what she did, he imagined she wore it well.

"Funny, but trust me, there is no Superman in my life," she said as if without thinking, her eyes filling with pain and confusion for a brief moment but then she seemed to catch herself and corrected her tone to one of a news informant. "I was walking along the coast when the tide was low and I saw something shining."

"Cat that ate the canary?"

"Something like that." Her lips tipped up a hair as if against her will.

"You know what they say about that cat, right?" He never lost focus on her hand as he continued to stitch.

Her tone sobered. "Curiosity can be deadly, I know, but hey, it's the nature of the job. Anyway, when I set out to investigate, I discovered an old bottle wedged between two rocks. I had to break the bottle to retrieve my treasure."

"Treasure?" This time he was the one to raise his brow as he looked up from his stitching to study her.

A flash of excitement swam into her eyes. She reached into her pocket with her good hand and pulled out a faded, yellowed map and held it up to him. It had a coded message written on it and at the bottom was signed, *Until Tomorrow*, followed by the name Kathleen Connor. The corner was cut off, but the rest of the map was legible.

"Interesting," he said as he studied the map. "Deciphering coded messages was a hobby of mine back in my college days when I took an art history class and got caught up in hieroglyphs." His curiosity piqued, but then he thought of something and his sensible doctor brain took over. "When exactly did this happen?" He went back to finishing with her hand.

She shrugged and seemed to contemplate that. "Maybe a half hour ago. I came straight here."

"That wasn't very smart." He was already shaking his head.

Her eyelids narrowed. "Bleeding hand, wet clothes, and hospital emergency room: what's not smart about that?" Man, she had a razor-sharp edge. Someone had wronged her big-time, if he wasn't mistaken.

"Treasure hunting at night when the tide is coming in." His gaze met hers once more, only this time he was far from enamored. "*That's* what's not smart." Wronged or not, she needed to face reality and start making smarter decisions.

She rolled her eyes. "I wasn't treasure hunting. I was walking. I can't help it if the journalist in me is wired to investigate strange occurrences. A sparkling object at low tide in an area not usually traveled by humans is worth checking out. I knew I might not get another chance at discovering what it was if I didn't react when I did."

He wrapped her hand while carefully considering his words. "Nothing is worth risking your life over." His voice grew quiet yet firm.

If he hadn't married Amanda and gotten her pregnant, she never would have died. He adored their son Trevor, but his wife had paid the ultimate price by being with him. He would never make that mistake again. Emma reminded him of Amanda: petite yet full of adventure. People like that didn't think first, they acted—consequences be damned.

Emma Hendricks was the most interesting person he'd met in six years, but he couldn't afford to be interested in anything except taking care of his son and his town. There was so much bad going on in the world: people fighting for their country, children starving, the homeless just trying to survive. He couldn't save the world, couldn't even save his wife, but at least he could try to make a difference in his town. It was his penance for what he had done, but it wasn't enough. It wasn't nearly enough. It would *never* be enough.

Because no one knew what had really happened.

MAY 1942: San Francisco, California (the Pacific West Coast)

Manning his station, Petty Officer Rutherford kept watch aboard the USS Tennessee as it patrolled the West Coast. It was early morning, the sea spray misting the sky, mixing with the daily fog that matched Joseph's gloomy mood. All was eerily quiet, leaving a soldier too much time to reflect on the past—a place he never wanted to go again but was determined never to forget.

All Joseph Henry Rutherford III had wanted to do was help people and get involved. He came from a small town in Maine called Beacon Bay, but his family was wealthy. They had made a name for themselves in shipbuilding and were pillars of the community. He could have been anything, but he'd chosen to enlist in the Navy in the summer of 1940.

His parents hadn't been happy with him joining the Navy and getting stationed on a battleship in Pearl Harbor, Hawaii, but he'd told them that was about as far away from the war as a soldier could get. It was like going on a beach vacation. After Hitler invaded Poland in September of 1939 and World War II started, he'd had so many friends go off to Europe to join the Allies in the fight against the Axis, never to be heard from again. Joseph hadn't felt right about sitting back and doing nothing except being a spoiled rich playboy. He'd simply wanted to grow up and do his part.

He'd had no idea the war would come to him.

Coming from a family of shipbuilders, battleships had always fascinated Joseph. The lines and angles which allowed the iron giants to cut through the surface of the water as though they weighed nothing at all still drew him in, which was why he felt so at home on the USS Tennessee. He felt powerful, almost invincible while on board, even though many people thought of battleships as sitting ducks out in the middle of the ocean. Joseph had thought they were crazy...

Until the attack on Pearl Harbor.

In times of peace, battleships were involved in training, maintenance, and readiness exercises such as competitions in gunnery and engineering performance. Yet during times of strife and confrontation, these sleek vessels became a commanding and intimidating presence to the enemy. Joseph had missed participating in the Fleet Problem XXI—a battleship competition that was conducted in Hawaiian waters during the spring of 1940. At the end of those pseudo-war games, President Roosevelt shifted its base of operations to Pearl Harbor, hoping to deter the Japanese Empire from expanding into the Orient.

The USS Tennessee arrived at her new base in August 1940 with an eager Joseph on board, but the next set of war games was cancelled due to increased hostility throughout the world. Joseph remembered feeling cheated at being confined to smaller scale operations in those final months of peace. Now that he realized *real* war was anything but a game, he'd give everything to go back to simpler times.

He scanned the Pacific Ocean, but didn't see anything except peaceful waters. After Pearl Harbor, he couldn't help but be jumpy, even though the Tennessee had proven to be one tough ship. She was the lead ship of her class and nicknamed the Rebel. Her underwater hull had better protection than earlier ships, and both her main and secondary batteries had two heavy caged masts supporting large optical fire-control systems to assist a weapon in hitting its target. It performed the same task as a human gunner, but fired a weapon much faster and more accurately. And since the turret guns could be elevated as high as 30 degrees, her heavy guns could fire an additional 10,000 yards, providing great value since battleships were starting to carry airplanes to spot long-range gunfire.

None of that had mattered or helped on the morning of December 7th, 1941. A day that would haunt Joseph for the rest of his life. The Tennessee was moored starboard side to a pair of masonry mooring quays on Battleship Row. During the attack, Joseph manned the ship's anti-aircraft guns along with his fellow crewmen, attempting to defend the harbor and their warship the best they could, to no avail. The Tennessee was struck by two armor-piercing bombs during the air raid.

When the first one hit the center gun of turret two, it made all three guns fail to work, leaving the crew feeling helpless. Debris from the bomb hit the command deck of the West Virginia, mortally wounding her commanding officer. The second bomb went through the roof of turret three, damaging her left gun. Debris showered the Tennessee when the Arizona's magazine exploded and flames engulfed her stern from the ship's burning fuel oil. Wedged between the sunken West Virginia and her mooring quays, the Tennessee was trapped at her berth for ten days of hell, its crew reliving the nightmare, before finally being freed. Four days later after minor repairs she set sail for the West Coast to be fully repaired, and that was where Joseph resided today.

Before leaving Hawaii, Joseph remembered staring out at the harbor still full of battleships that had been destroyed by Japan. Buildings were demolished, the destruction and devastation so huge he didn't know if the harbor would ever recover. The surprise attack had been so sudden, while most of the harbor slept, and everyone was left in shock and disbelief. All eight U.S. Navy battleships were damaged, with four being sunk.

He could still hear the piercing whine of missiles being dropped, the rapid fire of guns pelting everything within view, the agonizing sounds of men screaming and women crying. He squeezed his eyes shut, feeling sick all over again from the imagined smell of burned flesh and blood. It took a conscious effort not to vomit on a daily basis. He'd felt so helpless that day. He'd stood on the ship and had fired back at Japanese Zeros, taking down his share and killing more men than he wanted to think about. Yet he'd survived. He'd been one of the lucky ones, they all said.

Funny how he didn't feel lucky.

It took a man to do a soldier's job, but how could he do his job when he was only half a man now. A shell of his former self. Joseph didn't know if he would ever be the same, ever be able to help the people who needed him, ever be able to make a difference like he had once hoped. The nightmares haunted him every night. He would wake up screaming and sweaty and shaking. He was so homesick, the thought of Maine calling to his soul, but how could he go back there like this? With no other choice, he went into survival mode and focused on work.

At the Puget Sound Navy Yard, the Tennessee underwent permanent repairs and upgraded its anti-aircraft guns, as well as installing search and fire control radars and other modifications to improve its habitability. In February 1942, the Tennessee left the Sound and arrived in San Francisco, where she began a period of intensive training operations, creating Task Force 1, which consisted of the Pacific Fleet's available battleships and several destroyers. It was soon apparent that the older battleships like the Tennessee were too slow to keep up with the carriers for long-range duels, so Joseph spent his time patrolling areas of the Pacific in the expectation that part of the Japanese fleet might attempt an attack on the U.S. West Coast.

"Mail call," someone yelled.

Joseph blinked, realizing his shift was over. Everyone dropped what they were doing. It could take the mail months to reach the soldiers and months to send a letter back, providing nothing went wrong with the mail planes. Planes got shot down, mail got ruined, letters got lost. Whatever mail could be salvaged was delivered and sent to the recipient. Whatever couldn't be sent was returned to the soldier, if he was still alive, that is.

That was why getting mail was like opening presents on Christmas morning. It was special and something to be treasured. And when a soldier didn't get any word at all from back home, it was heartbreaking. People didn't realize thoughts of home were a soldier's lifeline. The smells, the sounds, the memories conjured by simple words on a page were the things that grounded a soldier and kept him from going crazy. It made him realize he wasn't stuck in the devastation forever, and there was hope that one day the war would end and he would go home. It was the only thing that kept most soldiers going when surrounded by so much death and devastation.

People thought he was brave, but if they only knew the truth. He wasn't brave. He was lonely and scared and felt like a coward on a daily basis for wanting to go home. The letter he held in his hand was so important to him. So precious. No matter who it was from, it was a gift.

Joseph took his lunch break, more concerned with opening his letter than eating in the mess hall. The fog lifted and the sun made an appearance, increasing the temperature to seventy degrees, almost as if sensing his spirits needed lifting. He wandered to a deserted part of the ship in his undress blue service uniform, consisting of button fly woolen trousers, a simplified jumper without piping or neckerchief, and a white cotton hat. He leaned over a deck rail and stared toward the shore at the impressive redwood and sequoia trees, taking a moment to clear his head before pulling out the cherished piece of mail from his pocket. Opening the envelope, he took a deep breath and read the contents.

• • •

My dearest son,

We miss you so. Your father and sisters and I worry about you every day. War is such an awful thing. I wish you had stayed home where you belong. My only son, my sandy blond-haired, sky blue-eyed angel of a boy, you should have stayed with your family and taken over your father's business. It's not too late. When you return, God willing, we will be waiting for you to help you pick up the pieces and get you back on the right track. You've had your fun, now it's time to grow up and be responsible.

Joseph's hands jerked, and the letter he held nearly fell into the ocean. He clenched his jaw. *Fun? Grow up? Be responsible?* He almost stopped reading her letter altogether. She had no idea what he had done was about the most responsible grown-up thing a person could do. He couldn't blame her really. There was no way she could know what he had been through and that it had changed him forever. It wasn't fun. It was awful, and he wasn't going to come home the same person. With a deep sigh of regret and resignation, he kept reading, his desperation for home and human contact running that deep.

Speaking of the right track, I have some wonderful news. I've found you the perfect woman to marry. Beverly Sanderson is of impeccable breeding; her family having made their money in real estate. She is a beautiful, agreeable, charming young woman and has already been informed of your impending return when your tour of duty is over. She loves a man in uniform and thinks what you're doing is so heroic. If anything, your little adventure has made you the most eligible bachelor in town. You're a perfect match socially, so it would

behoove you to propose upon your return. Please don't let us down
again. We want what's best for you, and for you to be happy, my son.

Until I see you again,
Your loving mother

JOSEPH FOLDED the letter and slipped it back into his pocket with
a soft chuckle and a sad shake of his head. *Little adventure.* His
family had always thought of themselves first. They never
thought about what might make him happy, but right now they
were all he had left. He didn't like his family intruding in his
personal affairs, but at the same time he knew they meant well.

Maybe getting married was what he needed to make him
whole again. He had never met Beverly, but he had heard of the
Sandersons. They lived at 37 Coastal Ridge Road, in the wealth-
iest part of town. His mother would not be happy unless he
married someone with the right background and social standing. The only problem was he didn't know if Beverly would be
happy with him.

He needed to write to Beverly and let her know what to
expect upon his return. He wasn't due to end his tour for
another two years, and he had no idea if he was even going to
survive long enough to make it home. If he did survive, he didn't
know how he was going to mentally last reliving this nightmare
for that long. Somehow, he had to find a way to get through the
rest of his time in one piece. All he could do for now was take
one day at a time, which was becoming more and more difficult.

It would take a special person to love a broken man. He had
no idea if Beverly was up to the task, but there was no one else
and only one way to find out. He pulled out pen and paper and
decided to write her a letter back.

How she responded would tell him everything he needed to
know.

3

PRESENT DAY: BEACON BAY, MAINE

After Emma left the emergency room of Beacon Memorial Hospital, she couldn't stop thinking about Dr. Logan Mayfield. He was a big, burly man with a heart equally as big, no matter how hard he tried to hide it. This strange connection hummed between them, which was crazy. Her life was a mess right now. She was an impulsive woman who was hurt and angry. Not a good combination. But still, there was something intangibly there with the doc. What, she had was no clue, which made it much more difficult to know what to do about it.

Being a good judge of character with a knack for reading people was a strength of hers. It was plain to see Dr. McGiant cared about his job, and helping people was in his nature. He'd obviously been through something major to cause him to put up the humongous wall he was hiding behind, but then again, who hadn't been through something these days? Maybe she wasn't a good judge of character after all. She hadn't read Mark right, or she wouldn't be in the predicament she was today.

Shaking off her train of thought, she focused on her present situation. She couldn't believe the message in the bottle had been a coded map. Curiosity gnawed at her, especially over the inscription: *Until Tomorrow, Kathleen Connor*. Why the secrecy in using a code? What was the code and how could she decipher it? What was supposed to happen on that day so long ago? But mostly, who was this woman with the gorgeous sweeping penmanship? There was something in the way she moved her pen that called out to Emma. The grip was firm and decisive in the way she pressed down upon the paper, yet the flowing way she crafted her letters was poetic and heart-wrenching.

A burning need like she'd never known propelled Emma to the library. She wasn't exactly sure why, but she had a strong desire to uncover this woman's story. Maybe because using her skills as a journalist to research Kathleen Connor was the only way Emma knew how to forget the past and move on with her life, which was imperative if she was going to save her career. So here she stood later that evening in the archives, reading up on a woman who had led a tumultuous life and then literally disappeared, never to be heard from again.

The library was eerily quiet now that school was out, with only a few patrons browsing the shelves. Probably most people in town were home with their families, significant others, or even friends. Emma felt alone as usual, her work her only companion these days. The archives didn't have a whole lot of information on Kathleen Conner. All Emma could find was Kathleen had started out as a teacher but ended up an outcast.

She was the daughter of a fisherman father and artist mother, with one brother who went on to marry and have children and grandchildren. Emma didn't get it. Kathleen had married William Connor, yet it said she lived alone in a cottage on the outskirts of town and then vanished one day. While her husband was listed as having never remarried, dying a heart-broken victim after her leaving him at their family home, surrounded by loved ones.

Something doesn't add up, Emma thought, filled with irrational anger for a woman she didn't even know and circumstances she didn't have a clue about, but she'd learned to trust her gut over the years. Why did the men always win? There was a reason Kathleen had left him. Emma would bet her career on it.

"What in the world happened to you, Kathleen Connor?" Emma said softly to herself.

Emma needed to find out what had gone wrong in Kathleen's life. Women didn't leave their husbands in those days. Where did she go? What happened to her? Did she ever find happiness? Emma couldn't seem to find any Connors left in the area, but she did find the address for Kathleen's nephew. Emma decided to reach out to him first thing in the morning.

Maybe then she could figure out what had gone so horribly wrong in her own life.

THE NEXT MORNING a soft rain misted Emma's window as she drove down the coast in her Mercedes. The road traveled along the jagged, rocky cliffs overlooking the powerful waves of the vast ocean below. Big summer beach homes like the one she had rented gave way to smaller cottages the further away from town Emma got. Stairs led from the top of the cliffs down to the rugged shoreline for those adventurous souls who dared to brave the power of the sea in the surge of the waves as they crashed against the shore. The cut on her hand throbbed beneath the bandage, reminding her she was brave, no matter what the doc said. He didn't know all she'd been through.

Maple and oak trees were scattered about, swaying softly in the sea breeze, changing over to pine the further inland a person traveled, eventually leading to the forest and all the dark secrets it had to offer. This rain was a sign of the marigolds and lilies that would soon blossom, followed by the gorgeous colors of the wildflowers that would sprout in the warmer days of summer. Emma had a good feeling about Beacon Bay. Spending the summer here and immersing herself in her quest was exactly what she needed.

"Benjamin Reynolds." Emma tested the name on her tongue.

Connor was Kathleen's married name. Reynolds had been her maiden name, and Benjamin was her great-nephew. Further research had revealed the family house in town had long since been sold. Ben used the cottage by the sea that Kathleen had lived out her days in as a vacation home every summer.

Finally, Emma reached her destination: 137 Coastal Ridge Road.

As she parked her car, the rain suddenly stopped and the sun came out. Emma's lips parted as a breathtaking rainbow arched across the sky above the sea, looking glorious in all its vibrant splendor, yet somehow solitary and lonely. Emma couldn't help but revel in the beauty of it and take it as a sign she was on the right track.

She climbed out of her car and shut the door, staring at the small one-story cottage by the sea. There was something inspiring about it. It was simple yet quaint. A small yellow building with white shutters and flower boxes in the front. A wooden deck sat on the edge of the cliff, looking out over the farthest end of the bay, with an ancient lighthouse way off in the distance. It was peaceful and still. Emma could see how Kathleen might have been happy here. Happy but alone, leaving Emma with so many unanswered questions.

Just then a man who looked to be in his sixties, wearing a plaid flannel shirt and a ball cap, walked outside carrying a box to his car. He stopped when he saw her, his eyes widening in surprise. "May I help you?"

Emma donned her game face as she walked over to him and

held out her hand. "Benjamin Reynolds, I presume. I'm Emma Hendricks."

He set down his box, his gaze skimming over her curiously as he shook her hand. He eyed her Mercedes. "What brings you to this end of the bay? This place isn't for rent. I think you'd be happier with one of them fancy beach houses at the other end of Coastal Ridge Road. You can't miss them."

He'd read her well. "I've already rented one of those beach houses for the summer, thank you. I actually wanted to talk to you about a story I'm doing."

His ears perked up. "A writer, huh? If you're looking to buy a nice little summer vacation home, I was planning to put this gem on the market. No one will bother you way out here, that's for sure. Great place for a writer to get inspired."

"I'm actually a reporter," she said carefully, not wanting to scare him off and make him clam up.

His smile slipped a little and shadows darkened his features. "Ah, one of those kinds of writers." He narrowed his eyes in suspicion. "What exactly are you reporting on?"

"Well, I'm looking into doing a piece on your great-aunt, Kathleen Connor. I'm researching the war, and she's listed as one of the local schoolteachers." Emma tried to appear bookish, as if she were researching his great-aunt from a purely literary standpoint. She was afraid he would shut her out completely if he knew she was mostly interested in his aunt's personal story.

"You don't fool me, missy. You're here about the scandal. I figured as much." He sighed, sounding defeated. Obviously, she hadn't been the first journalist to inquire about his aunt.

"What I found in the archives about your great-aunt wasn't much. I was hoping you might know something more about her or her husband? She vanished so mysteriously. I'm trying to figure out what happened."

Benjamin rubbed his jaw and shrugged. "Not much to tell.

The story I've heard through my family for years was they got married late in life, had a falling out, then lived the remainder of their days apart. Some sort of scandal caused by her. Poor chap must have been in love with her something fierce. He never did divorce her or marry anyone else or have children. He was the last in his line, so his name died with him, while she took off Lord only knows where." Ben's expression was one of pity and disapproval. "Not much was said about my aunt other than whatever she did was scandalous, and no one ever really forgave her for hurting him. Not to mention, she tarnished the family name."

"What happened to the rest of your family?"

"I heard tell they moved away over the shame of it all, and well, this here cottage is all there is left. They say she was selfish, always wanting something more. Don't know whatever became of her, but I hope she got what she deserved. There's nothing left but this cottage, which reverted back to the family after she disappeared. This place has been nice for my grandkids, but I'm getting too old for the crazy weather Maine has to offer, and I'm headed south. Gonna take 'em to Disney World. Now that's a real vacation."

Emma smiled the obligatory smile, when all she wanted to know about was Kathleen Connor. She couldn't understand why he would want to sell the cottage. It was adorable and perfect and part of his family's past. She instinctively knew Kathleen would be so disappointed. Emma hid her disapproval well from years of experience. "What's in the box?" she asked, trying to bring the discussion back around to his aunt.

"Just a bunch of old junk I found in the attic."

"Would you mind if I looked through it?" Emma asked.

He stared at her, perplexed as to why anyone in his or her right mind would want someone's old junk. Emma knew most people would feel that way, but there was something about

Kathleen she couldn't explain to anyone. It was like they were kindred spirits. She felt as if her entire future was connected to unraveling Kathleen's past.

"I want whatever you have that belonged to Kathleen Connor."

"Why? I've been through this stuff. There's nothing in here that can tell you anything more about her."

"I'm a journalist. My job is to look at things in a different way than most people. What you deem junk, she must have valued as treasure. If anything, it might shed some light on her personality."

"Why you would want to is beyond me, but I don't much care one way or another. Keep what you want, chuck the rest. Just be respectful and don't bring any more shame to my family name. That's all I ask."

"Thank you, and I can assure you, Mr. Reynolds, I am always professional." Emma took the box from Kathleen's great-nephew before he could change his mind and quickly stored it in her trunk.

He saluted her, bid her good day, and then disappeared inside the cottage once more as if to sever all ties to his aunt once and for all.

Emma started driving back to her beach house as fast as she could, but halfway there, her burning curiosity got the best of her. She pulled off into a lookout with a stunning view. Quickly retrieving the box, she carried it to a bench, the fresh air making her feel invigorated. The box contained a couple of old lesson plans, a few drawings of nature, and several sheets of random facts Kathleen must have discovered about various things. There was also a journal that drew Emma's attention. Opening the cover, she began to read.

The first entry was on Kathleen's wedding day, when she was so full of hope and excitement, but things quickly changed. Her words were so moving, Emma felt the sting of tears behind her eyes, knowing what it was like to invest everything you had in a relationship only to be let down. Her nephew was wrong. Kathleen's husband must not have loved her at all.

Emma's suspicions were confirmed. He wasn't the victim; Kathleen was. Why else would she speak of horrors and being deceived and failed expectations, yet later she also spoke of love and loss? Did she love her husband despite the monster he obviously was and mourned the loss of love when he refused to change? Emma could feel her pain so deeply, she could relate to what she must have been going through—alone and hurting with no one to talk to.

Looking back through the box, there were small little trinkets that looked like keepsakes or gifts maybe her husband had given her. There were also dried and pressed flowers, pine sprigs, fall maple leaves, and other various things that made Emma think of Maine during its four seasons. And lastly there was a beautifully decorated small wooden box. It looked delicate as if it had been whittled and crafted by someone with great skill, patience, and a lot of love. It was confusing to figure out. Her husband almost seemed like two different people. Regardless, Emma smiled with excitement over her discovery and quickly opened the top. Her smile slipped and her heart fell. It was empty inside. Just when she felt like she was getting ahead in figuring out the mystery of Kathleen Connor, Emma hit another dead end.

With a deep sigh, she set the wooden box on top of the other things and lifted the cardboard box to carry it to her car. She opened the trunk and set the cardboard box inside, but not before the ancient wooden box tumbled to the blacktop. The hard pavement was no match for the delicate wood. It cracked and fell apart. Emma dropped to her knees beside the box and picked it up with a heavy heart. She felt horrible for ruining it.

She blinked, and her lips parted. She hadn't ruined it at all. She'd made another discovery.

A secret compartment.

Her hands shook as she opened the secret compartment. Sucking in a sharp breath, she pulled out another coded message signed with the same insignia by Kathleen. There was also the code to the map, but it was ripped in half. With half the code, Emma just might stand a chance of deciphering the messages. These maps led to locations, Emma was sure of it, but she had no clue how to read them, especially with only half the code. Journal entries of love and loss, secret messages written in code, so many questions. She had no idea how she was going to discover the answers, but she had a pretty good idea where to start.

Dr. McGiant.

~

June 1942: Beacon Bay, Maine

Kathleen Connor didn't set out to cause a scandal. She couldn't go on living with the abuse. Her hopes for a brighter future had turned into a nightmare. William had hit her every time she said a word to contradict him. He would explode into a fit of rage, turning into a monster, and then snapping back to his apologetic self. He was a coward. And he always made sure to hit her in places where it didn't show. The last time he had beaten her nearly to death, his final blow missing its target and hitting her in the face.

That was when she'd found the courage to leave him.

She'd slipped away in the dead of night to her parents' house. They had taken her in, shocked over what had happened. Yet the next day when news of what she'd done spread around town, they had let her down, scandalized over the possible repercussions to them. Kathleen had brazenly marched straight through town so everyone could see exactly why she had left her husband of three months. To her horror, the folks in town had seen her husband as the victim and her as the free-thinking woman who had broken his heart. They said she was much too strong-willed for her own good and had brought what happened upon herself.

That hurt the most. Who on earth would willingly bring upon themselves a beating that would nearly kill them? Yes, she was strong-willed, but she wasn't a martyr. She didn't ask for any of this. No one deserved to undergo what had happened to her.

In the end, her parents had crumbled under pressure from the town and turned their backs on her as they focused on her brother, who had married respectably and given them grand-children. Not totally heartless, they gave her their old fishing cottage on the poor end of the coast. School was out for the summer, and the town added another blow by informing her they didn't want her back as a teacher in the fall. Teaching was all she knew, and it was the one way she could honestly express herself. With no support from anyone, Kathleen withdrew into herself and accepted her fate as a ruined woman and spinster.

Stepping out of her new home, she wrapped her blue clutch coat around her shoulders and let it hang open, as there were no fastenings. Smoothing her hands over her handkerchief skirt with its many panels, insets, and pleats, she walked out onto the deck and leaned over the rail. The lighthouse across the bay flickered like a steady heartbeat, guiding sailors home. Loneliness filled her being, yet a peaceful tranquility hugged her soul.

She was safe.

This powerful ocean would provide her with strength, and the beauty of her surroundings would heal her heart. Just the thought of William Connor so big and powerful and strong, capable of crushing her with a single blow, filled her with terror.

Her own town, the parents of the children she had nurtured and taught, had sided with him. All because she'd had an opinion and a mind of her own. They could see the damage he had inflicted upon her, yet it didn't matter.

They had turned a blind eye and had forsaken her.

The pain of that alone was almost unbearable, but the worst pain of all was having her parents and brother shut her out. She was truly alone and always would be. Her husband refused to divorce her. Divorce was unheard of, and he kept begging her to come back, promising he would change. But she knew deep in her gut if she went back, he wouldn't stop. He never did. And the next time she wouldn't make it out alive.

She tipped her face up to the sky, and warm rays of the waning sunlight caressed her cheeks, trying to help her forget, but she never would forget. The nightmares would haunt her for the rest of her days on this earth. She was broken physically, but she wouldn't let any of them break her spirit. A shadow settled over her, bringing with it a familiar chill. Opening her eyes, she jerked back a step and let out a cry.

William.

"Please don't look at me like that," he said, his face twisted in agony as he stared at the yellow and purple fading bruise surrounding her eye. "I miss you. My life is empty without you. I promise I won't hurt you again."

She swallowed past the dryness in her throat and stepped away from the railing. "I know you won't," she said carefully.

Hope registered on his face. "Does that mean you'll come home where you belong? Our house is not a home without you in it."

She forced her voice not to tremble. "No."

His gaze hardened. "What do you mean no?"

"That house is your home. This house is mine. We don't

belong together. We never did, and I am never going back. Not after what you did to me."

A muscle in his cheek twitched. "I told you I was sorry. You brought this pain upon yourself with your defiance of me. I've let you have your way, but you've pouted long enough. You're making a fool of me in town."

"You made a fool of yourself." She raised her chin a notch, unable to contain the part of her that was her very nature and always had been.

"Careful, darling. I might stop caring and leave you all alone out here like you ask. That can be dangerous, living on your own." He shook the railing hard, and it wobbled violently. "I would hate to see anything bad happen to you like falling over this shaky deck railing to the sharp rocks below." He took a menacing step toward her.

Her stomach leapt to her throat and her heart started beating furiously, but she stood her ground. "And I would hate to see something bad happen to you when the whole town finds out what you've done." She refused to step back this time, knowing if she didn't stand her ground and fight now, she never would. No matter what it cost her, she couldn't let him win.

"They already know I hit you." He shrugged nonchalantly. "They understand because you drove me to it. Everyone can see that but you."

"I'm not talking about you hitting me," she said, and that gave him pause. The first real look of doubt and fear crossed his face. "I've been writing a lot in my journal these days since I don't have a teaching job to go back to," she continued. "I've hidden some very interesting pieces that will surely be found if anything *bad* happens to me. Don't come near me, William." She actually stepped forward, and relished the look on his face as he took a step back. "I know what you did," she hissed through clenched teeth. "I promise you the whole town will know, too, if you ever touch me again."

"You're bluffing," his voice rumbled deeply, the expression on his face warring between fury and fear.

"Am I?" She thrust her face right up into his. People knew he was capable of violence, but they had no idea what he was capable of. She did. Oh, yes, she did. "Something tells me you're not willing to risk finding out." She didn't know how or when, but one day she would find a way to let the whole world know the truth and set the record straight.

"Thank you, Rebecca, I really appreciate you taking Trevor with you again this summer," Logan said to his mother-in-law on Saturday morning when she stopped by his two-story colonial house in downtown Beacon Bay to pick up his son. She was a darker shade of blonde than her daughter, but just as tiny. It was enough of a reminder to make every day difficult, yet a gift he wouldn't squander. He was lucky to have her in his life. It was like having another piece of Amanda still with him.

"Nonsense. We love spending time with our only grand-child," Rebecca said with a beaming smile, and he knew she meant it. She and her husband Barry were good people. That was part of the reason why Logan had kept his secret and suffered alone. They would be devastated if they knew the truth.

"And Trevor loves spending time with you both," he replied. "You're all he has for family."

"We're your family, too. I wish we were watching our little munchkin because you were going out for a change and having some fun instead of working your life away. You don't always have to offer to work the on-call weekend hours, you know. I hope you use some vacation days and do something for yourself this summer." She squeezed his hand. "Amanda loved life. She would want you to go on living."

"I know," he said, but in his heart, he knew the real truth. Amanda *did* love life. That's what made what had happened that much harder to accept. Punishing himself was the only thing that made him feel better. If she couldn't go on living, then why should he get to? "I will," he lied.

"You say that every summer when Barry and I take Trevor to our summer camp, but you never follow through with it. It's time, Logan. It's not too late for you to go with us, you know."

"I can't get away from the hospital for the entire summer, you know that," was all he said, but he couldn't quite meet her eyes.

"What about part of the summer?"

"It's too late. Everyone already put in their time. We would be short-staffed."

"What are you going to do all by yourself?" she asked softly.

"I'll find something to do that doesn't involve work," he looked her in the eye this time as he finished with, "I promise."

"I certainly hope so." She reached out and cupped his cheek. "Don't you think you've punished yourself long enough?"

He blinked, and for a moment he was terrified she knew why. She could never know because it would kill her.

"Daddy, Daddy, wait!" Trevor bolted into the room like the Tasmanian Devil and launched himself at Logan in the nick of time, saving him from having to respond to a topic he had been dancing around for over half a decade.

Logan scooped up his bear of a son and threw him over his shoulder as if he weighed nothing at all. At six-years-old Trevor was a tank already—a chip off the old block, so to speak. Logan spun him around until he lapsed into a fit of giggles, then he kissed his son's baby-soft cheek, inhaling the scent of lotion and donuts and the outdoors all rolled into one precious package as he hugged him tight. Damn, he would miss him so much.

"What's wrong, buddy?" he asked when Trevor didn't let go.

Trevor buried his face into Logan's neck, his blond curls tickling Logan's skin. "You're not going to be sad if I leave you this summer, are you?"

Logan took a moment to swallow past the lump in his throat before pulling away to look his son in his innocent sky-blue eyes. "When am I ever sad?" he bluffed.

"I miss having a mommy sometimes, but you're sad all the time." The answer was so honest and forthright, it was like looking into his deceased wife's eyes and seeing the pity and disappointment and regret. His son was too smart for his own good and way more intuitive than Logan had given him credit for. "I don't want to have fun if you're not."

Logan's stomach twisted into knots, and he was pretty certain he was developing an ulcer. Hearing those words was like a sucker punch to the gut. The last thing he wanted was for his self-imposed misery to rub off on his only child. He took a deep breath and said with determination, "I promise I will have fun this summer like you."

Trevor's face, still so young and angelic, brightened with hope and excitement. "You mean you're going on a big adventure too?"

"How about I do my best to find one this summer and tell you all about it when you get home. Deal?"

"Deal. That makes me feel lots better, Daddy."

"Me too, and I don't want you to worry about me. I really am okay, buddy." He kissed his son again and set him down, vowing he would find a way to be. He owed him that much at least.

LATER THAT NIGHT, Logan was once again in the hospital emergency waiting room on a slow evening. It brought him back to the night he'd met Emma Hendricks. She had only been passing through, but she'd been interesting for sure. A mixture of class and sass that intrigued him. He thought of his son, Trevor, asking him not to be sad this summer. Logan hadn't realized how perceptive his son had become. He didn't want his little boy to grow up too fast because he was worried about his father. Logan had to stop letting the whole world see what a mess he still was. There had to be something adventurous he could do in this quiet little town.

The front door opened and Logan's jaw fell open. Emma Hendricks walked in once more, followed by a whirlwind of possibilities. Maybe it was a sign.

"Well, it's too early for your stitches to come out. I take it you had another mishap?" he asked, trying to fight his grin.

She smirked. "Funny, but no. Don't you have a life, or do you live here 24/7?"

"Something like that," he responded. "You still didn't answer my question. Why are *you* here, Ms. Hendricks?"

"I'm actually here to see *you*, Dr. Mayfield." She crossed her arms, and the corners of her lips tipped up.

She was good. She knew exactly how to build anticipation for her audience. She wore a soft looking green sweater that made her amber eyes pop, with a pair of snug-fitting black leggings and knee-high boots.

"I'm listening," he responded, his curiosity piqued as he leaned against the edge of a chair.

"You have something I want." She strummed her perfect, French-manicured nails on her arm.

He blinked. "I do?"

"Yes...your expertise in map decoding skills, of course." Her lips twitched. She knew exactly what she was doing.

"Ah, your treasure, *of course*. I remember now, but what does that have to do with me? If I recall, the map was written in code and the corner was ripped off. That's not very promising if you ask me." He crossed his feet at the ankles.

"That's what I thought too, but then I found another map." She waited a beat after casting her line. "I have a proposition for you."

"Really now?" He tried not to let on that he was nibbling, but she was damn good.

She wiggled the line by adding more bait. "I didn't just find a map. I found half the code for deciphering it."

He sat up straight, feeling her set the hook before he knew what had hit him. All teasing aside, he was genuinely interested now, and she knew it. "Go on," the words came out of his mouth of their own accord.

She handed him the map and what she had of the code, and he studied the markings while she talked.

"I looked into the name written at the bottom of the first map, Kathleen Connor. She was actually from here. A local teacher who caused quite the scandal back in the day. I find her fascinating. I want to uncover the truth of her past as my next story, but I can't do it alone. With my investigative skills and your code-deciphering ability and knowledge of Beacon Bay, I think we would make a great team."

"What's in it for me?" His eyes met hers, and he studied her carefully, already knowing he would say yes but wanting to at least appear to put up a fight as she reeled him in way too easily.

"Gee, I don't know. How about a little thing called truth and justice for all? Something's not right with this story. Don't you want to be a part of the fame of having set the town records straight?"

He thought of Trevor, and realized this might very well be the kind of adventure he'd promised his son he would have. If he couldn't tell him the truth, the very least he could do would be not to lie to him again and keep his promises.

"I'm in," Logan said with conviction as he handed the map and code back to her.

This time *she* blinked. "Seriously? You are? Just like that?"

"Just like that."

Her gaze dropped to his wedding ring. "But what about your family? This will take up a lot of your time."

He found it odd his heart didn't ache quite as much as it normally did when someone brought up his dearly departed wife. He frowned over that thought. He didn't deserve for the pain to go away. That was why he still wore his wedding ring as a constant reminder.

"I'm widowed," he replied with honesty as he met her gaze, "and my son left this morning with his grandparents for most of the summer at their camp. Time is something I will have way too much of. Consider me at your disposal."

Emma's face looked stricken. "I'm so sorry. I didn't know."

"It's okay." He wanted to put her at ease, even if he himself wasn't okay, and he didn't know if he would ever be. "It's been six years, and there's no way you could have known." He looked at her bandaged hand. "I couldn't help notice a white tan line on your ring finger when I stitched you up. "I'm taking it that has something to do with this quest and your visit to Beacon Bay?"

"I'm not widowed. I wasn't even married, if that's what you're wondering," she answered with a bit of her own honesty, her bitterness shining through. "I might or might not be engaged because I have no clue where my fiancé is at the moment. All I know is he cleaned out his bank account, took off with no word, and missed our wedding. And yes, that has everything to do with why I am in Beacon Bay."

"Wow," Logan blinked, "now I'm the one who's sorry."

"You and me both." She threw her hands up in the air. "Frankly, Doc, I'm through with being sorry and feeling sorry and looking pathetically sorry. How about you?"

He admired her candid approach to life. Too many people skirted around the truth, dancing around his feelings, tiptoeing over the thought of bringing up anything that might cause him more pain. Yet they couldn't disguise the constant pity in their eyes, which was far worse than being honest and real.

His mouth twisted. "While I don't think either of us look pathetic in any way, I get what you're saying."

"So, Doc, are we going to do this thing, or not?"

He chuckled, enjoying her personality. It was damned refreshing. Talking to her was the most entertainment he'd had in years. Well, hell. He suddenly realized *pathetic* was actually the perfect word to describe him. Maybe it was time he did something about it.

"I think the map is a mix of Morse, radio, and the Greek alphabet. I'm familiar with all of them. When do we start?" He stuck out his hand with determination.

"Yesterday," she responded, sounding emphatic as she slipped her tiny hand within his own.

The electricity that hummed between them had them both staring at each other in surprise. This might be a whole lot more than an adventure, he feared, and his never-ending seed of doubt had him wondering what exactly he'd gotten himself into.

THE NEXT MORNING Emma stepped out of her fabulous beach house that sat right on the shore of the Atlantic Ocean. It was brand new and full of all the amenities, including a hot tub and pool. While it was gorgeous, there was nothing unusual or charming about it, and there were several others like it in a long row down the flat beach. Not like the quaint small cottage on the edge of a rugged cliff that led down to the rocky shore below at the other end of Coastal Ridge Road.

Now *that* place was inspiring.

Emma could see why Kathleen had been so taken with it, but Emma didn't fully understand why Kathleen had lived there instead of with her husband. What exactly had been the catalyst that made her move? Speaking of unanswered questions, Emma was excited to start her quest. Dr. Mayfield was on his way to pick her up. He'd recognized the code and made out enough of the map to know it led to some hiking trails in the woods on the outskirts of town. It was a beautiful, sunny day in the beginning of July and starting to warm up a little, but this was Maine after all. Layers were a must.

Emma wore a soft pale pink zip-up hoodie over a light blue ribbed tank top and a pair of designer skinny jeans tucked into hiking boots. Her hair was bobbed but it was all one length, which meant it still fit into a short ponytail at the base of her neck, minus a couple strands at the side of her face that kept escaping. Conceding defeat, she let them hang as she slipped on a pair of sunglasses. She slung her small purse filled with necessities like a mini-cassette recorder, notebook and pen—and yes, okay, lip gloss—diagonally across her body and then looped her camera over her neck.

The doctor pulled up in a big black pickup truck as dark and rugged as himself. Figures. He *was* McGiant, after all. She didn't expect him to drive anything less than a McBeast of a truck. He cut the engine and stepped out, not seeing her yet. She took a moment to study him. Tall, broad shoulders, and massive legs— good Lord, he really was a giant. She'd been able to tell he was a big man through his scrubs. But now that he wore jeans and boots with a soft cotton forest green t-shirt that hugged everything beneath it, her jaw had no choice but to fall open. His arms were huge, and who knew those pecs had been hiding beneath his clothes?

His gaze met hers and he arched a brow, so she snapped her

jaw closed and smiled wide as she met him halfway. "Dr. McGi ... uh, Dr. Mayfield, you're right on time."

"Punctuality is my middle name." One corner of his lips hitched up lopsidedly as he eyed her curiously. She could tell she amused him. "Now that we're treasure hunting partners, don't you think it's time we called each other by our first names, *Emma*?" he went on. "No, I'm not a stalker, in case you're wondering. I saw your name on your chart. My name is Logan, by the way."

Her stomach gave a funny little flip over the sound of her name spoken with the rich baritone of his voice. She rubbed her stomach, deciding not to put hot sauce on her eggs again. It had to be indigestion because anything else was unthinkable.

"I'm game if you are, Logan." She walked beside him back to his truck. "Where's your coat? Didn't your mother teach you any common sense?" She laughed, unable to stop herself from teasing him.

"This is a heat wave after the winter we've had, and I didn't have a mother. I was an orphan." His tone didn't give anything away, but he looked straight ahead.

Her smile slipped. "Open mouth insert foot again," she muttered.

"Your chariot awaits." He opened her door when they reached his truck.

"Thanks." She hopped in without looking at him and chewed her bottom lip, hoping the day picked up from here.

He jogged around the truck and climbed in, then started her up. McBeast roared to life, and Logan put her in gear.

"Do you know where we're going?" Emma asked.

"Sure do," he responded as he navigated the roads like the back of his hand. "I like to run that trail when I need to get away and think."

"You run? Of course, you do. You're a doctor. I hate to exercise." So much for the day picking up.

"No worries, Lois." Amusement laced his words. "We're not going to run. We're going to hike."

"Is there a difference?" She let out a short laugh. "Just kidding, but seriously, can't we stroll? There's no way I'm going to be able to keep up with your pace."

"No worries. I'll go easy on you." He pulled into a fairly empty parking lot near some campgrounds on the outskirts of town with a big wooden sign that had a map of many trails. "We're here."

They both climbed out of the truck and went to check out the trails. He held up the map and studied it, comparing it to the sign.

"Wow, you're like a regular Daniel Boone. I'm just glad to have you on my side."

"I have my moments." He shook his head at her, wearing an amused grin. "Reading a map and hiking are pretty much it, though."

"Somehow, I doubt that. Either way, I'm glad you decided to help me. I'm not sure I could do this on my own." She eyed the woods with wariness.

"I take it you're not exactly the outdoorsy type?"

"He's smart, too." She laughed. "However, I'll do almost anything for a story. I'm a quick study and not afraid to try most things. But if we get lost, I draw the line at eating bugs." She held up her hand, letting him know there was no discussion on that matter.

"Duly noted." He started walking. "Follow me."

After a half-hour of walking through the dark forest with rays of sunlight streaming through like spotlights, highlighting the pinecone and needle-covered stage of a forest floor, Emma was ready for a break. Logan had pointed out various flora and fauna, but it was the spooky wildlife that freaked her out. She kept jumping at every sound, terrified a bear or moose would pop out at any moment. Finally, they broke through to a clearing in an open meadow. It was stunning. The grass was a rich shade of green, dotted with wildflowers in vibrant colors of the rainbow.

"Why are we stopping?" She tried not to seem as out of breath as she was. He had attempted to keep his pace slow for her, but his stride was two to her one. She'd caught herself before bouncing off his back when he stopped and couldn't help but notice he wasn't breathing hard or sweating. In fact, he smelled incredible, like soap and aftershave and the outdoors.

"This is where the map ends." He looked around the clearing. "Years ago, this park wasn't here with all these hiking trails. It used to be private, probably just a few man-made trails from hunters. I'm sure the creators of the map chose this place for its beauty as well as its isolation."

"Can I see the map for a second?" She reached out her hand.

"By all means." He handed the ancient, yellowed paper to her.

Emma studied the markings carefully, looking for clues he might have missed. In her line of work she had learned to be observant, look for things people normally didn't see. Her smile came slow, and the sweet feeling of satisfaction filled her. Yes, there was an X, and it ended in the clearing. But if you looked closer, it covered two trees that crossed each other and looked almost like they were hugging.

"What is it? Do you see something?" he asked curiously.

She showed him the map, pointing to the spot above the X. "See those hugging trees?"

"Hugging trees?" His face puckered comically, but then his eyes widened. "Oh yeah, I didn't even notice that before."

"I guess I have my moments, too." She shrugged and couldn't

stop the goofy grin from tipping up the corners of her lips. She hadn't met anyone this easy to talk to in a long time and had to admit she was enjoying herself, which also hadn't happened in way too long. Feeling a bit uneasy, she shook off that unsettling thought and refocused. "Look at the other side of the clearing," she said, needing to keep her mind on what was important. Their quest, not flirting with hunky doctors. "What do you see?"

"Well, I'll be damned. Hugging trees." He rubbed his whiskered jaw. "Lead the way, Sherlock."

They walked over to the set of trees and searched the area but didn't see anything at first.

"Here, on the other side," she said excitedly.

Logan came around to stand beside her, and she traced the letters carved into the tree in that same sweeping handwriting she'd come to know so well.

KC + JR

"Kathleen Connor is KC, I take it, but who is JR?" he asked.

"I'm not sure," she admitted.

"So, the map led to a secret rendezvous place for these people to meet in private," Logan said. "I guess that's all there is to our adventure. Huh. Well, that's kind of a letdown, I must say."

Emma shook her head. "That can't be all there is to it."

He ran a hand through his thick black curls, looking pensive, and then finally snapped his fingers and eyed her with excitement. "Why did we not see this? X marks the spot in every treasure map."

Realization dawned. "Oh, my God! You're so right. Most treasures are buried. That has to be it. Why didn't I think of that first?"

He shrugged. "I guess my moments are bigger than yours."

"Funny." She looked around, wishing she'd brought a shovel. "Maybe we can find a stick. Whatever is buried can't be deep."

After searching the area again, Logan brought back a couple of sharp sticks that were thick enough not to break. They both started to dig. After several minutes and plenty of holes, Logan hit something.

"No way," he said in awe. "I can't believe I was actually right. Do you think there's really buried treasure here?"

"Only one way to find out."

They unearthed an ancient looking box that actually resembled the wooden box she'd found the code and the map in. With trembling fingers, she opened the lid and carefully unfolded a piece of paper that was decades old.

"What is it? Gold? Jewels? An Artifact?" Logan's face was shining with anticipation he didn't even attempt to hide.

"Better," she said. "I think we've found the greatest treasure of all." Her gaze met his.

"*Love* is the greatest treasure of all." Logan's face softened.

"I wouldn't know." Emma sighed in defeat. "I've never had it, and I'm starting to think I never will."

"Nonsense." His gaze softened. "This of all things should give you hope."

"You should listen to your own words. Who says love only comes along once in a lifetime?"

"What's in the box?" He skirted her question.

She let it go. "Another map and a letter from Kathleen's lover." Emma scanned the letter once more and then looked at Logan. "I'm beginning to think I know what the scandal was about."

"What's that?"

"Kathleen Connor was having an affair because JR aka Joseph Henry Rutherford III was most definitely not her husband."

5

JULY 1942: BEACON BAY, MAINE

It was July 4th, Independence Day, but Kathleen's freedom had come at great cost. She'd been on her own for a couple of weeks now. William had left her alone, as promised, but every time she ventured into town, she felt his eyes watching her. She knew he wouldn't risk her revealing his awful secret, so she held her head high and refused to cower no matter how much she was shaking on the inside. Everyone had condemned her anyway. Why did it matter what they thought?

That was the part that got to her the most. People would cross the street when she was walking on the same side, or they would stare and whisper and point fingers. Her parents had taken pity, supplying her with fish they caught and vegetables from their garden, but they still wouldn't be seen with her in public. After that, she'd refused their help, learning to fish and planting her own garden. With what little money she had left from teaching, she'd placed an order in a catalogue for the essentials she was running out of, refusing to shop at the main store in town—her husband's store.

Kathleen would rather live simply on her own terms, alienating everyone in town, than to live in fear with a monster just to

be accepted. If that was what it required to be socially acceptable, then she would gladly die an outcast. But that didn't mean
the loneliness hadn't hit her hard. Her days weren't bad with
summer wrapping its warm embrace around Beacon Bay. She
would go for long walks, fish, tend to her garden, and write.

Oh, how she would write.

Putting pen to paper in her journal, she poured out her soul
and let everything she was feeling emerge: her anger, her fear,
her acceptance, her determination, her peace, her sadness, her
secrets. The nights were the worst. That was when she would let
her tears fall, in the quiet stillness where no one would judge
her, and she could be free to be herself in all its ugly beautiful
glory.

She walked around her small, one-story cottage consisting of
a kitchen/living room combination with one bedroom and a
single bathroom. She'd painted the white walls a sunny yellow,
and added some lace curtains and a couple of throw pillows to
make it feel more like home, but she was still isolated at this end
of the coast.

A noise outside had her running through the front door.

The mail was here. She never got mail, but she knew her
package of supplies was due to arrive soon. She hadn't thought it
would come this soon and was impressed with how quickly the
postal service had worked, especially given the demands of the
war going on. Cargo planes were brimming with supplies for
soldiers, so supplies for citizens took longer.

Everyone was aware of how important the mail had
become for both soldiers and their families back home, but
space was limited. V-mail—short for Victory Mail—was
created as a hybrid mail process. Letters were censored, copied
to microfilm to save room, and then printed on paper once
they reached their destination. Kathleen could relate to the
soldiers in a way. She felt completely cut off from life as she

knew it, left on her own to make the most of her dire situation and survive.

She reached her front yard just as the mail truck disappeared from view. Her heart sank. He wasn't very friendly toward her, but at least he was a form of human contact. Sighing heavily, she reached down to pick up her box of supplies but stopped short. A letter lay on the top, clearly marked V-mail.

Her brow knitted, puckering her forehead.

She didn't know anyone in the military. Picking up the letter, the name of the recipient was blurred. The only part of the letter that was visible was 137 Coastal Ridge Road, which was Kathleen's address. It was a federal offense to open someone else's mail, but she knew how the system worked. If she sent the letter back to the post office unopened, they would return the letter to the soldier who had sent it—providing he was still alive. It would take a long time to reach him, and even longer for him to resend it until it reached its proper recipient. She suspected he needed to hear from someone back home, even if that someone was a virtual stranger like her.

With no idea who the letter was intended for, Kathleen had no choice. Her heart went out to the soldier who had sent this letter. It was a lifeline for him she didn't have the heart to cut. Maybe if she opened the letter, she would figure out who it was meant for and she could deliver the letter herself. It was obviously meant for someone in Beacon Bay. She told herself that was the only reason she would ever open anyone's mail, but even she wasn't convinced. A part of her was desperate.

She needed a lifeline herself.

Carrying her box of supplies into her cottage, she set the box down on the kitchen table. Pouring herself a glass of iced tea and pacing the room for several minutes, she finally gave in. She lifted the letter as if it was fragile and took it out onto her back porch overlooking the ocean. Inhaling a calming breath, she turned the letter over and opened it. Carefully pulling out the precious cargo nesting inside, she slowly unfolded the letter and read the words that would change her life forever.

MY DEAREST BEVERLY,

I hope this letter finds you well. I know we have never met, but I have heard of your family. My mother has told me the good news. You are agreeable to meeting me upon my return. That is good news indeed, for I long to come home to Beacon Bay and my old life. I fought in this war in the hopes of doing my part for the greater good. I am glad the United States has joined the war, though I must confess, I was naïve. I thought I could make a difference.

I had no idea I would barely make a dent.

I feel I must pour my soul out on these pages so you are fully aware of what you are getting yourself into if you agree to become my wife. I am damaged goods. This war has changed me. I will not be coming home the same man as when I left, and I can't promise I will find my way back to him. You have no idea what it's been like being in this war. The things I've seen would break your heart, for they have broken mine beyond repair, I fear.

I knew war was violent, but to actually bear witness to the destruction and pain and suffering of those around you is not something I prepared for properly, though I'm not entirely sure one can prepare for something like that at all. To see the fear in a man's eyes when he dies right in front of you is something that will haunt my dreams forever. And seeing the resignation and acceptance of death in the eyes of a man I am preparing to kill is something I will have to live with for the rest of my days.

I'm not trying to scare you away. Quite the opposite, in fact. I selfishly don't want to be alone if I make it back. I want to be fair to you. I don't understand why I'm still alive. I sometimes think death would be easier. Maybe with your help, this will be something I can overcome. I certainly hope so. The last thing I would want to do is to make you care about me and then let you down. I couldn't handle hurting anyone else. I hurt enough all by myself.

The weather in Hawaii was balmy and the lava rocks and tropical flowers stunning. I can't tell you where I am now, but it's cooler, although growing warmer every day, although nothing compares to home. I miss Maine. The smell of pine from the forest, the sight of deer running across the wildflowers in the meadow, the feel of the crisp salty air as it stings my face, the taste of fresh snowflakes melting on my tongue, and the thought of the many lighthouses shining their beacons and guiding me home. My dreams of home are the only things keeping me going.

I would give anything to be in Beacon Bay right now, and that makes me feel like a coward. I don't understand why I was spared when so many souls much braver than I were taken or maimed in ways that will change their lives forever. I might not be physically injured, but mentally, I am a wreck. I don't know how I am going to survive the rest of my time over here. I still have two years left.

Every little sound makes me jump, and the nightmares are relentless. They leave me disoriented and drained, which is something I can't afford to be right now. This war is far from over. All Japan did was wake a sleeping giant. I fear how we will retaliate and how much more death and destruction have to happen before the war will end.

Anyway, I've probably given you many reasons to walk away, and I wouldn't blame you if you did. But if you're still willing to give us a try, it would fill my heart with joy to hear back from you. Even if you're not, please write to me. I need to hear from someone back home.

Yours Truly,
Joseph Henry Rutherford III

KATHLEEN REREAD the letter three times before finally refolding it gently and slipping it back into its envelope. *Beverly*. There were many Beverlys in town, as it was a common name. She had no idea which Beverly this was meant for. Her heart ached at the mere thought that this poor soldier named Joseph must have witnessed the attack on Pearl Harbor first-hand and lived to tell about it, expected to be strong and fight on, wherever he was. No wonder he wasn't the same man. How could he be? Anyone who expected him to be was naïve and foolish, and quite frankly, not very compassionate.

His words had moved her more than she'd ever imagined. She longed to comfort him in some way and let him know it was going to be okay. *He* was going to be okay. He'd made it this far. He only had to hang on for a little while longer. He was so lost and alone, the same as she was. It somehow made her feel a connection to him she hadn't thought possible since becoming an outcast. She was married, and he was intended for another, but that didn't mean she couldn't write him back. She had to help him in any way she could, even though it probably meant she would never hear from him again.

Maybe by writing him back and explaining what had happened, he would correct the situation and get the happy ending he deserved. She would sleep better at night knowing she had done the right thing, but that didn't mean she would stop thinking about him anytime soon or stop wondering if he was okay or stop worrying about him. A man she didn't even know who had somehow changed her with his words.

Maybe her words would do the same for him.

~

August 1942: Pearl Harbor, Hawaii

Joseph paced the deck of the USS Tennessee, nervous at being back. He wore his summer uniform of white button-fly trousers, white jumper, and white cotton hat since he was back in the warmer climate of Hawaii. They had sailed from San Francisco, and after a week of exercises, they went to the South Pacific to escort the carrier The Hornet back to Pearl Harbor while the rest of the task force supported the invasion of Guadalcanal. The Tennessee and the other older battleships were due to return to the Puget Sound in two weeks for modernization because, not only were they slower than the carriers, they burned a lot more fuel.

Joseph whittled away at another small wooden box. He'd taken up the habit to keep himself focused on anything other than the devastation around him. Staring out over Battleship Row was still just as heartbreaking. The Tennessee had sustained relatively minor damage during the attack by Japan on Pearl Harbor, but the damage had been repaired since February, unlike the Arizona and the Oklahoma which had sunk and were total losses. He remained a gunner, but he had a hard time even touching the weapons without bringing on more nightmares.

Joseph kept checking his watch, knowing the mail was coming soon. He'd heard there had been a problem with the cargo plane last month when he'd sent his letter to Beverly from San Francisco. By the time the mail was loaded onto a new plane, the sacks had been damaged by torrential rain. Any letters that were legible were sent out, with the rest being returned to the soldiers who had sent them. He hadn't received his back yet, so he had assumed it had made it to Beverly's house. He prayed it had, as he needed to hear something from anyone at this point.

"Mail call," someone finally yelled.

A mixture of relief and dread filled him. What if his letter was never sent after all? The post office did a good job of tracking down soldiers wherever they were and keeping their families informed since they weren't allowed to tell their loved ones where they were stationed, but damaged mail complicated matters. Or worse, what if it had been sent, but Beverly decided it was all too much for her and decided she didn't want anything to do with him? But worst of all, what if no one bothered to write to him? He could take almost anything, even bad news, but he couldn't handle not hearing from someone at home.

With slow agonizing steps, Joseph made his way to the mail room. Everyone's name was called except his own. At the last possible second when he was at his worst and giving up, someone yelled his name. He took the letter and slipped it into his pocket, holding it close until he was free to read it at the end of his shift.

A couple hours later Joseph bypassed the barracks and made his way back up the hill far from the harbor to sit under his favorite palm tree. He could see the ocean, but up here he could focus on the waves instead of the devastation. The rain hadn't come yet, but the sky looked stormy. The wind picked up, making the waves swell into large crescent moons before rolling into balls and crashing against the shore as if the gods were bowling.

He smiled slightly, thinking of home, fighting down the wave of longing that always came with it. With that thought, he pulled out the letter that had been burning his flesh through his pocket, searing his heart and soul. A sprig of dried pine fell onto his lap, and he sucked in a sharp breath. With shaking fingers, he lifted the sprig to his nose and inhaled deep. He squeezed his eyelids closed and fought back a surge of tears.

Home.

He'd been so homesick. To have a simple small token from the place dearer to his heart than any other meant more than he could possibly put into words. Maybe things with Beverly would work out after all if she could read his needs this well already. He fought to get his emotions under control and opened his eyes to read the words that would seal his fate.

. . .

DEAR JOSEPH,

Please don't be angry with me. I have no idea how you feel about the war or what you were expecting, but I have to tell you I received your letter. I must say your words moved me beyond what I can ever write in a return letter, but you must know before you read any further, I am not your intended.

My name is Kathleen Connor. Your letter was addressed to a woman named Beverly. If I had known her last name, I would have gladly given her your letter. But the message was sent to my address at 137 Coastal Ridge Road. I'm not sure how that happened. It looks as if part of the address was blurred.

I had to respond to you because I didn't want you to think you were alone and that no one back home cared about you. I think you're so brave. Wherever you are, know that what you're doing over there, fighting for your country and standing up for what you believe in, is important to us all. You are making much more than a dent. You're making a difference by being there. I know it must be difficult, but you can do this. This might sound crazy because I don't even know you, but I believe in you.

It's hard being isolated. I know first-hand what it feels like to be cut off from everything you thought was important to you and everyone you loved who you thought loved you back. You see I'm married, but my husband isn't a very nice man. He hurt me, yet the whole town blames me and sees him as the victim. I'm only telling you this because you bared your soul in your letter. I thought if I bared mine, it might help.

I too think about giving up at times, but I'm not a quitter and I refuse to let the enemy win. It's the same with you, I suspect. I can tell you're not a quitter, and you can't let the enemy win either. Maybe you survived so you could make sure your comrades didn't die in vain. I know you're lonely. I'm very lonely too.

Please don't give up on yourself. You might not believe it, but you do make the world a better place by being in it. It's people like you who give those of us back home hope. I have hope this world will be a better place because of you someday. I sincerely wish you the best of luck and hope your Beverly can see what a great catch you are. Keep your chin up, Joseph. Tomorrow is another day, and maybe your happy ending will be right around the corner.

Until Tomorrow,

Kathleen Connor

JOSEPH REREAD the letter a couple of times and then slowly folded the paper and placed it back in his shirt pocket right above his heart. He sat there in stunned surprise. He had thought the letter would be from Beverly or his parents or his sisters, but never in his wildest imagination had he expected it to be from a complete stranger.

Kathleen Connor.

Who was she? Beverly Sanderson lived at 37 Coastal Ridge Road in the upper-class section. Kathleen lived at the other end at 137 Coastal Ridge Road in a much lower-class section, obviously surrounded by scandal. His mother would have palpitations if she knew he was even speaking to someone like Kathleen, but he didn't care what his mother or anyone else might think. Kathleen was the one who had written him back at a time when he'd needed it the most, and she'd given him the most precious gift of all.

A piece of home.

Granted, Beverly didn't know he had written her first, but still. She could have written to him on her own accord, and his parents and sisters only wrote when they wanted something. They never wrote to cheer him up or see how he was doing or lift his spirits. Kathleen didn't have to write him back at all. She certainly didn't owe him anything and had nothing to gain. Yet she had written to a complete stranger because she cared about how he was feeling when he didn't think anyone else did. He needed to thank her, he thought, trying to justify his strong urge to write her back.

Joseph would still reach out to Beverly because his mother was counting on him and had probably already said something to her, but that didn't mean he and Kathleen couldn't still be friends. She was married to a monster by the sounds of it. People could be so cruel. He was embarrassed to think he was fighting for a town that didn't care enough about its own people to support them.

Anger fueled him on her behalf. He wished he was there to protect her. He would damn sure fight for her and show her husband the proper way to treat a woman. He felt helpless this far away because the reality was there was very little he could do. Her words had given him hope and the energy to carry on. Maybe he could do the same for her.

What harm could possibly come from that?

6

Later that evening Emma and Logan sat across from each other to celebrate finding their very first treasure earlier that day by eating a bucket of clams at Salty's Shack. It was a hole in the wall down by the ocean in a small little nook you would miss if you blinked, but those were always the best kinds of places. The décor was rustic, weathered wood, the seafood fresh, the clientele even fresher. Salty himself had been a fisherman for years until he retired and opened his shack.

Emma had taken off her pink zip-up hoodie and placed a paper bib over her light blue ribbed tank top. She couldn't stop the corners of her lips from tipping up. She licked the salty melted butter away and went back to eating more delectable clams, having no shame that she looked as if she hadn't eaten in weeks. Her parents' idea of a celebration would have been lobster and king crab legs at a five-star seafood restaurant, while Logan's suggestion of clams at a dive was much more Emma's speed, she was discovering.

Emma might have been born into money, but that didn't mean she agreed with all that it stood for. Granted, she enjoyed her luxury apartment and her Mercedes and even her beach house, because up until now the finer things in life were all she had known. But those things were material things that didn't have any meaning or history to them. After seeing Kathleen's quaint cottage and discovering this culinary treasure, Emma was beginning to appreciate looking at the world in a whole new way.

"What are you smiling about?" Logan asked, reaching for a clam, which stretched the fabric of his soft cotton dark green t-shirt. The play of the muscles in his arm was impressive as they flexed and released.

Her eyes met his and she blinked. "Huh? Oh, yeah. I was marveling over how delicious these clams are. This place is the best kept secret."

"Why do you think we keep it that way? Can't have rich, touristy outsiders crowding in, eating all our food and making a nuisance of themselves." The deep timbre of his voice was laced with a teasing tone.

Her jaw fell open. "Hey, watch it. I'm not a rich tourist."

"Okay, rich journalist then. It's obvious you come from money."

"You're one to talk. You're a doctor. You can't tell me you don't have money of your own."

"True, however, I didn't always have money." He transformed his face into a pensive frown. "I came from nothing and had to work hard for everything I've ever gotten." He blinked. "And I have no idea why I'm telling you this. Sorry."

"No need to be sorry. Getting people to open up is my job." She shrugged. "I can't help the situation I was born into, but believe me, there are no free rides." She sat up straighter. "I've had to work my ass off to get taken seriously in my profession."

"I bet." He nodded. "Listen, I didn't mean to imply you weren't a serious journalist. I simply meant it's obvious we come from different worlds, but you hiked the land and became one with Maine's soil today, digging in the dirt with your bare hands, communing with nature. I'd say that makes you a part of this place. The way I see it, you're no longer an outsider. You're a temporary towny."

"Nice save, Doc." She snickered.

"I thought so, Lois." He winked.

Thinking of Lois Lane, Emma pondered the story she was investigating. "I still can't believe those letters." They'd taken time to read them together while waiting for their food. "Kathleen's husband William *hurt* her. It doesn't take much to read between the lines and know by hurt she meant hit. She wouldn't have run away unless she feared for her life. The town records don't say anything about that. They make him out to be the victim and her the scandal-causing outcast. Even her own family thinks that. It's so sad."

"I have to admit I judged her unfairly when I heard she'd had an affair," Logan said with chagrin. "Back then divorce wasn't acceptable. But to think her husband might have abused her and the whole town turned against her, taking his side, is just plain wrong."

"It *is* wrong and sad and makes me furious on her behalf." Emma shook her head. "I really feel a connection to her, like we're kindred spirits or something. I am free to say and do whatever I please, yet she wasn't free to be the strong independent woman she so obviously was. I'm sure her husband was trying to punish her by making her stay married to him. I wonder if he hurt her further. It had to be hard to stay safe on her own. There had to be a reason why she survived. She must have had something pretty big on him. Then again, she disappeared, so maybe she didn't survive after all. I need proof. All this speculating is driving me crazy."

"Me too. The letters say she and Joseph were just friends and that he was getting ready to propose to someone else, yet they carved their initials into the tree like lovers would. I'm thinking at some point they must have come to care for one another as more than friends." Logan wiped the butter from his large hands and then took a sip of wine, looking thoughtful.

Emma sipped her beer and came to a decision. "Whatever happens, we can't stop looking. We have to follow the new clue we found with the map and see where it leads. Maybe there are more letters and more clues. I need to know the rest of their story."

"Agreed," he said. "You need to set the record straight, and I need to have an adventure to share with my son."

Curiosity spurred Emma to ask, "Speaking of your son, how old is he?"

Logan's whole face lit up when talking about his little boy, bringing an endearing softness to his rugged features. "He's six, but he looks more like he's nine."

"Ah, he must take after you, McGiant," she said without thinking. She had a bad habit of doing that. Speaking out loud whatever random thought was passing through her mind at that moment. Probably from a lifetime of talking to herself as she worked through a story. It used to drive Mark crazy with embarrassment and disapproval.

"McWhat?" Logan's brows drew together in an amused arch, looking anything but embarrassed or disapproving.

"Whoops." She laughed and hoped her face didn't flush as pink as it felt. A firm believer in an honest and direct approach, she decided to spill it. "That's what I first thought of when I saw you in the emergency room," she admitted. "Here I was scared enough after having gone through my near-death ordeal with King Triton trying to turn me into fish bait, then I see you standing there, looking like Dr. McDreamy meets the Jolly Green Giant." She shrugged. "What can I say? McGiant was born."

"McDreamy?" His eyes widened, and he looked genuinely surprised.

Of course, he would have to focus on that part of her admission. "Come on, Doc. You're a doctor and you've got all that going on." She swept her hand up and down, gesturing from his head to his toes. "You can't tell me you don't get this all the time from the single women in town. I bet they don't even have to be single. I bet you get this from the entire female species in general. I'm surprised you're still single."

His face looked comically confused.

"Wow, you really are out of practice." She chuckled. "How long has it been?" Well, crap, there she went again.

This time a telltale flush crept up *his* face. "Pretty much six years." That warranted a big sip of his wine.

She couldn't help but gape at him. "You're kidding."

He winced. "Do I look like I'm kidding?"

"Actually no, you look like you're in pain."

"You don't have any filters, do you?" He stared at her with amazement.

"Unfortunately, no. Sorry," she said with a sheepish expression. She took a big sip of her own drink to shut herself up, but her incessant curiosity won out again. "I'm sorry, I can't help myself. I don't want to pry, but do you mind if I ask why? I'm only asking because you have so much going for you. You seem like a great catch. I find your situation fascinating."

"It's okay," he finally said with a quiet tone as if he were seriously pondering her question. "I'm not sure why I'm still alone. I guess it's hard not to blame myself for my wife's death."

Emma's heart melted. "Survivor's guilt. I've heard of that." She softened her tone. "But you shouldn't blame yourself." She put her hand over his and squeezed gently. "You're a doctor, not God. From what you've said," and what she'd read, "It was a tragic accident. There was nothing anyone could have done to stop the bleeding in time." A funny look she couldn't quite read crossed his face, but he remained silent, staring down at their hands. "Look at what a fantastic job you've done raising your son. I say it's time you put yourself out there again."

His gaze met hers. "I say maybe you should follow your own advice."

She pulled her hand away from his and played with the napkin in front of her. "Kind of hard without closure. My...I don't even know what to call him. Ever since Mark disappeared, he took my trust along with him. Trust in myself, trust in men, trust in love. And that was only six months ago. I can't imagine six years. I don't even know if I believe in love these days anyway."

"Oh, it exists. I had it." Logan sighed, sounding wistful yet full of regret. "Amanda was my soul-mate. I'm pretty sure you only find that once."

"Like I said, you never know unless you try." He really did seem like a great guy. She felt bad he was still punishing himself.

"About this Mark of yours." Logan steered the subject back to her in a classic avoidance tactic she knew all too well. "I don't want to alarm you or anything, but how do you know something didn't happen to him?"

Her heart squeezed painfully. "Believe me, I looked into every possible lead," she managed to get out. "All I know for certain is that he cleaned out his bank account and disappeared. It was obviously panic driven." She swallowed hard, still having a difficult time processing it all. Was she really that bad to live with? "I don't get it. We were fine. Everything was good. If he didn't want to be married to me, all he had to do was say so. I would much rather he have officially ended our engagement than leave me hanging, wondering what happened to him and whether or not we are still engaged."

"The way I see it, it's his loss. It's not like Lois Lane is a serial killer, so don't sell yourself short." He nodded sternly, and she shook her head on a small laugh. "I hope I'm not crossing the line by asking this," he added almost hesitantly. "If you're not officially un-engaged, then where's your ring?"

"You're fine. You certainly haven't crossed the line any more than I have." She shrugged. "The more you get to know me, you'll discover I tend to be a bit impulsive. I was so angry when I first got here, that I threw my ring in the ocean the night I found the bottle. As far as I'm concerned, we're un-engaged, but I'm afraid I will never have closure and be free to move on with my life without telling him that to his face."

Logan nodded in understanding. "There's so much I wish I could say to Amanda. I never even got to say goodbye. At least your Mark is alive."

"He won't be for long if I ever find him." She downed the rest of her drink in one gulp.

Logan studied her for a moment before asking, "What if he comes back with a good excuse someday? Have you written him off completely?"

"First of all, that's highly unlikely. Secondly, I don't forgive or forget easily. It would have to be one hell of an excuse. What about you?"

Logan's face took on a sad expression. "I don't think my wife is going to come back from the dead."

Dammit! She mentally smacked herself. "I didn't mean that. I know she was your soul-mate, but she doesn't have to be the only wife, girlfriend, or whatever you ever have. You deserve to be happy, Logan, whatever that entails."

"I could say the same thing to you." He pointed at her knowingly. "I still have some unanswered questions of my own. Guess I'm not ready to move on until I get closure, either, which will probably never happen." He stared off into the distance. "I guess we're both screwed."

"Well, we're quite the messed-up pair, aren't we?" She blew out a breath that fluttered her hair.

"Which is exactly why this adventure is so important." He stared at her with intense eyes that unnerved her.

"Agreed." She nodded with conviction while returning his stare, no matter how unsettling it was.

"We're going to do this again on my next day off, right?" he asked with hopeful excitement ringing loud and clear in his voice, as if he had a lot riding on this. In a way, she guessed they both did.

"Was there ever any doubt?" She grinned wide, and he matched her smile-for-smile. Her stomach flipped like it had this morning, but some nagging voice in her brain told her she was fooling herself if she thought it had anything at all to do with indigestion.

A FEW DAYS later dawned sunny and calm. The days were getting longer and the mid-July temperatures finally warming up. Logan hadn't seen Emma for a few days since he'd had to work, and she was researching Kathleen and Joseph's story. He had to admit he'd missed her company. She was so easy to talk to. He had shared more with her in the short time he had known her than he had with anyone. At times Logan found himself opening up before he even realized what was happening.

He couldn't stop smiling as he carried their supplies onto his father-in-law's boat. Barry kept his thirty-five-foot red and white express cruiser in the marina. The motorboat was meant for entertaining but was capable of having a fishing outing onboard, as well as being fast enough to pull a water-skier. Logan's son Trevor loved going for boat rides with Grandpa Barry. Sometimes they spent the night on the boat with its social cockpit and roomy salon.

Logan turned on the radio as he waited for Emma to arrive. He stored some essential supplies like extra blankets and flashlights in the maple finished interior cabinetry, as well as a few snacks, then he secured the cooler in a corner out of the way. The boat was a beauty, with its fully enclosed fiberglass head with shower, mirror, vanity and sink with storage below. Making his way back to the helm seat with flip-up bolster, he admired the molded fiberglass sport spoiler and overhead lighting.

He thought of his son once more, his mind never far from him, and felt a pang of longing. If Trevor were here now, he'd be out on the extended swim platform or the forward deck sun pad, peeking through the rails. If Logan didn't know better, he'd swear Trevor had been born with fins and gills. That was definitely a trait Amanda had possessed, same as her father. Living near the water, Logan had learned how to operate a boat, but that didn't mean he was all that fond of the ocean. Not after nearly drowning as a child. Logan had never been the best swimmer and he'd seen first-hand the damage a jellyfish sting could do to a man, let alone a shark attack. Eying his medical kit secured in another corner gave him reassurance.

"Am I late?" Emma hopped on board the *Mandy Marie.*

Barry bought this boat after Amanda died, naming his new baby after his only child. He adored this boat almost as much as he had her. He never minded when Logan borrowed it, but that didn't mean Logan didn't feel the pressure to make sure he brought it back in one piece without so much as a scratch.

"Not at all." Logan focused on the task at hand. Taking Emma's windbreaker, he set it on one of the seats and then handed her a life vest that matched his own. He spotted her hand as she took the vest from him. "What happened to your stitches?"

"I took them out. It's not the first time I've had stitches, and I could tell they were ready to come out. Several had come loose and my skin itched as it was healing. You did a good job, Doc. See?" She held out her hand for his inspection.

He studied her palm and had to agree it looked fine, but still. "You're a piece of work. Has anyone every told you that?"

"All the time." She winked.

He shook his head. "Are you ready to get going?"

"Absolutely." She slipped the vest on over her blue and white striped shirt and white cotton shorts, looking every bit the sailor and just as comfortable. This obviously wasn't the first time she had been on a boat, which eased his mind a little. "At least the weather is cooperating. It's a beautiful day for boating."

"I checked the weather. It's supposed to be sunny all day, the southwesterly winds only five miles per hour, so we should be good." He double-checked his own vest that he'd secured over his black polo shirt and tan cargo shorts. He glanced at her feet, making sure she had rubber bottomed shoes on that would be appropriate when walking on the deck. "I packed some extra survival supplies just in case, and we can always turn back if things start to look sketchy."

"Relax, Captain Worrywart." She patted his shoulder. "The island we're supposed to be going to doesn't look that far from what I could tell in my research."

"It's not," he confirmed, "but it's small and uninhabited. Besides you can never be too careful. I'm a doctor. I always take the necessary precautions."

"You can also never be too curious. I'm a journalist. I go where the story is, which can mean leaving at a moment's notice. Sometimes you have to be spontaneous. Have a little fun." She swatted him on the butt. "You can't always play it so safe."

He sat there, stunned for a moment, then laughed. "You're going to be the death of me yet, Lois."

"I'm hoping to be the *life* of you. You seriously need to loosen up and have some fun, Doc."

He sighed in resignation, knowing he wasn't going to win this debate, but he couldn't help chuckling. She sure made life entertaining, which is something he hadn't experienced in way too long. At least it would make the summer go by much quicker. Through their conversations, they were learning more and more about each other. They were two very different people with one common goal: seeing this adventure through. Even though she came from money and he'd had to work for everything he'd ever gotten, they had become unlikely friends.

He supposed he could relax a little, but it was hard. A while back, he'd gotten sick with a rare bacteria he'd picked up from the hospital. He'd slipped into a coma, and they weren't sure he would survive. He fought his way back and did survive, but that had changed him. He couldn't help thinking his son would have been left with no parent at all. Because of that, he took it upon himself to be extra careful, protecting himself, his son, his town...pretty much everyone. It was exhausting at times.

"Grab that line," he said, while shaking his head with a wry grin. She did as he requested, and moments later they were on their way.

"This is awesome," she shouted while standing beside him with her face lifted toward the warm rays of the sun as the wind whipped the auburn strands of her hair wildly about.

Just watching her enjoy herself made him relax, and soon he found himself laughing along with her. He sped up and went over waves just to hear her squeal. It didn't take long before they reached their destination. According to the map, this small island is where Kathleen and Joseph had secretly met. Beacon Bay was surrounded by a lot of small islands, many of which were uninhabited like this one. Logan pulled in as far as he could and cut the engine. The rocky bottom grew shallow and dangerous so they couldn't travel any closer, but he had a blowup dingy.

He said, "Drop that anchor while I blow up this dingy so we can go ashore."

"Okay," she replied with a snappy salute while he got busy.

When he was done blowing up the dingy, he set the anchor, and then, leaving everything on board except the map, a small shovel, and a couple bottles of water, he helped her into the small boat. Fifteen minutes later they rowed up on shore. Logan climbed out of the dingy and pulled it onto dry land, then reached out and helped Emma step from the boat.

"Thanks." She smiled, looking around in awe and a bit of fear if he wasn't mistaken. "This place looks so primal."

"I know. I can't imagine meeting here in the middle of the ocean in a place so remote. It remains uninhabited today, probably because it's so small. Its privacy had to be its appeal. Kathleen and Joseph's chances of getting caught would have been cut down drastically."

"Trust me, after what I read, privacy was a necessity. From what I gathered during my research, Joseph was the only son with three sisters. His parents were prominent members of society, having made their money in the shipbuilding business. In fact, they are the ones who started the company that made your father-in-law's boat."

"No kidding?" Logan marveled. Small world. "What a coincidence."

"I know, right?" She shook her head. "Anyway, they came from the upscale end of the coast, if you know what I mean. They would never have allowed their son to associate with someone like Kathleen. After the scandal she caused and where she lived, there's no way they would have made things easy for them. Hence, this desolate rendezvous spot."

"Desperate times call for desperate measures, and all that, I guess."

"Exactly. So where to now, Doc?"

He pulled out the map and studied it. "Well, it looks like we make our way inland."

She eyed the woods, the humor from her face all but gone and major trepidation taking its place. "Oh, the woods again. Yay me."

"It's okay, Emma. I'm here, and you can bet I damn sure won't let anything bad happen to you." That had pretty much been his mantra since his wife died, but with Emma, it somehow took on a whole new meaning and he was too afraid to examine why.

"You know what?" Emma studied him, the fear in her eyes all but gone, as a calm yet eager expression took its place. "I believe you."

That made him smile. "Good. Because the last thing we need is a *Misses* Worrywart."

Their eyes met briefly and something indescribable passed between them, then they both quickly looked away.

"No problem there, Doc. I'm the cool one, remember?" Emma's laugh sounded forced, as if she was just as much freaked out as he was over the bizarre chemistry humming between them. "Let's get going before our daylight is gone."

"You won't get an argument from me there." He led the way with the map in hand, excited for the first time in a long time to see what was around the bend.

7

PRESENT DAY: BEACON BAY, MAINE

L ogan and Emma came to a small, rundown cabin not far from the shore, and the first doubts of the day crept through her mind, though she'd never admit it to Dr. Worry-wart. The island was uninhabited, but obviously someone owned it. There was a sign that read condemned, do not enter on the front door.

"This must be the place," he said. He carried the map and shovel while she carried the water.

"I repeat, it's very primitive," she responded, still trying to figure out their next move. Maybe the treasure was buried outside like before, but that would mean the area they would have to dig would be that much greater. The map wasn't clear. It showed an X where the cabin was built.

"Primitive, yes, but it's also been *how* long?" Logan pointed out logically. "I think the cabin has held up fairly well, given the circumstances. Though as you can see it's not safe, given the sign on the door."

"Joseph must have built this one room shack for the two of them to meet in." Emma walked around the log cabin that was barely more than an enclosed bedroom, trying to put herself in

Kathleen's shoes. What must it have been like for her, so lonely and desperate for human affection? Emma imagined she would have done just about anything for someone she loved. In fact, she had. She'd searched high and low for Mark, and she wasn't even sure she had ever really loved him. At least not like Kathleen had loved Joseph or Logan had loved Amanda, she realized, shooting him a quick glance.

He was traipsing around the cabin, looking for a spot to dig to no avail. Emma paused. There was what had to be an outhouse next to the cabin that had caved in long ago, and Lord knew what resided in it these days. She shuddered, avoiding that contraption at all costs. Taking a deep breath, she set down her bottles of water and reached for the door to the cabin. Maybe their answers lay inside the lovers' cocoon.

"Are you crazy?" Logan appeared by her side instantly as he dropped the shovel and grabbed her hand.

They both looked at their entwined fingers and dropped their arms.

Emma cleared her throat, both frazzled and frustrated. "You're out of your mind and obviously don't know me if you think I would come all this way, through the forest no less, and *not* go inside."

"Oh, I'm beginning to know you all too well. You don't think before you act, do you?" He looked exasperated with her. "That sign is there for a reason. This place is probably a death trap. Yes, we came all this way for some answers, but we certainly didn't come here to die. You obviously don't know *me* because I would never risk your life."

"Good Lord, you really are uptight, aren't you?" she responded, because she hated admitting when she was wrong. "I know exactly who you are, so trust me, okay? We're not going to die. I'm an adult. I can compromise. We're just going to peek inside. See what we can see. Maybe that's what the X means."

A muscle pulsed in his rugged jaw, but then he sighed. "And if we see nothing, we dig outside, deal?"

"Deal."

Logan stepped in front of Emma and carefully opened the door. A whiff of musty air greeted them, followed by the scent of maple and pine and a faint lingering of something flowery. Peeking inside, they saw a solid bed and a sturdy dresser and a beautifully crafted rocking chair.

Carpenters of long ago obviously took pride in their work and spent the time necessary to make their creations stand the test of time. That aside, there was nothing treasure worthy in that cabin. Or at least nothing she could see from outside. She needed to get inside and look around.

Emma set her jaw with determination. "I know the treasure's in there, buried somewhere. You know we have to go inside, right?" she said, not really asking.

He sighed. "Of course, Lois. Your wish is my command." Logan bowed at the waist. "Because if I say no, you're not going to listen to me anyway, are you?"

"You're finally getting it, McGiant. Be glad we didn't live back then because unlike Kathleen, I probably wouldn't have been able to keep my mouth shut, and they would have stoned me to death"

"I don't doubt that at all." He chuckled and laughed harder when she playfully swatted him on the arm. He turned to her and pointed his finger in her face, removing the smile from his lips. "I'm doing this for you, Emma. So please promise me you won't follow. I need to know someone I care about will live to tell my son why I was such a fool."

She blinked. "Well, when you put it that way, I have no choice. Don't die, you big lug." She gave into impulse and kissed his cheek.

Now he was the one to blink and then cleared his throat. "I don't plan on it. Someone has to get you home in one piece."

"Not to mention your father-in-law's boat," she couldn't resist adding.

He groaned. "Thanks for reminding me."

"Call it life insurance." She shrugged.

Logan painstakingly made his way throughout the cabin, searching every nook and cranny with Emma looking on. He seemed like he was about to give up and head out, when Emma noticed the headboard. She'd seen one of those before on another story she'd covered not long ago. Her heart started beating with excitement.

"Logan, wait."

He looked at her curiously.

"Check the headboard. I've seen this type before on a story I covered about storage wars. There was a big fight over an ancient headboard found inside one storage unit. The panel on the front was a door to a secret compartment inside. This might have the same thing, and maybe our treasure got overlooked."

"The odds of that are slim, but I'll give it a try."

Logan tapped all around the panel and jiggled the front until finally it moved an inch. He shot her a look of surprise, and Emma's heart started pounding with excitement. This had to be it. He shoved harder and the front slid open just enough. She couldn't control the gasp that slipped out as she stared at another intricately carved wooden box like the one they'd dug up under the tree in the woods.

Logan lunged and grabbed the box then darted outside as if his heart was pumping furiously and he was totally freaked-out. "I made it!" he breathed out on a whoosh.

She snorted. "Sorry, I can't help it. You're so dramatic. This isn't an Indiana Jones movie. The cabin isn't going to cave in because you stole its treasure." She doubled over into full-blown laughter.

"You're so bad." He couldn't help but laugh right along with her.

She rolled her eyes. "You have no idea, Doc. Something tells me you need to be a bit *bad* yourself." She grabbed the box from him without even asking. "You never know, I might rub off on you."

"Help yourself." He stared at his empty hands, ignoring her last comment.

"I already did," she responded absently, fully focused on the treasure she cradled in her palms.

Joseph mentioned in his letters that he started out whittling and carving as something to do to take his mind off what he was going through, but it was clear by the boxes he'd carved for Kathleen that his hobby had turned into a labor of love. Each box had something different on the cover: a pine tree, a light-house, this cabin. Emma traced the cabin reverently and then carefully opened the box. Sure enough, there were more letters inside and another map.

"Thank God." She breathed a sigh of relief.

"More like thank King Triton for letting us pass his waters unscathed," Logan pointed out.

"You really are worried, aren't you?" She looked up at him with a serious expression, all kidding aside.

"I kind of have to be. I'm a widower and a father and a doctor. What in the world did you expect?"

"Honestly? A beast of a giant who looks like he would take no prisoners. I bet that was someone you once were, especially having been an orphan who had to work his hardest for every-thing he's ever gotten." She could tell by the way he was looking at her that she was right. "I'm close, aren't I?"

"Too close," he answered truthfully. "That was exactly who I used to be. There was a time I wouldn't have second guessed anything. I would have just acted and reacted and lived, kind of like you do. But the harsh reality of life taught me to be more cautious. First my wife died, and then I almost died. Can you imagine what that would have done to Trevor?" Logan's words said one thing, but the expression on his face revealed doubt, as if for the first time ever he wondered if he was doing himself and his son a disservice.

"Don't worry, Doc." She relented, her heart melting for the big, tough softy with a boatload of responsibility that made him worry way too much. "I can tell you're a great father, Logan." She touched his cheek. "You'll work through your issues; I know you will. And the way I live hasn't worked out so well for me, so maybe you're on to something. Maybe I need to take a page out of your book." She laughed out loud over the horrified look he gave her. "On second thought, probably not. I'm honest enough to admit I would never survive, so I guess I'm doomed to a life of chaos and loneliness."

His lips twisted. "I've never quite heard it put that way, but thanks for the vote of confidence. And I'd say you've done pretty well for yourself by the looks of things." He tucked a strand of her flyaway hair behind her ear, and she sucked in a sharp breath. "Chaotic loneliness beats boring loneliness any day, but at least my son's safe. I'm sure you'll work through your issues as well."

"We're good for each other. Who knows?" She cleared her throat and shrugged. "Maybe this summer will help us both."

"Maybe so," he responded, though his face said he doubted it. "In the meantime, I'm starving. Let's take our treasure back to the boat and read the letters over lunch."

"Now there's something we can agree on." She relaxed, feeling more like herself.

"Will wonders never cease?" The crow's feet at the corners of his eyes made him look even more handsome. "Maybe we stand a chance of surviving this summer after all."

～

"I was wrong. We're never going to survive this summer because we're never getting off this island." Logan stared at the empty ocean before him. "Where the hell is the Mandy Marie? She's not exactly a small boat. She couldn't have just disappeared." He dropped the shovel they hadn't even needed this time and took a swig of water, trying to fight the anguish he felt over possibly losing his father-in-law's boat. The waves had picked up. There was no way they were taking the dingy out into that.

"I lowered the anchor like you told me. Did I do something wrong?" Emma looked devastated over the thought she might be at fault.

"No, it was my fault," he was quick to reassure her. "I didn't set the anchor well enough, apparently. I use a plow anchor because it's good for many types of bottoms, from rock to sand, but it must have come loose. Dammit, I shouldn't have been in such a hurry to get to shore. I should have made sure the anchor was secure."

"We both were in a hurry. It's no big deal. I'll use my phone to call someone." She set down the treasure box and pulled out her smart phone from her back pocket and held it up triumphantly.

"Except it *is* a big deal." He plunged a hand through his tangled curls. "All of our supplies were on that boat. Not to mention if any damage happens to that, my father-in-law is going to be devastated. I can't do that to him."

"Uh oh." Emma chewed her bottom lip which he was coming to realize was never a good sign.

"Yeah, uh oh." Logan laughed harshly. "He's going to have my head."

"Not that kind of uh oh. I mean, *Oh no, uh oh!*"

Logan frowned. "What could be worse than losing the Mandy Marie?"

Emma winced. "Um, being stuck on this creepy, deserted island with no cell service."

"Oh shit." Logan could feel his face drain of color.

"No shit." Emma joined him.

"Okay, let's not lose our heads over this," he said, knowing one of them had to be strong and not freak out.

"Easier for you to say. That jungle looks scary enough in the daylight. I'm not going in there at night." Her almond-shaped, amber eyes were wide with fright.

"We won't have to." He grabbed her shoulders and looked her in the eye, hoping to sound reassuring. "We'll stay out here on the shore."

"Animals come out at night, and it still gets cold after dark. Oh my God, I'm so stupid. This was such a bad idea."

"It wasn't a bad idea, and you didn't make it alone." He squeezed her arms gently until she looked at him. "I'll build a fire. It will keep the animals away and keep us warm."

"How? We don't have matches." Her eyes weren't so wild-looking now, but fear still laced her words.

"I'll build it with my bare hands, some sticks and moss. My son Trevor started Cub Scouts this year. I'm the proud father of a Tiger Cub and went a little overboard on my research." He shrugged, a little embarrassed, but it must have worked because she no longer looked afraid.

"A man after my own heart." She inhaled a few deep breaths, nodded with determination, and then said, "What can I do to help?"

"That's my girl." He laughed when she curtsied. "Well, first we need to find some tinder. That's basically anything that is dry, fibrous, and will take a spark or "catch" and ignite. Pocket lint, feather down, dried mosses, and shredded plant fibers such as cedar bark would work. Use your imagination. I'll gather some firewood while you do that, okay?"

"Okay. It's not dark yet, so I'll be fine, right?" She looked at the setting sun with its beautiful yellows, oranges, and reds reflecting off the rolling waves of the ocean lapping at the shore, and trepidation rather than admiration filled her gaze.

"You've got this, Lois." He rubbed her back. "Don't go far."

"You don't have to worry about that." She grunted and ambled off reluctantly.

Logan tried to remember everything he'd learned from his research. He knew he needed to avoid laying the wood on the ground since it might be damp, especially from the tide and the ocean spray. Searching the area, he found some dead branches that had broken off big trees but got caught in the lower branches and never hit the ground. He snapped off a few that looked dead, but a couple were bendy which meant they were still alive. Those he left alone because they wouldn't be dry enough. When he had his stack, he made a makeshift pallet to hold his supplies.

Next, he went in search of several handfuls of kindling. Avoiding green wood because he knew it wouldn't burn well, he chose tiny pieces of wood in various lengths and thicknesses and placed them on his pallet. Then he went in search of firewood. Lots of pieces about as thick as his arm.

Emma returned with her arms full. "No pocket lint in my stylish outfit, Doc, but I did find some featherdown, dried moss, cedar bark, cattails, and dead leaves."

"Excellent." Using the small fiber of cattail, which would ignite his tinder, and the thicker fiber of dry leaves on the outside as shelter, he made a nest. Then he made a cotton ball size piece of the tinder and set it aside, leaving a hole in the center of the nest for the coals he would make.

"I'm impressed." She stood with her arms crossed, looking down at him.

"Don't be. I've never actually done this before. I just read about it."

"You're smart. How hard can it be?"

"Harder than you think." He got to his feet and headed for the woods once more.

"What are you doing?" Her voice sounded panicked again.

"Making a bow. I won't be long, I promise."

"What can I do?"

"Make a fire board. Make sure the wood is light and dry and doesn't have sap. It should be soft enough to dent with your thumbnail without gouging. We'll need a piece about an inch thick, a couple inches across and about a foot long."

"I'm on it." She disappeared into the woods as well.

Moments later, Logan found the perfect piece of green, bendable wood that was slightly curved for his bow. He'd read a lighter bow would be easier to control and would take less strength to push back and forth. Sitting by the fire pit, he pulled a shoelace from his sneaker and attached it to his bow, leaving a little slack in the lace so he would be able to twist the drill into the bow.

Emma came bounding back out of the woods, looking only a little freaked out, but curious and exhilarated. "Voila! Will this do?"

He took the board from her and inspected it. "This looks like it will work."

"So does your bow. You should be a Den Master. I bet you'd be good at it, and I'm sure your son would worship you."

"Trust me, I'm not Den Master material...yet." He winked. "I hope this works. Now time to make the drill."

"That sounds scary and difficult."

"Nah. This part should be the easiest." He'd found a straight piece of Maple that was one inch thick, which was better for a smaller person like Emma, but it would have to do for a big guy like himself. The top was shaped like a pencil head while the bottom was flat to gain the right amount of friction.

"What else can I do so I don't feel helpless?"

"Trust me, you're not helpless. You're doing great and I couldn't do this without you. We need to make a socket. Look for a rock that's about the size of a fist. Not too small if possible because it can heat up very quickly. Try to find one with a deep dimple and smooth sides if you can."

While Logan waited for Emma, he made a teepee out of wood over his nest. He layered the tinder, then small sticks, followed by larger sticks, putting them at right angles with spaces between so the coal could breathe.

"How's this?" Emma squatted down beside him. She handed him the rock and studied what he'd done. "You might just pull this off."

"Well, here goes nothing."

He found a spot on his fireboard with a notch in the side that would work as a chimney. Then he threaded his drill through the shoelace on his bow and then placed his drill next to the chimney and rested his foot on the board to hold it in place. Setting the rock socket on top, he pushed down and held the drill in place while he pulled back and forth on the bow, sawing faster and faster to burn a hole into his fireboard.

When black powder and smoke came from the bottom of his bow, she said, "It's working!"

He stopped and grabbed the bark to catch the coals. Putting it under the chimney, he placed his drill in the burnt hole again. He started pushing and pulling on the bow, and pushing down on the socket until he got into a rhythm, and then he went faster.

"You've got it. Keep going. You're doing great, Doc."

Black powder started collecting in the chimney, so he kept going until he saw smoke.

"Oh my God, I think you've done it." She shook his shoulders in her excitement.

His lips tipped up slightly as he moved the drill and the fireboard and sure enough an ember lay on the bark. Carefully lifting it, he gently blew on it until it burned brighter, then he transferred it to his tinder and kept blowing until the tender ignited. He added his twigs until the wood finally caught.

"I can't believe that actually worked," he said in wonder.

"I can't believe you did that from memory," she said in awe. "You're more than smart. You're a genius!" She held her hands over the warmth of the fire. "Now what?"

"Now we eat."

She frowned and gave him a hard look. "I'm not a vegetarian or anything, but I am *not* eating squirrel, I can tell you that much."

He fought a grin. "Well, I'm not much of a hunter, so I'd say you're safe. I saw some berries we can eat when I was looking for the wood."

"Berries sound great."

They took their waters and walked together until they came to an open spot inside the woods. Sitting down in the berry patch, they ate their fill of the wild raspberries and blueberries because they didn't have anything to carry them back to the fire with. Finishing their water, they looked at each other and laughed. Her white shorts and striped shirt were stained with grass and berries, while his black polo shirt was ripped and sweat-stained and his tan cargo shorts were covered in dirt and ash.

"That should hold us for the night." He got to his feet and reached out to help her up.

She took his hand and stood, looking around the nearly dark area warily. Birds weren't chirping as much as they settled down in their nests for the night, but other animals were starting to scurry about, snapping twigs and rustling leaves. "Now to find a bathroom. It's getting too late to go back to the cabin, and I highly doubt the outhouse I saw is equipped for humans."

Logan pointed to a tree. "Mother Nature's finest."

She looked horrified for a moment but then straightened her spine like the trooper she was. "If Kathleen could do this, then so can I." Emma paused long enough to thrust her finger in his direction. "But if I get poison ivy on my nether regions, you're a dead man."

"Lucky for you, I'm a doctor."

"A doctor who's not getting anywhere near my nether regions, thank you very much." She spun her finger, gesturing for him to turn around. "No peeking."

He turned his back, fighting another smile. "Poison ivy's the least of your worries. I'll keep watch for critters."

She gasped.

He couldn't stop the chuckle this time, so he coughed hard to cover it up. "You'll be fine."

She did her duty in record time and then charged past him, clearly on a mission. "Meet you back at camp."

"Wait," he hollered after her. "Who's going to watch out for me?"

"Why, Mother Nature, of course. I'm sure you'll be fine." She didn't miss a beat, not so much as sparing him a backward glance.

When he was finished preparing for the night, he returned to camp to see she had covered the ground next to the fire with some ferns she'd found. "Not bad," he said with a smile. She'd known enough not to use the dingy in case a spark burned a hole in it. As much as he didn't want to take it out on the ocean and try to row all the way back to Beacon Bay, it was their only means of escape if it came to that. He glanced around, assessing the situation as realization dawned with a bit of dread. "Now, where's my bed?"

"We're sharing one. I'm no doctor, but even I know without blankets, we need body heat to keep warm. It still gets pretty chilly at night. Besides, I don't bite."

His smiled slipped. She was right, of course, but he hadn't snuggled up to a woman in a long time. And dirty or not, Ms. Emma Hendricks was one fine-looking female, and he was a heavy sleeper. He still dreamt about his wife often. Emma might not bite, but he couldn't guarantee he wouldn't.

8

PRESENT DAY: BEACON BAY, MAINE

E mma was dreaming about Mark at some point in the wee hours of the morning, her brain foggy with sleep. She was warm and toasty, wrapped in a pair of strong arms with her head resting on one shoulder and bicep while the other arm was draped over her mid-section. Her back was pressed against a hard chest and flat stomach while her bottom was snuggled tight against an even harder part of his anatomy.

Her lips tipped up in her sleep and she wiggled her fanny more snugly against him. He slid his hand up her stomach and cupped her breast. Oh, how she'd missed this. The intimacy and closeness. The feel of being held in a man's arms. The feeling of being safe and protected. Yes, she was all about being independent and taking care of herself, but not at the expense of loneliness. It felt wonderful to be cradled and cherished. Mark had been gone for so long. She couldn't remember where he went, but he was back now and better than ever.

He'd put on size and was bigger than she remembered. He kissed her neck and kept alternating between gently kneading her breast and stroking her nipple with his thumb. Shivers ran through her as incredible sensations traveled down her stomach to pulse deep within her womb. Stretching in his arms, she rolled over and kissed him. He responded immediately by tipping her onto her back and slipping his tongue between her lips to dance with her own.

Fireworks went off and feelings more powerful than any she'd ever felt exploded throughout her body. She spread her knees and wrapped her legs around him, holding on tight as he ground against her. He tasted of berries and smelled faintly of wood smoke, she realized, as her arms snaked around his neck to slip into his thick curls. *Curls?* Two things suddenly hit her: she wasn't sleeping on a bed and this sure as hell wasn't Mark.

She pulled her lips away and opened her eyes to lock with a set of shocked dark espresso ones.

"What's up, Doc?" She choked on a laugh. Humor and sarcasm were her defense mechanisms when she was nervous, and right now mortification wasn't a strong enough word for how she was feeling.

"I'm pretty sure you can tell exactly what's up," he muttered as he rolled off her and sat up to plunge his hands through his hair and scrub his face. "I am *so* sorry."

"Don't be." She sat up next to him. "I'm the one who attacked you," she admitted grudgingly, feeling her cheeks heat.

His hands stilled. "Are you sure? Because I was having one incredible dream."

"Me, too." Her eyes met his. "Only I thought it was about Mark."

"Guilty. I thought I was making love to Amanda, and if you hadn't woken up, I most definitely would have made love to you." His gaze dropped to her swollen lips, and the look of longing he gave her nearly had her jumping back into his arms.

"Lonely people do crazy things, Doc." She swallowed hard, desperately trying to get the feel of his hands caressing her body and how good it had felt from her brain. "Guess we dodged a bullet with that one."

"For the record that was, um, the nicest way I've woken up in a very long time." Sincerity rang through in his kind voice, his tone gentle as though trying to ease her embarrassment.

He really was so easy to be around and talk to, she suddenly couldn't imagine spending this summer alone. He'd made her realize she needed a friend. Even though under different circumstances she probably never would have been friends with someone like him, she now couldn't imagine spending this summer with anyone else.

Except it was going to be hard not to keep reliving that incredible *dream*.

"Thanks, Doc." She winked, feeling more like herself with a little teasing. "Same here, but it's probably best we don't share a bed again unless you want another child. I'm not on the pill anymore. Up until this morning, I didn't think I needed to be." She laughed, trying to lighten the mood.

That sobered him up in a hurry, and his amusement faded away. "No, I don't want any more children. Not now or ever."

She frowned and stared at him curiously. "Can I ask why?"

He raised a brow at her. "Can I stop you?"

"Probably not." She shook her head, unable to stop her grin.

"I didn't think so. Let's just say children are a gift but a hazard to one's health. At least my children are. Amanda was small like you, and like you love to point out, I'm a giant. Medically speaking that doesn't equal a good mix when delivering a baby."

"Oh, I don't know. I've always heard it depends on how wide your hips are, not on how big or small you are."

He smiled despite himself. "I think you mean your pelvis. Not your hips."

"And there's always a scheduled C-section, so there's still

hope for you, Doc," she said, glossing over his comment. "I mean if you wanted a brother or sister for Trevor, that is."

"I grew up an only child and so did Amanda. We turned out just fine."

"That's debatable," Emma couldn't resist adding but then admitted, "although, I grew up with a brother and a sister, and I'm just as messed up as you are." She sighed. "I didn't know if I wanted children because I've always been so focused on my career, but getting stranded out here has made me see I don't want to die without leaving a legacy behind me. I know, stupid, right?"

"Not at all." He was a great listener: looking her in the eye, not trying to interrupt, and actually caring about what she had to say. He nodded in agreement. "I get that. This kind of experience can be life-changing. I see it all the time in my line of work. Makes a person want to put down roots, marry, and have a family."

"I could care less about having a husband. I haven't exactly had much luck with men and don't really like them at the moment. No offense. But maybe I'll adopt a baby someday, or go to one of those sperm banks and have my own child. I could pick out a gorgeous, smart guy, who has an adventurous spirit." She eyed him, thinking he fit the bill perfectly, now that she thought about it, but then she sighed with resignation. He was too damaged to ever entertain the idea; besides, she had a career to save and they were just friends. At least she thought they were. Actually, she didn't really understand *what* they were.

"You should do it," he said with encouragement in his tone. "Like I said: children are a gift, and you certainly don't need a husband to have one these days. I can't imagine my life without Trevor. I never dreamed I'd have to imagine my life without his mother."

"Speaking of Amanda, I hope the Mandy Marie is okay. I'm

going to see if I can find a signal to call for help." Emma stood up and pulled out her phone.

"I'll pick up around camp. Holler if you find anything."

"I will." She wandered off down the beach, holding her phone high with no luck.

There had to be a way to get a signal. She glanced around and saw a tree that looked like she might be able to climb it. Anything for a story, she reminded herself. No, she was not the outdoorsy type, but how hard could climbing a tree be? Tucking her phone in her back pocket, she started grabbing branches and pulling herself up. Finding footholds and new branches to grab, she kept climbing and climbing and climbing until she reached the top.

It was breezier up here, and the view was spectacular: miles of ocean with white caps from cresting waves in one direction and miles of treetops in various shades of green in the other direction with a cloudless baby-blue sky above. Grinning triumphantly, pride filled her over accomplishing her goal. Glancing down to let Logan know where she was, she let out a little yelp.

She'd had no idea the tree was that high. It had to be twenty-five or thirty feet. Terrified, she didn't have a clue how she was going to get down. Dr. Worrywart was going to kill her if she didn't die by her own hand first. She took several deep breaths and told herself she could handle this. She'd made it this far; she might as well make the best of it.

Carefully pulling out her phone, she held it up and relief surged through her. She had a signal. A weak one, but a signal no less. She quickly called 911 and told them what happened and to send the Coast Guard. She had no clue where they were. She tried to describe the island and then she heard her battery beep several times before it went dead.

"Emma?" Logan called her name from down below, over and over.

She closed her eyes for a moment and then let out a breath of resignation, knowing this wasn't going to be pretty. "I'm up here."

She heard him stop walking. "Up where? I don't see you."

Holding tight to the branches, she inched her way down to a better vantage point and peeked through the leaves. "In the tree above you."

He looked up. "I still can't find you."

"Look higher."

"Higher? How much higher could you possibly go?" He shaded his eyes with his big hand and squinted. It took him a moment, but then he spotted her. His eyes sprang wide and he cursed. "You really are insane."

"Not insane, just impulsive, remember?"

"That's one word for it," he muttered, clearly not amused.

"The good news is, I got a signal and called for help," she went on, ignoring his comment that had carried on the wind. "I tried to describe the island but then my phone went dead. Hopefully I gave them enough details to find us before I die up here."

"That's not even funny."

"Seriously, Doc, I'm not trying to be funny. I'm actually terrified. How am I going to get down from here?"

"Same way you got up there. Climb."

"I can't," she snapped, even though she knew it wasn't his fault.

"Why not?" he sounded exasperated.

Nothing but silence hovered between them for a full beat. "I'm afraid," she finally admitted.

His whole face softened, making him look adorable and sweet and oh, so heroic. He seemed to think about that for a moment, and then he nodded more to himself, suddenly looking determined. "Okay. I'll come up and get you."

Heroic or not, she couldn't let him risk his own life because of her impulsive stupidity. She only had herself to think about. He had Trevor, and she knew how important that was to him. "Now *you're* the one who's talking crazy," she responded. "You're too big to climb trees. You'll kill us both."

"Well, someone didn't leave me much choice, now did she, Lois? Besides, I'm a Den Master in the making, remember?" He started climbing and the whole tree shook. Slipping a few times, he finally got a rhythm going.

"Be careful." She held on for dear life, reminding herself to breathe.

"I always am."

It seemed like forever before Logan reached her. "You okay?" He searched her eyes as he touched her cheek. She nodded, too afraid to speak. "Climb onto my back and hold on tight."

"Oh God, what if we're too heavy and the branches break?" she managed to get out, though she hated how weak her voice sounded.

"I'm strong. I've got you." His deep baritone was so reassuring, she clung to that for all she was worth.

Emma did as Logan asked and wrapped her arms and legs around him tightly, feeling his heart beat against her chest. It was up to her to hold on because he needed his arms and legs to climb down. No worries there. She plastered herself to him like a second layer of skin. He started to move, and she closed her eyes and held her breath, burying her face in the crook of his neck and not saying another word until they reached the bottom of the tree. Only when she knew they were safe, did she lift her head and let out an explosion of air and open her eyes.

"You can let go now," he said in a strangled voice, carefully peeling her death grip from around his neck and crouching down until her feet touched the ground.

"I'm sorry." She reluctantly released him and shook out her wobbly limbs.

"For what?" He eyed her curiously when he stood back up to face her.

"For being so stupid again."

"Impulsive, remember?" He tipped up her chin. "Besides, if you hadn't climbed that tree, there's no way you would have gotten a signal and we might have been stuck here forever. You might not think so, but you're a hero, too, Lois."

She knew he was being dramatic for her benefit. They did have the raft still, after all, but she would play along to reassure him she was okay even though she still felt shaky. "In that case, you're welcome." She couldn't help herself.

"Don't push it." He grunted in mock frustration, but couldn't quite hide the slight upturn of his full lips. "Let's go back by the fire and wait for help."

"Okay." She followed him but couldn't stop her hands from shaking.

They both sat by the fire he had rekindled. Ever the observant doctor, he must have recognized the signs of how rattled she was because he said, "We need a distraction."

"Like what?" she asked warily, wondering for an insane moment if he meant picking up where they'd left off this morning. Good God, her body had already started to respond at the mere thought of him touching her again. She prayed he wouldn't notice.

"Let's read the letters." He handed her the treasure box.

She blinked, completely having forgotten about why they were on the island in the first place. "Good idea." Relief slumped her shoulders and caused her to wilt. It had to be relief because if it wasn't relief, then it felt suspiciously like disappointment.

And disappointment meant she already cared about him more than she should. And caring about him equaled a whole new world of trouble she wasn't ready for.

OCTOBER 1942: *Beacon Bay, Maine*

Kathleen finished sealing the last of her canned goods for the winter with a sense of pride and satisfaction and then stored them on the shelves in her root cellar. Making her way up the stairs, she closed the door behind her and allowed herself a small smile. She'd grown her own food in her garden, caught her own fish, mended her clothes, and repaired her cottage all by herself.

She'd done it. She'd survived the summer on her own.

At times it had been lonely, but other times she'd felt a sense of peace and acceptance. This was her new life, and she was safe. She could wither up and cry her life away, or she could accept her fate and find a way to survive. She'd always been a fighter. In preparation for the winter, she'd canned seafood, fruits and vegetables, insulated her house the best she could, and cut down a massive amount of firewood. Her palms had the hardened blisters and calluses to prove it.

She walked outside onto her back deck and stared out at the ocean. The days were growing shorter, the temperatures colder, but the view was breathtaking. Fall was her favorite time of year. She loved the crisp air and the trees on the small islands just offshore were vibrant and beautiful with shades of orange, yellow, red, and burgundy dotting the landscape as if an artist had splattered the hillside with paints from a pallet.

It made Kathleen think of her students. She missed teaching those bright, eager faces and briefly wondered who her replacement might be and if they would care as much. But she'd long since given up on pining for things she had no control over. Shooting her favorite lighthouse one more look of appreciation, she went out front to get the mail.

Stopping short, she sucked in a breath. "Mother, what are you doing here?"

Sarah Reynolds was a replica of her daughter with sea-green eyes and caramel-brown wavy hair, only her eyes were faded and sad and her hair was now streaked with gray and hung to her waist. She left it long and free, in true artist fashion, and opted for flowing dresses and soft sweaters than more tailored skirts, blouses, and jackets like Kathleen. Today she wore a burnt orange, while Kathleen wore a sensible gray.

"I miss you," her mother said softly, wrapping her sweater more securely around her to ward off the chilly breeze. "We all do."

"Then you shouldn't have thrown me out," Kathleen responded, refusing to shiver over the cold or what her family had done to her. At her mother's stricken look, she relented by adding, "I miss you, too."

Sarah wrung her hands, not quite meeting Kathleen's eyes. "We didn't throw you out, dear. We couldn't have you living with us under the heavy weight of the scandal. You understand, don't you? We're not like you. We're simple folk. We have to live in this town. What will happen if no one buys our fish or our fruits and vegetables or my paintings anymore? We'll starve. It's not that we don't love you."

Kathleen wasn't angry anymore. She'd forgiven the townsfolk, her family, and even William. Holding onto her anger and resentment was toxic. It wouldn't do her any good, and it would only let them all know they had won. They had defeated her. She refused to be defeated. Letting all those feelings go had opened her up to a whole new world of possibilities.

"I understand perfectly, but it's fine, Mother." She tried for a smile.

Her mother's eyes watered. "Are you okay?"

"I'm surviving. It hasn't been easy, but I am learning more every day and surprising myself." Kathleen rubbed her arms through her cape. As confident as she might appear, she would be fooling herself if she didn't admit she was worried. "The real test will be getting through a harsh Maine winter."

"It's not too late you know."

Kathleen blinked and then narrowed her eyes. "For what?"

"To go back where you belong." Her mother took her hands in her own, and Kathleen smelled a mixture of baked bread and paint, making her long for home until the words her mother was speaking sank in. "William told me he's changed. He asked if I would speak with you on his behalf. He wants you back. He's willing to forgive you. He's a good man, Kathleen. You could do worse."

Forgive her? Kathleen pulled her hands from her mother's and fought the bile rising in her throat. "He's not a good man," she finally got out. "He's a monster just like his father. He might not like what he's become, but he can't help himself. He'll never change, and I'll never forgive him." She stared hard into her mother's eyes. "I can do better."

"But he loves you."

"He doesn't love me. He loves another. I wasn't his first choice, he settled for me because she's gone. I was his last hope for a family."

Sarah's brow puckered in confusion. "Do you mean Evelyn Baker the woman he dated in high school? But they were just children, and she left him to run off with that drifter. She broke William's heart. The whole town knows that. How does that make him a monster?"

"She didn't leave him for another man. She left him because

he beat her just like he did me. William couldn't handle it and tried to get her back. When she refused, he killed her in a fit of rage, and his father helped him cover it up." Kathleen confided in her mother because she knew she would be too afraid to say anything to anyone else, and she couldn't stand her family thinking highly of William. Maybe now they would understand why she'd left him and would never go back.

Sarah gasped and covered her mouth.

"William's father told everyone that Evelyn ran off with someone else so they would see William as the poor victim and have pity on him. Her parents had to move away from the shame of it all, never knowing the truth about what really happened to their daughter."

"That can't be right." Sarah was shaking her head and backing away from Kathleen as if she were the crazy one. "If that's true, then why hasn't William tried to kill you?"

"Who says he hasn't?" William standing over her, threatening to push her off her deck flashed through Kathleen's mind, and she tried not to flinch and cower.

Her mother's lips trembled, and she placed her fingertips to her mouth.

Kathleen relented enough to say, "And he won't." She knew her mother didn't want her dead. She was just a coward and would never stand up for her only daughter against the town. No matter how much she might think she loved her, the town was more powerful than she was. They both knew it. Sadness filled Kathleen because too much damage had been done. Even if her parents accepted her, she could never go back now.

"What makes you so sure William killed Evelyn?" Sarah asked on a whispered sob.

"Because he talks in his sleep, and I know where the body is buried," Kathleen reassured her as well as herself. Not a day went by that she didn't look over her shoulder in case William was crazy enough to kill her anyway.

"You must never tell anyone this. It will ruin you."

"More than I already am?" Kathleen laughed harshly. "Don't worry, Mother, I'm not going to cause more of a scandal than I already have for daring to stand up for myself. However, I will never go back to William, either. Please don't ask me to again, and you can tell him as much. If that's all you came for, I think we're finished here."

"No, I don't suppose you will go back to him, and now that I know the truth, I don't blame you." Sarah touched Kathleen's cheek as if for the last time, like she knew there was no going back now, either. Too much damage had been done. "If it's any consolation, I'm sorry. I wish I could be as strong as you, but I'm not. Please take care of yourself, my darling. I hope you find what you're looking for out here and be happy, or at least at peace. Goodbye, dear one."

That was the last time Kathleen Connor would ever speak to her mother.

9

K athleen watched her mother walk away with a heavy heart, feeling more alone than she ever had. She'd held on to a small grain of hope her family would welcome her back someday. She now knew that wasn't a possibility unless she took William back, and that was never going to happen. It was hard letting go for good.

She wished things could be different, but she knew they would never be. She had never felt like she belonged in her own family, but she wasn't ashamed of who she was. She wasn't sure what she was going to do with the rest of her life, but she somehow knew she was meant for something more. She wrote in her journal every day, hoping to be inspired. Now more than ever she needed to make a plan and move on with her life.

Opening her mailbox, Kathleen's lips parted. She was afraid to breathe.

Another letter.

She hadn't thought she would ever hear from Joseph Rutherford again after he knew who she was. Her hands trembled as she pulled out his letter and held it close to her aching chest like a lifeline. He had no idea how much she needed him. She hadn't even realized it until now. She might be lonely, but she somehow knew she wasn't alone anymore. That was enough to keep her strong and keep her going through what was sure to be tough times ahead. Taking the letter back out onto her deck, she sat in the wooden rocking chair her father had carved and assembled by hand and slowly opened it.

Dear Kathleen,

I cannot express my gratitude for you choosing to write me back when I'd needed someone the most. You have no idea how much hearing from home means to me. Your inclusion of the piece of pine from Beacon Bay was so thoughtful. Every time I smell it, I think of Maine, which now makes me think of you. It brings back so many memories of hunting with my father, playing in the woods with my sisters—I have three—when we were young, and inhaling the scent of my mother's homemade candles during the holidays. I can't help but anticipate maybe someday meeting you in person.

I know my family loves me in their own way, but they have a hard time showing it now that I am an adult. I live a life of luxury and ease, taking for granted all I have and admittedly thinking only of myself too often. I went against their wishes and chose not to work in my father's shipbuilding business, joining the navy to fight for my country instead. I simply wanted to grow up, become a man, and do my part. I've had friends who have died when they went abroad to help the allies. I couldn't live with myself if I stayed home and did nothing.

You asked how I felt about the war. Even after everything I've been through, I still believe the United States needed to get involved. Hitler and his Axis can't be allowed to keep doing the deplorable things he's done. I wasn't prepared when the war landed on my doorstep. I might forever be ruined because of my decision, but at least I will go to my grave with no regrets.

I don't know Beverly Sanderson but I know of her, and she comes from the same cloth as my parents, caring more about social standards than what's right or wrong. I will give her a chance to get to know me because it's the right thing to do, but that doesn't mean you and I can't be friends. I hope you don't mind my being frank, but I need you. Not in a physical way, but a spiritual way. You seem to understand me like no one else ever has, and your encouragement for me to keep going is inspiring, especially after everything you have been through.

Your words touched me deeply, and I wept for you. You are an amazing woman. So strong and independent. I know most people don't appreciate that. At one time I wouldn't have either, but after what I've seen and been through, I now realize how naïve and shallow I once was. The value of passion, honesty and the right to speak one's mind is invaluable.

Life is too goddamned short!

Pardon my language, but I feel as though I have known you since forever, and you will forgive me for the outburst. I don't even know what you look like, but you have a beautiful spirit. Don't let anyone try to stifle that or hold you back. You can and should do anything you want to. This is me encouraging you to keep going. Don't let them win. I know it's hard when it seems like the whole world is against you, but you are special. You have so much to offer. Please hold on to that and follow your dreams, whatever they may be.

I'm not due to come home for leave until next summer and not for good until the summer of 1945. There was a time I wondered if I would be able to make it until then, but you gave me the will to try. Only you. I will owe you a debt of gratitude for the rest of my life. You are a gift in my life, and I shall never take you for granted. I don't know what the future will bring with Beverly. I did send another letter to her at the correct address this time. We will see if she writes me back. I hope you are safe and well. If I see your husband upon my return, I honestly don't know what I will do to him for the harm he has caused you.

Be careful, my friend. Enjoy every day as if it were your last, and whatever you do, please don't stop writing to me.

Until tomorrow,

Joseph

KATHLEEN FOLDED the letter and couldn't stop smiling. She was startled to realize she had tears running down her cold cheeks. Joseph had not only written back; he had filled her with a newfound assurance that she wasn't the one in the wrong. She hadn't caused her marriage to crumble. She hadn't done a goddamned thing wrong, as he would say.

And he was right!

She hadn't deserved to get beaten. If she had stayed, she would surely end up dead and buried with no one the wiser, like poor Evelyn. No matter how long it took, Kathleen would find the courage to live out her dream. And she would have Joseph to thank. And to thank him, she would start by writing him back. He was her friend, and he wasn't officially taken yet.

She was a gift to him. That thought filled her heart with joy. The thought that she had made a difference in his life was incredible. It made her feel like she did have a purpose in this world. She could touch people's lives with her words. It gave her an idea. She didn't know if she could pull it off, but she sure could give it a try. She suddenly knew what she was meant to do....

And she owed it all to Joseph Henry Rutherford III.

∼

DECEMBER 1942: *Puget Sound Navy Yard*

Joseph stared up at the bunk above him, barely a foot above his head. When he first joined, he'd been claustrophobic, thinking he would never be able to handle the close quarters of living on a battleship. And it didn't help he'd been in his bunk when Japan had dropped their bombs on Pearl Harbor. It was hard to sleep and not worry that it could happen again.

The United States had positioned their battleships like sitting ducks in Battleship Row because the waters were shallow. They thought no torpedo could get through to sink their ships. The problem was, they didn't anticipate the ingenuity of the Japanese. Japan was smart. They figured out a way to make their torpedoes float until they struck their target by building wooden planks and attaching them to the bombs.

Problem solved.

Now that the attack was over, many ships had been upgraded. The Tennessee bore little resemblance to her former self, much wider and more modern. The interior had been rearranged and improved with the addition of a new compact super structure designed to provide control facilities while offering less interference to anti-aircraft guns. Upgraded anti-aircraft guns and fire-control radars were also installed. She now had a single funnel—or chimney—instead of her original twin funnels in a super structure tower. She was a force to be reckoned with.

The ship might have been rebuilt, but its crew had not. The disillusioned and damaged soldiers were expected to carry on as if business as usual. It didn't matter that Joseph wasn't the only one to scream out in the night. If he wasn't having a nightmare, he would be awakened by someone else who was. They all lived in a constant state of fog and fear.

It was December. One year after the attack on Pearl Harbor. How was he supposed to get through reliving the horrible tragedy and the lonely holidays on his own? He clutched the letter to his chest. Kathleen had become a lifeline to him. His own family hadn't written him back. Beverly had written him a short letter, sounding just like he'd feared: shallow and selfish. She didn't have depth and not once did she ask about what he had gone through. She went on about herself and what their life would be like when he returned and took over his father's ship-building business.

She sounded exactly like he used to be.

Only Kathleen seemed to genuinely care about him, and yet she had nothing. People had treated her horribly. She should be so angry at the world, at people like him, yet she wasn't. She was still so full of compassion and sympathy. She truly cared about what he thought and how he felt and what he was going through. Everyone else back home expected him to man up and be okay. They had no clue he might never be okay again.

He carefully opened her letter as if it was the most precious Christmas gift of all. To him it was. She was just a friend, but his inner voice screamed he was fooling himself. She had become so much more than just a friend in such a short amount of time, yet their situation was impossible. His family would never accept her because of where she came from, but even more so with the scandal surrounding her. He swallowed the lump in his throat and read her letter, needing to feel close to her.

DEAREST JOSEPH,

I am so glad you took the time to write me back as well. You have no idea how much your words have meant to me and how much I needed you in the moment your letter arrived. Knowing I am not crazy, that someone else believes in me means everything. You are the gift, and I will treasure your friendship always. I have doubted myself immensely, thinking maybe William's abuse, and the town's shunning, and my parents' betrayal were all my fault. You, and you alone, have made me realize it wasn't me. It was them. I can't make them take ownership for what they have done, but I can forgive them and move on with my life, and I owe it all to you.

Now, the great question is, what do I want to do with the rest of my days? I feel free for the first time ever to do what I want. To be whom I want to be. To say what I want and not be punished for it. With my background in teaching, I have always loved the written word. And you yourself said my words were poetic. There must be something I can do. I'll keep you posted.

In the meantime, I know how much you miss home. I thought you might enjoy another little piece of it. And fear not, I know you are promised to Beverly—PS I hope you hear from her soon—and I am married, but I agree. There is no reason we cannot be friends. You take care of yourself. Be safe and keep your spirits up. If I can get through the holidays alone, then you can too. Look up at the stars. There is only one sky. Know I will be thinking of you as I look up at the stars as well. You are not alone, and I will never stop writing you so long as you'll have me.

Until tomorrow,
Kathleen

KATHLEEN HAD SLIPPED the most brilliantly colored dried leaves inside the envelope. They fell out onto Joseph's chest as he lay on his back in his bunk and reread every word of her letter once more. Holding each leaf up one at a time, he studied the small intricate lines like roads on a map and wondered if they led to anywhere but here. The colors were faded but still rich, the texture beginning to turn brittle.

A whiff of her perfume drifted to his nose, and he closed his eyes, picturing her. He suddenly had a strong urge to know what she looked like. He needed something real to hold on to. A vision to go to sleep to every night. An image of hope to chase the nightmares away. When she sealed that letter, she'd sealed her fate. He might not have a clue what the future held for him, but one thing he was certain about. Somehow, someway...

Kathleen Connor would be in it.

~

FEBRUARY 1943: *Beacon Bay, Maine*

Kathleen put another log on the fire and sat down to look at Joseph's picture one more time. In fact, she hadn't stopped looking at it since his letter had arrived the day before. It was black and white, but he had told her he had hair the color of a sandy beach and eyes the color of the sky. His hair was cropped short in standard military fashion. The picture must have been taken recently because he looked tired, his cheeks sunken in a bit as if he hadn't been eating like he should. He was handsome in a classic way, but the war had taken its toll on him. It was clear he had been through a lot, but his eyes drew her in and wouldn't let go.

He looked so sad and lost and broken down. Her heart melted and she longed to hold him in her arms and heal him, letting him know everything was going to be okay. But he wasn't hers to hold. They were friends, but she knew deep in her heart she felt so much more for him. She didn't dare express that to him for fear of scaring him away. He said he needed her, but she wasn't naïve enough to think he meant it as anything other than a pen pal.

He was due to come home this year, but he wasn't sure when. His family and Beverly and a whole new life awaited him. Kathleen would never deny him the chance to be happy, and being with her would only cause him more pain. He'd asked for a picture of her so he would have something to see in his dreams other than blood and death. How could she say no? She wasn't much on pictures or spending a lot of time on her appearance, but she did have a picture of her on her wedding day. It was the only picture of her alone, right before she became William's wife.

She studied the picture. It was a good one of her, but she realized for the first time that even then, on what should have been the happiest day of her life, she hadn't looked happy. That should have been a sign. If only she had followed her instincts and walked away, she wouldn't have traveled down this rough path in life. Although it was this very path that led her to live in the cottage and receive Joseph's first letter. Fate was a strange beast. Before she could change her mind, she slipped the photograph inside the envelope with her letter and headed into town to the post office.

It was so cold out; her hat and gloves and cloak were no match for the harsh Maine weather they'd been having. The road was snow packed and barely passable; the trees heavy with carrying the load of their burden on their empty branches. Everything was cold, stark and white. Small little puffs of smoke filled the air as Kathleen's warm breath escaped and her breathing picked up to match her rapid pace. The sooner she arrived at the post office, the sooner she could return to her cottage by the sea.

She missed the sunshine and flowers and the sound of the waves lapping the shore. Even the water was hibernating beneath the top layer of ice and the sunshine nestled beneath a blanket of gray overcast. Her food had been holding up, but next year she would need more. She'd lost weight in trying to ration what she had left to get her through to the spring thaw.

Finally coming around the last bend in the road, she reached town. It was a Sunday, so most people were at church. Kathleen had taken to worshipping at home as everyone, including the priest, had made it clear she wasn't welcome at mass. That was why she had chosen this time to go to the post office. It was easier to avoid reality than have to face its ugly condemnation.

Heading inside the office, she handed her letter over to the clerk. The woman didn't know who she was, much to Kathleen's relief. She paid the fee and then left the office to head for home as quickly as she could. She stepped onto the sidewalk and stopped in her path, her breath freezing in her lungs.

"Kathleen," William said with a note of desperation in his voice. He towered over her, blocking out her view and stealing her voice to cry for help. Not that anyone would come to her aid anyway. "I'm not going to hurt you. I just want to talk." He touched her arm with his gloved hand, but she still felt the heat and it gave her a chill.

She stepped back carefully until his hand fell away so it wouldn't look like she was repulsed by his touch, even though that's exactly what she was. She would rather freeze to death than be touched by him. "We have nothing to talk about, William."

"I know your mother told you I've changed. Why won't you give me another chance?" He shook his head, genuinely looking confused. He really didn't see that what he had done was so wrong.

"You know why." She stood straighter, knowing she needed to appear confident and strong, not showing any weakness. Snow started to fall softly and stick to her eyelashes, but she refused to blink first.

A shadow of fear crept into his haunted muddy brown eyes. "I never meant for that to happen. You've got to believe me. It was an accident. She fell off the cliff. I would never let that happen to you."

"Really, because the last time you were at my cottage, you insinuated that very thing might happen to me." She shook her head at him and let her disgust and disappointment plainly show. "How could you let her family think she ran off with another man?"

He stared at his feet, his face filled with shame and regret. His voice trembled as he said softly, "I loved her, and I knew how much losing her hurt. I thought it would be easier on her parents if they thought she was still alive."

Kathleen believed him. He wasn't born a monster, his father had turned him into one, and sadly there was no cure. While she might believe him, she still feared him. He was like a bomb, ready to go off, and she was tired of treading lightly. "You need to tell them. Set the record straight."

His razor-sharp gaze snapped up to hers. Gone was the sadness and shame, replaced by anger and determination. "They've been gone for years. No one is going to tell anyone anything, you hear me? If you do, you will live to regret it. No one will believe you." He looked at the post office behind her and scowled. "I saw you mailing a letter. Who was it to? Your boyfriend? It won't take much to make the town believe you're a whore too."

And this was exactly why she would never go back to him. "I'm not afraid of you," she lied, lifting her chin for good measure and staring him down. "I have proof hidden away. If anything happens to me, it will come out. It won't matter if they believe it or not, they will always doubt you and your reputation will forever be damaged. I know where you buried Evelyn, and I know that your father helped you. That's the trouble with sharing a bed. You never know what you might say in your sleep."

He squeezed his eyes shut over the sound of Evelyn's name spoken out loud. "Stop, just stop," he growled, then his voice faded to an agonizing whisper, "please."

Kathleen tried a different tack. "I know you regret what you did, or you wouldn't still have nightmares about it. I won't tell anyone, William. You'll have to live with what you've done for the rest of your life. But I won't give you the chance to do it to me. Stay away from me. I mean it."

She didn't give him a chance to say anything more as she quickly walked around him and headed home as church let out. Glancing over her shoulder, she watched people come out and greet William with smiles as if he were some upstanding citizen to be looked up to. It made her stomach turn. No, she wouldn't say anything. She wouldn't have to. Somehow, someway the truth always came out.

10

MAY 1943: ALASKA (THE ALEUTIAN ISLANDS AND TARAWA)

Joseph Henry Rutherford III stood on the deck of the USS Tennessee—part of the new and improved Battleship Force Pacific Fleet—staring out over the Alaskan waters, headed toward a fight in the Aleutian Islands. The waters were home to the humpback whales and the majestic cliffs and mountains reminded him of Hawaii, except the peaks were snow-capped, there was no lava, and grizzly and polar bears roamed the forests.

Pulling his wool coat tighter, he admitted the temperature left much to be desired. But he wasn't here on vacation, he was here for war. Providing sea protection to the landing forces was a job of major importance. Joseph had feared repercussions by Japan, but the Japanese Navy did not challenge the American forces, much to his relief. Instead, the Tennessee spent her time using her formidable guns to support the ground troops by bombarding enemy land positions. That didn't mean he still didn't witness horrible destruction and people dying. War was still war. The only thing that kept him going was looking at Kathleen's face in her photograph and dreaming about the day he would finally get to hold her in his arms.

In three months, Joseph was going home to Beacon Bay, Maine on leave. He wasn't due to get out of the Navy until the following summer, but he hadn't been home in so long, this leave was desperately needed. His mother had already planned a big welcome home party. She fully expected him to meet Beverly and propose marriage to her, allowing her to plan the wedding over the next year while he returned to war, and then he would pick up where he left off in his father's company upon his return. She had no idea he didn't intend to marry Beverly. How could he when he was in love with a woman he'd never met, who was all wrong on paper for him, yet more perfect for him than any woman he had ever known.

Kathleen Connor was his soul-mate.

He knew it as sure as he knew he needed air to live. He would die without her. He would have died already if it wasn't for her. He pulled out the picture she had sent him and held it in his hands as if it was the most precious gift. And it was. She hadn't come out and said so, but he was pretty sure she had given him her heart as well.

She wasn't the most beautiful woman, but she was more beautiful to him than any woman he had ever seen. She was captivating. She said her hair was the color of melted caramels, and her eyes a sea-green. In the picture he could see the soft waves coming just to her delicate shoulders in a simple style, but they framed her too-long face, making the overall contrast lovely. Her mouth was small but shapely. She was pretty in a natural, mysterious, haunting way. Her eyes were what had hooked his heart and held it captive. Big, almond shaped, and mesmerizing. He could see the intelligence shining within and the determination lurking beneath as if afraid to show itself.

He knew no one would accept her and they would all be angry at him for his decision, but he didn't care. She was the only thing that had kept him going this past year, and truth be told, he'd given her his heart as well. He wanted to tell her how he felt, but decided to do it in person. He couldn't tell her he was in Alaska, but he could let her know he was coming home soon.

Let her know he wanted to meet her face-to-face.

She had left her husband, but the bastard refused to give her a divorce. He did however promise to leave her alone. After what he had done, Joseph wanted to protect her from him. Protect her from them all. Life was precious. Whatever time they had left on this earth was meant to be cherished, and he knew he wouldn't be happy unless he spent his time with her. Everyone would just have to accept his decision. They would have a year to get over it and move on. After all he'd been through, that wasn't too much to ask.

Then why did he have a sinking feeling war was just the beginning of the hell he would live through?

Present Day: *Beacon Bay, Maine*

"You ready?" Logan asked Emma as they prepared to step foot off the Coast Guard boat and face the music back at Beacon Bay Marina. It was a small marina with rows of docks that had mostly personal cruisers, sailboats, and a few speed boats tied up in slots the local citizens had rented for the summer. It was also home to seasonal fishing vessels of various sizes, but cruise ships and tour boats frequented the bigger harbors with better accommodations.

The water had grown rougher after they'd finished reading Kathleen and Joseph's letters by the fire. Kathleen was a remarkable woman. She'd stood up to her husband, who'd turned out to be a real animal, even when the entire town was against her. Logan didn't know how she'd handled that, especially given the time period she'd lived in. He had a feeling Joseph played a big part in her perseverance. Joseph was one hell of a man. He was a real hero, even though he didn't think he was. He'd fought for his country and lived through unspeakable times, yet he still put others first. Kathleen was lucky to have him in her life, even if they were just friends.

Logan stole a glance at Emma and couldn't help thinking how lucky he was to have her in his life. The wind had picked up several knots since this morning, and Logan was grateful the Coast Guard had found them when they did. Rowing off the island back to shore in ten-foot waves wasn't something he'd wanted to even think about, yet the thought of spending another night in Emma's arms had been even more terrifying. He didn't think he could handle a repeat of the "dream" and not do something stupid. Whatever the sacrifice, he wouldn't jeopardize their friendship. She'd become too important to him; a lifeline he hadn't even known he'd needed.

He couldn't lose her, too.

"No, I'm not ready," she answered on a laugh, but she held out her hand to him anyway in a show of trust that warmed his heart.

His connection to her wasn't just physical. They had been through quite an ordeal getting stranded on that island, but had somehow come through the experience closer than ever. He was relieved to see the Mandy Marie safe and sound in her spot at the marina without a scratch on her from what he could tell. He'd called Barry to let him know he was okay because he was afraid news of the rescue would leak, and he didn't want his in-laws or son to worry. Especially since the Coast Guard had notified them shortly after that, that their boat had been found floating on its own. Emma had phoned home as well. She must have called her sister, because the woman on the dock bore a striking resemblance to her. As tough as their ordeal had been, a nagging feeling told him the toughest part of their adventure was yet to come.

Logan and Emma thanked their rescuers once more, and then he led Emma onto to the dock. All eyes turned toward them and immediately dropped to their joined hands. Logan and Emma glanced at each other. It had become second nature to touch each other without worrying how the other might take it. They'd needed each other to survive, plain and simple, but now reality had slapped them both in the face. They weren't on the island anymore. They were home and under close scrutiny. No words were necessary.

They both let go immediately.

Trevor ran down the dock to greet them and vaulted into Logan's arms, hugging him tight. His blond-headed tyrant looked up at him with wide-set blue eyes filled with fear. Knowing enough about the water, it was clear he realized the Coast Guard didn't just rescue people, they were the water police.

"Did you get into trouble, Daddy?" Trevor whispered loudly.

Everyone chuckled, Logan being the loudest. Man, he had missed his baby boy. "No way, buddy. I was on an adventure like I promised."

The worry left Trevor's face, replaced by buzzing excitement and anticipation. "You were?" His voice was full of wonder.

"Yup." Logan nodded in an exaggerated way.

"What happened?" Trevor shook Logan's shoulders over and over in a silent plea of, *Tell me, tell me.*

"I can't tell you because it's not over yet." Logan winked, making it clear he knew exactly what his son wanted. He'd promised him a full adventure, and the summer wasn't over with yet.

"Oh, man." Trevor stuck out his bottom lip, perfecting his pout, but then his eyes turned to Emma with curiosity sparkling bright. "What was *she* doing there?" He thrust his finger toward her.

"She was on the adventure with me," Logan said in a conspiratorial tone. "She's my assistant."

"Partner," Emma interjected.

"Helper," Logan clarified with a hushed tone and his hand cupped over his mouth as if he were speaking for Trevor's ears only, though he knew his whisper was loud enough for them all to hear.

"Don't let him fool you." Emma shook her head, fighting her own grin. "*I* brought the adventure to *him*."

"Okay, fine." Logan rolled his eyes in mock annoyance, but he lost the battle and tipped his lips up. "We're part of a team."

"Like me and Grandpa Barry?" Trevor asked, his eyes darting between the two of them, clearly not wanting to miss anything.

"Sort of," Logan said, thinking they weren't anything of the sort. The way he had kissed Emma was a whole lot different than the way Trevor kissed his grandfather. Logan shifted uncomfortably, thinking about it. Clearing his throat, he said, "Trevor, this is my friend, Ms. Hendricks." He set his now squirming son down.

Trevor, who at only six nearly reached a short Emma's shoulders already, gave her a high-five. "Cool." He wrinkled his nose. "You guys got dirty, too. Awesome."

"It *is* cool, isn't it?" Emma laughed. "You can call me Emma. All my friends do." She couldn't stop smiling at him, and every ounce of her smile was sincere, endearing her even further to Logan.

He sighed, repeating *friend, friend, friend* to himself, hoping like hell his traitorous body would listen.

"Wait until you hear about the things we've done," Emma went on. Her sister had taken her private jet as soon as Emma had called her. Now she eyed Emma with a raised brow, and

Emma's smile slipped a little. But like Kathleen, Emma was a remarkably strong, independent woman. Ignoring her sister, she added with her own conspiratorial tone, "Maybe I'll get to see you at the end of the summer when your dad tells you all about our adventure. You know, to make sure he gets all his facts straight."

"His facts?" Trevor blinked up at her in confusion.

"It means the details. I'll make sure your father gets the story right and doesn't try to make up anything or make anything seem more exciting than it is."

Trevor's eyes dawned with realization. "Like when Grandpa Barry and me fish, and sometimes the fish gets away. Grandpa likes to tell people he caught a fish that was *this* big." Trevor spread his arms as wide as he could, then let out a huge huff as he rolled his eyes and shook his head, worthy of a Tony Award on Broadway. "I have to tell everyone the real truth—er, the straight facts." He beamed proudly.

"Exactly." She tweaked his nose, and he giggled. "How about I watch my partner and you watch yours, then we'll compare stories later. Deal?" She held out her hand.

"Deal." Ignoring her hand, he threw his arms around her and hugged her hard, making her lips part in surprise. She barely had time to hug him back before he ran off to check on the Mandy Marie with his grandfather, their exchange probably already forgotten.

"He's not shy," Logan said by way of apology. Not everyone was comfortable around children. He'd seen that firsthand from a few women who had been interested in him. All he'd had to do to deter their affections was sic his bumbling bundle of joy on them. He frowned. Why wasn't it working on Emma? Every time he thought he had her figured out, she kept surprising him, and that was more disturbing than anything he'd faced in years.

"No, he's definitely not shy." She stared off after his son with a tender expression on her face. "He's adorable."

"Thank you." Logan studied her profile, softening toward her. *Well, hell.*

She must have sensed his gaze because she locked eyes with him, but then her eyes widened and her gaze quickly turned to the woman next to her. "Dr. Mayfield, this is my sister, Stacy Dresher."

"Please call me Logan." He held out his hand. "It's nice to meet you."

Stacy gave him the once over, raising her perfectly waxed eyebrow in contemplation over the word doctor, but she obviously wasn't quite ready to give her approval as she shook his hand weakly almost as if she expected him to kiss it. She might look like her sister, but they were worlds apart. He knew Stacy's kind. Doctors, lawyers, and CEO's were a dime a dozen where she came from. It would take more than a mere title to impress her, like having the right lineage and ranking at the top of his class. One out of two wasn't bad, but once she learned of his humble beginnings, it would all be over with Emma. Not that he planned to get anything started with Emma in the first place, he reminded himself, mentally shaking his head.

What was wrong with him?

She smiled cordially, yet it looked stiff and fake as she responded with the obligatory, "Likewise."

"Well, it's been real. Thanks for the crazy night, Doc." Emma stepped between them. "Stacy and I have some catching up to do. We'll talk soon." She didn't wait for his response as she took her sister's arm and walked away.

"My, my, my. She's certainly interesting," Rebecca said, startling him into realizing he was still staring after Emma, a part of him not wanting to let her go. It had been so nice having someone to talk to, someone who really listened and was going through pain of her own. For the first time in a long time, he hadn't been lonely, which shocked him.

He looked at his mother-in-law, saw her expression, and crossed his arms. "Oh, no you don't. Don't even think of going there."

"Going where?" Rebecca tried to look innocent, but he knew better.

"We're partners." He scrubbed his face. "Or, maybe friends. Hell, I don't know what we are, but we're not what you're thinking. That's all."

"Whatever you are, apparently that's enough." She squeezed his arm gently. "You've changed."

"How do you mean?"

"You're not so sad anymore."

She had been trying to fix him up for years to no avail. But she also knew him too well. She could see the way he looked at Emma was different than how he had looked at any other woman in a very long time. If he could erase the touch of Emma's silky, soft skin from his fingertips and the sweet honey taste of her kiss from his lips and the feel of her warm, pliant body pressed firmly against his, he might stand a chance of returning to his normal life. But she'd awakened something inside of him he'd thought would never stir to life.

And he feared nothing would ever be *normal* again.

A COUPLE HOURS LATER, Emma and her sister Stacy sat out back on the patio of her oceanfront beach house, watching the sun set over the rolling waves, drinking sake and eating Chinese food. Emma had showered and changed into yoga pants and a tank top, leaving her feet bare. The breeze had finally died down, and the warm July evening was heavenly. Speaking of heaven, Emma couldn't stop thinking about Logan. He'd been so heroic and manly and attentive in taking care of her, which went against everything she thought she was. But she could no longer deny she liked when he did chivalrous things for her. They made her feel special and appreciated and cherished.

She'd come to the conclusion it was okay to be a strong, independent woman and still enjoy the chivalry of days gone by. Kathleen would have given anything for treatment like that, and she was the strongest most independent woman Emma had ever known. Not that she had actually "known" her, but she felt like she did. Like they were one and the same in many ways, except Kathleen had had to fight so much harder for everything she'd ever gotten.

Emma was obsessed.

She had to find out what happened after Joseph came home on leave. He was so kind and caring and encouraging. It was like reading a great novel you couldn't put down, except Emma had no choice. She couldn't keep reading if they didn't find more letters. If there weren't any more, she didn't know what she would do. It would be like watching a TV show you love suddenly get cancelled and there's no closure. She'd always felt that wasn't right. The network should have it in their contract when a show is cancelled that they will film enough episodes to wrap up the story and give their fans closure.

Emma frowned. The thought of closure made her think of Mark. He had hurt her deeply. Maybe not physically like Kathleen's husband William, but Mark had scarred her emotionally and she wasn't sure she would ever be the same. Would she ever be free to move on from him? She didn't even want to think about Logan, because he reminded her way too much of Joseph. He too loved to help people and was always trying to make the world a better place, but he also had been through great tragedy. Was he even in a place to move on himself?

Everything was such a mess, and kissing him had only made things worse. Now she knew how wonderful it felt to wrap her legs around his hard, massive body, and smell his manly scent and taste his mouth that left her begging for more. Don't even get her started on what his big, muscular hands had felt like as they'd roamed over every inch of her. Emma shivered and earned a curious look from her sister, which snapped her back to reality and common sense.

"Thanks for coming, Stacy. I know how busy you are with the kids." She had married an older, wealthy man, had given birth to twin girls and then divorced the boring, selfish lug, taking him for half of what he was worth. Her ex had the girls on vacation for a couple weeks, so the timing had been perfect.

Stacy waved her hand in the air. "Don't be silly. We're sisters. I might not always agree with you, but I will *always* be there for you." She sipped her sake from a crystal glass, wearing designer loungewear and sandals. Her hair was the same shade of auburn as Emma's but it was much longer. Stacy had hers scooped high in an artful messy bun she must have spent hours perfecting to appear as if she had thrown it up, when in reality, she looked perfect.

There was a time Emma had been jealous of her sister, but she knew everything Stacy did was calculated for appearance's sake. Once Emma realized she wanted no part of that world, she let the jealousy go. That was when she'd noticed the sadness surrounding her sister's beautiful amber eyes. Stacy might have gotten everything she'd ever wanted, but she wasn't happy. While Emma was content with her life. Or at least she had been...

Until Mark had come into it.

"Still, I'm glad you're here. It's been too long. I miss you." Emma reached out and squeezed Stacy's hand. At times their relationship had been strained in the past, but neither one had ever doubted they loved each other.

"Me too." Stacy held her hand a moment and gave her a sincere smile—not like the one she'd given poor Logan—before letting go.

"That reminds me, why the frost treatment toward Dr. Mayfield?" Emma raised a brow at her sister in disapproval.

"Hello, he's a married man." Stacy scoffed. "Didn't you see the ring on his finger? Not that it would matter to me, but I know you." She pointed at Emma. "You have scruples. You're not the kind to steal another woman's husband."

"He's widowed."

"Oh." Stacy frowned. "Still, he's so...big, and manly, and...I don't know. Common."

"He is big and manly and gentle and kind and compassionate and caring and...passionate." Emma was horrified to feel her face flush pink. "Maybe common is exactly what I need."

"Oh my God, you're blushing." Stacy curled her legs beneath her. "What exactly happened on that island?"

This time Emma waved her sister off. "Nothing."

"Don't you dare tell me nothing. My life sucks. I want the scoop. I'm talking details, darling."

"There is no scoop." Emma's flush deepened. "We kissed. That's all."

"That's plenty, apparently. You need a cold shower, honey." Stacy laughed softly. "I'm curious. Mark was anything but common."

"Exactly my point." Emma felt her anger rise all over again. "After what he did, I don't want anything to do with the men from our world. Maybe common's a good thing. Not that I'm looking to start up anything with a man from *any* world."

"Oh, please. Are you kidding yourself? I saw the way you looked at him, and don't even get me started on the way he worshipped you with his eyes. And that, my darling, is why I gave him the frost." Stacy stared down into her drink with a wince. "I hate to admit it, but I was jealous of you."

Emma gasped. "Jealous of me? What on earth for?"

Stacy met her eyes. "I have been jealous of you my whole life."

"Oh my God, why?" Emma stared at her sister, seeing her in a whole new light. "I'm the one who has been jealous of you. You're so perfect."

Stacy laughed harshly. "I'm not perfect. I'm plastic. Fake in every way possible. I'm a Barbie Doll creation of what they all expect me to be. You, on the other hand, are real." She looked at Emma with such pride and admiration, it brought a lump to Emma's throat. "You don't give a shit about what people think. You don't care about living up to Mom and Dad's expectations, you do what you want. I envy that. I landed the perfect husband like I was supposed to, but not a single day of that was happy. The only joy I got out of my marriage is my girls."

"And half his fortune." Emma held up her glass, not knowing what else to do or say.

"Cheers to that." Stacy clinked her glass against Emma's with a soft laugh. "Still, no man has ever looked at me the way the doctor looked at you."

Emma had filled Stacy in on everything that had happened since she'd arrived in Beacon Bay. "He's not over his wife, and frankly, I'm not over what happened with Mark. I feel like I'm stuck. Like I can't move on until I find out what happened to him. I don't understand what went wrong between us that made him want to pack up and take off, ditching me and our families and our future."

"I know it might be hard to understand now, but trust me, darling, you never looked at Mark like you look at Logan. Maybe Mark did you a favor by walking away. Don't be like me and settle. Don't wait around for your happy ending. Make your own."

"Maybe." Emma shrugged, and then looked at Stacy. Really looked at her in a way that she never had. "You're not a fake Barbie Doll. You're a smart, beautiful, strong woman, and my sister and I love you." She leaned over and hugged her. They stayed that way for a while, before finally pulling away with tears in their eyes. "Maybe you should take your own advice. Go find your happy ending. You deserve it, you know."

"I love you, too." Stacy wiped her eyes. "Does your doctor have a brother?"

They both laughed.

"Seriously, though, I think I'm going to try life on my own for a while." Stacy swirled the liquid in her crystal glass, looking pensive as she stared out over the rolling sea. "I have never once thought about what I wanted to do with my life or what might make me happy. I think I need to take a page out of your book and figure that out first. As you said, I can certainly afford it now."

"Good for you. That's why I'm so fascinated with Kathleen's story." Emma hugged her knees to her chest and leaned her head back, shaking it sadly. "She was so much like me, yet she was persecuted for being so. I can't imagine being in her shoes, yet she survived. If she can, I can. That's why it's so important for me to set the record straight. It's hard to explain, but I feel like I owe that to her. Like she's pushing me to continue."

"It doesn't sound strange at all. There are so many things that happen in this world that we can't explain. Maybe you ended up in Beacon Bay for a reason. I think you should stay here and finish what you started."

"You do?" Emma lifted her head and blinked in surprise.

Stacy laughed. "Yes, I really do. I know what you're thinking, and you're right. I told them you called me. They sent me here to convince you to come back home."

"I figured." Emma felt closer to her than she ever had before. She wasn't alone in any of this. She had someone who cared about her. A sister. And that bond couldn't be stronger.

"They aren't bad people, Emma." Stacy broke through her thoughts, speaking softly. "They love you; they just have a hard time showing it. I think you should definitely stay."

Emma closed her eyes for a moment, and then opened them and said with conviction, "Okay."

They clinked glasses.

"Finish your adventure and write your story, but when it's over, Trevor's not the only one who wants the facts. I expect to hear about all the juicy details."

"Done. And Stacy?"

"Yeah?" She looked at her curiously.

"Thank you."

"For what?"

"For being you and being my sister and being more special to me than you will ever know."

It was clear Stacy struggled to fight back emotion over Emma's words as she replied, "Ditto, babe."

11

I t was the end of June. One year had passed by since
Kathleen's life had forever been changed. She'd made it
through the winter. There was a time she feared she would
never survive, but Joseph's letters had kept her going. His
enemies were far more dangerous than hers. If he could make it
through the war enduring such hardships and sacrifice, then
surely, she could do the same.

His last letter had said he was headed off to parts unknown.
That was the worst. Not knowing if he was in safe territory or in
the middle of a battle, risking his life for the freedoms of others.
She prayed for his survival every day. He hadn't said she was
anything other than a friend to him, but he was her everything.
He had come to mean so much to her. This was what had been
missing from her marriage: tenderness and compassion and
kindness and caring and selflessness.

Kathleen's heart fluttered when she thought of Joseph. She'd
never imagined she could love someone so much. For the first
time in her life, she didn't care about what she wanted. All she
needed to know to be content and at peace was knowing he was
happy. If Beverly made him happy, then Kathleen could live with

that. She would be okay. After all that Joseph had been through, he deserved to be happy.

It would be hard to see him in person and not be able to talk to him and touch him and hold him in her arms like she had done in her dreams for so long now. She would give anything for just one kiss, but she knew once he came home for good, the letters would stop. She would no longer get to be his friend. This town wouldn't allow it. Besides, he wouldn't need her anymore, even though she knew she would need him for the rest of her days. His picture and his letters would have to last her a lifetime, but knowing he was getting everything he wanted in life would be worth it.

But first he had to make it home in one piece.

Kathleen walked through the park called Lighthouse Lane, tightening her Eisenhower jacket which was bloused at the chest and fitted at the waist with a belt. The sun was shining, but the temperatures were cool. At least the snow had melted after a long rough winter. The park was nestled further down from the marina on the shores of the Atlantic Ocean, with a breathtaking view of her favorite lighthouse. There was a gazebo and picnic tables and lanterns set up beyond the rocky shore—the park a favorite destination for both the locals and visitors of their small town. Preparations were in full swing for the Fourth of July celebration. There would be food and music and fireworks. Kathleen had loved this holiday when she was little and had attended the celebration for as long as she could remember.

Until now.

Last year had been a disaster. The whole town had shunned her when she'd made an appearance, in favor of a wounded William, though her bruises hadn't even faded at that time. So now she made sure to visit the park when no one was there. She hadn't realized the preparations would start this early. She was about to turn around and head home when she saw Joseph's mother and his future wife, Beverly Sanderson.

Kathleen froze by a tree, hoping they wouldn't notice her. It was silly. They had no idea who she was. They knew *of* her, of course. Everyone in town did, but they hadn't met her in person since they traveled in two very different social circles. She only knew who they were because her curiosity had forced her to seek them out a while back. She couldn't help herself. She'd had to know more about Joseph, to see the woman who had created him and the woman who would share his bed, bear his children, and share the rest of his days.

His mother, Hilary, was a sophisticated golden-haired, blue-eyed replica of Joseph and queen of high society. Prim and proper and perfectly poised—everything Kathleen wasn't. And Beverly was an angel. She had pale blonde curls that fell past her shoulders and the most beautiful lavender eyes set in a heart-shaped face. Of course, the two of them were dressed in fine clothes from the latest fashions. Attention being drawn to the arm, they wore butterfly sleeves and banjo sleeves with exaggerated shoulder pads and dresses made of rayon material with a viscose lining.

Kathleen couldn't compete with that and felt frumpy in comparison in her drab, simply-cut blouse and skirt she wore beneath her jacket. She'd never been one to care about such trivial things as her looks when there were far more important matters happening around the world. That was why she'd avoided running into Hilary and Beverly ever since first laying eyes on them. She didn't like how she felt or who she became when around them. Her mind told her feet to move, but some force she couldn't quite understand wouldn't let her leave.

"It's terrible. Just terrible, I tell you," Hilary said to Beverly, wringing her hands. "I told the foolish boy that joining the war was a mistake. He had no business being in that battle. Alaska is so wild and savage. He should have known a gentleman would be no match for the battle in the Aleutian Islands. Now he'll never be the same again after getting injured. And how embarrassing to the family name for him to get discharged from the Navy early. I don't know if we'll ever fully recover."

Kathleen's heart tightened and she forgot to breathe. She held onto the trunk of the old oak tree with both hands, feeling faint. Battle, injured, discharged—her mind tried to piece the story together, but all her brain kept repeating was, *Joseph*....

"An honorable discharge is still heroic; I just hope he's not horribly disfigured. Do you think he'll still be able to run Rutherford Ships?" Beverly asked, obviously caring more about her social standing and wealth than his well-being.

"Only time will tell. We'll have to wait until he comes home to assess the damage he's done to himself." Hilary shook her head, looking disappointed in her perfect son for allowing himself to be flawed in any way.

Kathleen felt the anger welling up inside of her, building pressure that made her shake in her effort not to explode. How dare they? Joseph was perfect no matter how he looked. They should be more concerned with his emotional state and any pain he might be in and what they could do for him, not the other way around. They were selfish, shallow people, and Kathleen let go of the tree to tell them so. She didn't care that it would expose that she knew Joseph. He deserved to have someone show compassion and that they cared about him and would do anything for him. She took two steps in their direction but stopped short, sucking in a sharp breath. She forgot to breathe as her eyes settled on a man who had just entered the park.

Joseph.

She would know him anywhere. He was walking across the rich green grass that was in need of mowing, straight for his mother and Beverly, but they hadn't seen him yet. He wore his dress blues—a four-piece woolen uniform with cap, jumper, neckerchief, and trousers. He'd described all of his uniforms and what each of them was worn for in his letters. Being honorably discharged would warrant his dress blues in his honor.

There was nothing wrong with being honorably discharged. He had served his country well and should be proud of that. Kathleen was certainly proud of him as she drank in the sight of him, right down to the last detail. The jumper had finished cuffs with white piping and a back flap consisting of the same white piping along its border, and the trousers had a thirteen-button broadfall front opening, and a lace up back, topped off with signature flared bottoms.

He looked so handsome and distinguished and heroic. His family would do well to recognize that and realize how lucky they were to still have him in their lives, especially when so many other poor unfortunate souls weren't so lucky. Other than a slight limp, he appeared to be perfectly fine, setting Kathleen's mind at ease. Her anger was gone, replaced with intense relief that he was okay and pure joy at seeing him in the flesh for the first time.

Joseph hesitated, and his steps slowed for a moment as he turned his head toward her as if some unknown force had compelled him to do so. Kathleen's lips parted when they locked gazes. His eyes widened, and neither one could look away. Her heart started to pound, and her breath grew choppy. He was home. He was here, alive, and in the flesh and safe. She hadn't thought she would see him until the end of the summer, and then he would be gone for another year only to come home and start a new life without her. A selfish part of her had wanted him to stay away so their letters would continue and a piece of him would still be hers. But she'd known that someday her fairy tale would end. She just hadn't expected it to end so soon.

Because the reality was, he didn't belong to her, and he never would.

His hand lifted slightly toward her as if he wanted to reach out and touch her, and he even took a step in her direction, but then his mother let out a cry and rushed toward him with Beverly floating casually behind her as if she didn't have a care in the world. Startled, Joseph faced his mother and caught her in a hug. After a moment, he looked back in Kathleen's direction, his eyes scanning the park for her, but she had hidden behind a group of trees. She thought she detected disappointment in his gaze, but that was probably wishful thinking on her part.

Joseph smiled at his mother as she stepped back and introduced him to Beverly who gave him a proper smile of her own, even if it did look a bit fake. Again, probably wishful thinking on Kathleen's part. When Joseph bowed slightly and bent over to kiss the back of Beverly's gloved hand like a perfect gentleman, Kathleen couldn't take any more. She slipped into the shadows and quickly made her way home, knowing what they had was over. Their friendship might be over and Joseph would never know how she truly felt about him, but he would forever hold a special place in her heart. He was her soul-mate, the love of her life, but now he was gone.

JOSEPH SCANNED the park one more time but still didn't see Kathleen. For a moment he wondered if he had imagined seeing her. He'd lost his vision in one eye, after all. The station on the USS Tennessee he had been manning was struck by ground fire from the Alaskan shoreline, knocking him to the deck and causing some equipment to fall on him. He'd lost the vision in his left eye and his leg had been injured, leaving him with a permanent limp. He was lucky to be alive and relieved to be sent home honorably, but a part of him felt guilty, as if he'd deserted his crew.

The only thing that had kept him going was knowing he would get to see Kathleen early and he would be able to stay with her forever. He'd longed to hold her in his arms and confess his love. The anticipation of their first kiss had helped him fight through the pain as he healed. He'd dreamt about laying eyes on her for so long, she had to be real. His heart still hadn't slowed its beating at spotting her standing there in the park like an angel. She'd stared at him with those haunted, mystical eyes of hers and captured his soul. He could have sworn he'd read the same love that he felt in her gaze, but maybe not. She hadn't stayed long enough for him to speak with her, so maybe she didn't feel the same way after all.

"What are you looking at?" his mother asked.

"Nothing, really, just the park and thinking about how good it feels to be home." Stifling his disappointment, he donned an expression he knew his mother wanted to see. She frowned at his limp and couldn't stop blinking over his cloudy eye. "I'm okay, Mother," he finally said, doing what he always did in putting others first and easing their worry over giving in to his own pain.

"I'd hardly say you're okay, but you're here and that's a start." She blinked back real tears and clasped her hands in front of her.

Joseph knew she loved him in her own way, but the hug she'd given him had been a rare occurrence. She wouldn't let it happen again, and she certainly wouldn't give in to the weakness of tears, therefore, neither could he. "I can still do everything I used to; it just takes me a bit longer with a bum leg. And as for the eye, at least I have two." He tried to ease the tension with humor.

She didn't so much as crack a smile. Instead, she stepped aside. "Joseph, I'd like you to meet Miss Beverly Sanderson."

Joseph smiled the obligatory smile as he bowed and kissed her hand, though she did not stir his blood or make his heart sing. She was stunningly beautiful, but there was no depth in her pretty eyes. She was a replica of his mother, in training to be the princess of high society. He bit back a sigh. There was a time he would have thought her perfect and him the luckiest man on earth, but he was a different person now. All he wanted to do was find Kathleen and sink into her embrace if she would have him.

"I'm so happy you're home, Mr. Rutherford. Now we can get properly acquainted, don't you think?"

If Beverly had bothered to write to him more than the obligatory first time like Kathleen had, she would already know exactly who he was, but she hadn't. She undoubtedly didn't want to waste her time in case he didn't return, but now that he was back, she was willing to play the game.

"Please, call me Joseph," he said in lieu of an answer, biding his time. He needed to tell them all what he intended to do, but now was not the time or place.

"Let's go home," his mother said, stepping between them and looping her arm through his in a show of affection, but he knew it was more likely to help disguise his limp from any onlookers as they walked away. "Your father and sisters will be so happy to see you."

Yes, he would play the game...but not for long.

LATER THAT NIGHT Kathleen couldn't stop thinking about Joseph. She stepped out on her back deck to look over the railing with longing. The brilliant sun sank over the horizon in a spectacular display of purple, red and orange, the faint hues still lingering as the stars began to twinkle. What she wouldn't give to go to her favorite lighthouse and disappear forever. She was wrong. It hadn't been better to see Joseph in person just one time because once would never be enough. But once was all she'd ever have.

Knowing she couldn't ever be with him was killing her.

How could she go on living alone without his letters? Never to hear his words of encouragement, or to know he was looking up at the same sky even though he was far away and thinking about her, or to have someone to share her hopes and dreams with was heartbreaking. She could live with her husband's abuse, and she could live with her parents turning their backs on her, and she could even live with being shunned by the town....

But Kathleen honestly didn't know if she could live without Joseph.

Suddenly she felt a presence behind her, but she didn't flinch or cower in fear. She somehow knew it wasn't a monster. It was an angel. It was Joseph. "You're here," she said without turning around.

"I couldn't stay away," he replied, his voice sounding rich and sweet like warm honey. Her eyes welled up over actually hearing it, which was something she'd thought would never happen after what she'd witnessed a few hours ago. "I saw you at the park earlier," he added.

"I saw you, too." She tried not to let her voice shake. He was here, in the flesh, as real as can be. She wanted to touch him so badly but was afraid if she did, she would never let go like she knew she should.

"Why did you leave?" he asked softly, and she could feel his breath on her neck as if he'd moved forward like he wanted to be closer to her as well.

She did turn around at that and lifted her face to look him in the eye. He stood so close she could almost feel the heat from his body. "I left for you." She swallowed hard. He was so handsome, even more so in person, his cloudy eye only making him more special as a reminder of all he had gone through for her and everyone else. He'd changed into gray trousers and a soft blue shirt that matched his good eye; the expensive fabric draped perfectly over his muscled torso.

He searched her eyes carefully, his hands in his pockets as if to keep from touching her. "I thought you left because you didn't care." A spark of pain and vulnerability flashed across his face.

She was already shaking her head and tears she could no longer control slipped out of the corners of her eyes to roll down her cheeks. "Don't you see? That's the problem. I care too much." She stepped away from him, needing distance for what she was about to say, and paced her deck. "More than I should. It's not fair to you or to me. I don't think I can be your friend anymore. It's too hard now that you're back. You're getting ready to start a new life."

"You're right. I *am* starting a new life, and I don't want to be your friend anymore, either." Her steps faltered over the pain his words invoked, and he reached out to grab her hand. She faced him, and he cupped her cheek with his palm then gently wiped a tear away with his thumb. "Don't you see? I can't be your friend because I want to be so much more."

Her lips parted and shock rocketed through her, rendering her frozen like a statue. A glimmer of hope blossomed and her walls began to crack, but she was afraid to believe in it, afraid to get hurt even worse than she had been. Unable to stop herself, she finally asked, "Y-You do?"

His hands cradled her face as if it were precious to him, his eyes so tender and misting up as much as her own. "I am completely and totally head over heels in love with you."

She sucked in a breath. "Y-You are?" Could he truly feel the same way she did? Was there actually hope for them after all?

"Yes, Kathleen Connor, I am. I guess I thought you knew even though I was afraid to say the words, but only because I didn't know if you felt the same way. I adore you. You're so strong and beautiful and independent. You've helped me in ways you will never fully understand. There were times I thought of taking my own life. I might have if it wasn't for you. You're everything to me. I want my new life to be with you. No, I *need* my life to be with you. I can't live without you. Please say yes."

That only made her cry harder. She wanted the fairy tale with every ounce of her being, but she thought about where they came from and who they were and the lives they led. She put her hand over the ones cradling her cheek and lowered them, holding them tightly in her own as if that alone would make him hers. "I'm married. It's impossible."

He actually winced over the word married, but then he steeled his features with determination. "Separated and nothing's impossible." He squeezed her hands for reassurance, holding on just as tight as if to let her know he wasn't going to let go now or ever.

While she appreciated the effort, she knew it was hopeless. "William will never give me a divorce."

Joseph was already shaking his head. "I don't care. That won't stop us from being together."

"He's a monster," she added, wanting to let him know exactly what he was getting into. Life with her would never be easy.

Joseph didn't look put off, he looked determined and passionate and ready to take on the world on her behalf. "I'll protect you."

Kathleen believed him. Sincerity rang through his every word, and she couldn't love him more, but she sighed and lowered her head to look at her feet. "Your family will never accept me."

Joseph tipped her chin up until her gaze met his. "Then it's their loss." That meant a lot coming from him because she knew even though they were flawed, he still loved them.

"What about Beverly?" She also knew he was a man of honor and would always do the right thing.

"From the moment I read your first letter, I knew I could never ask her to marry me." He traced every inch of Kathleen's face, making her feel cherished and special and loved. "She's not you, my love. You're real and you have depth and you have dreams and goals and aspire to be something more. I want to help you achieve that and be there to celebrate when that happens, and it *will* happen. How do I know? Because you are a special, rare, precious gem that I long to call my own. Now, are you finished?"

"No." She let a small smile tip up the corners of her lips. "One more thing, Joseph Henry Rutherford III."

"What?" He eyed her curiously with a slight smile of his own.

"I love you, too. Desperately, completely, wholeheartedly. And if you don't kiss me this instant, I'll never survive."

His smile turned tender as love and passion shined fiercely in his eyes. "God, yes! I thought you'd never ask. I've dreamed of this moment for so long now. It was the one thing that kept the nightmares away." He tugged on her hands and pulled her into his embrace as he wrapped his arms around her and lowered his head.

His wide full lips were firm as they pressed against her soft mouth respectfully, but she was having none of that. He wasn't the only one to dream of them being together in more ways than one. She'd learned life was too short to worry about doing the right and proper thing. She slipped her arms around his neck and pressed her body to his as she deepened the kiss and let her desire shine free in all its glory.

He only hesitated briefly and then poured every ounce of what he was feeling into that kiss as well. His pain and anger and fear ravaged her mouth, and she welcomed being a beacon of light for him. She would weather his storm and calm his seas with her reassurance and love. Soon his kiss turned to one of sadness and homesickness then to one of passion and love, leaving her breathless and aching for more.

When they finally broke apart, she stayed in his arms as he rested his forehead against hers and fought to catch his breath. She kept running her hands up and down his back, caressing him and letting him know she was there for him. "It's okay, Joseph, I've got you and I'm not going anywhere," she said when she felt his tears wet her cheeks. "You're home now, right where you belong."

12

JULY 1943: BEACON BAY, MAINE

"I'm not going to marry her, Mother," Joseph said a week later during dinner at his family home.

The massive colonial sat up the coast in the rich part of town down from the Sanderson place. The fact that Kathleen's simple cottage was the size of the servants' quarters or that he even *had* servants to begin with didn't go unnoticed by him. He smiled at the staff and served himself, longing for a simpler way of life, which definitely didn't go unnoticed by his mother.

His mother frowned, obviously disapproving of him fraternizing with the staff about as much as she had disapproved of his casual attire of khaki pants and a blue cotton button down shirt more suitable for day wear. She still very much believed in dressing for dinner. "You're not feeling well, dear, that's all. How could you be after all you've been through?"

Now she cared about what he'd been through? Since he'd been home all that had concerned her was finding a way to fix his limp and eye so he wouldn't embarrass her in public and whether or not he'd be up to starting work at Rutherford Ships anytime soon. He'd told her repeatedly there was no "fixing" his wounds, and frankly he didn't feel he deserved for them to be fixed since he still lived and breathed while so many others no longer did.

His daily nightmares should be proof of that.

She'd sent him to a psychiatrist after that and had kept him so busy with parading him around, he hadn't been able to sneak off and see Kathleen. He feared she would think he'd forgotten about her. That was why he'd decided to take control of his life now. He couldn't stop reliving what it had felt like to hold her in his arms and kiss her sweet lips and bare his soul, knowing she would never judge him. She would only love him. He needed that.

He needed her.

"You're right, I don't feel well, but not in the way that you think. I tried to tell you before I came home that I wasn't the same person as when I left, and I never will be." It was just the two of them at dinner. His father spent more and more time at work since Joseph had been home. His father claimed business was booming and that was why, but Joseph suspected he was having trouble coping with and connecting to the wounded *different* man his son had become. His only son and heir apparent to the family business, who had changed in so many ways.

"Beverly can help you get over the war," his mother broke into his thoughts. "You need her."

"No, I don't. She needs me, or rather she needs my last name. And the war isn't something you get over. She wouldn't be able to handle living with a wounded veteran who's half a man."

"You're not half a man, for goodness sake." He could clearly see his mother was getting frustrated with him and his new backbone. He used to pretty much give in to whatever she wanted. Now that he'd discovered he actually had an opinion and a mind of his own, she wasn't pleased to say the least. "You have a limp and can't see out of one eye. How does that make you half a man?"

"I was referring to my emotional state," he said dryly, quickly realizing that was an area that was off limits. She was uncomfortable dealing with emotions of any kind.

"Oh, well, you need time." His mother dismissed his concern with a wave of her hand. If only getting better was that easy. "How do you know Beverly can't help with that as well?" she added. "You haven't even given her a chance."

"I know." He stood and limped over to the window to stare out at the sea and immediately thought of Kathleen. "I don't love Beverly," he said quietly.

"You might in time."

"No, I won't," he said with conviction, hoping she would finally back off.

"I'll arrange for you both to—"

"Mother stop." He rubbed his temples wearily. He'd been a fool to think she would understand. She was on a single-minded mission.

She went on talking as if he hadn't even spoken. "There's the Fourth of July celebration you two can attend together, and then—"

Pressure built inside his head, and he could no longer stand idly by and let her take over his future. "Stop interfering with my life," he snapped, whirling around to face her. "I can't take it anymore."

She blinked, startled, then raised her chin a notch and looked at him disapprovingly. "Fine, spend your life alone. Your sisters will give me grandchildren. I only wanted for you to be happy. Is that so wrong of a mother? I'm trying to help you."

He sighed, feeling tired. Drained. War hadn't been much harder than trying to cope in a world he no longer belonged. "I'm sorry for snapping at you, but you don't have to worry about me. I'm not going to spend my life alone, Mother." Maybe the truth would set him free. "My heart belongs to someone else and has for a long time now. I'm happy, or at least I will be if you'll let me."

She perked up at this. "Someone else? But how on earth could you possibly have met someone else, and who in the world is it?"

He told her everything that had happened over the past year, hoping she cared about his happiness like she'd said. Her face had paled considerably, and she was looking at him with sheer horror in her eyes as if she didn't know him at all. Disappointment sucker punched him in the gut. No matter how old he got, it was painful accepting reality. His own mother didn't care about his happiness. She only cared about herself, the same as always. He'd made a big mistake in thinking she would understand.

She surged to her feet. "I forbid you to see that trashy woman. She is beneath you. The things she did to her poor husband were unspeakable. You are not to mention her name again in this house or anywhere. If you have anything at all to do with her, your father and I will cut you off. You will be left with nothing."

He didn't know why he was surprised. He should have expected nothing would be different after he got home, but he'd been away for so long and been through so much he had hoped his family would have changed. "I don't care," he finally said, making up his mind with ease. Kathleen was his family now, and that was all that mattered. "For without her, I am nothing anyway."

"You would rather live in poverty and shame in a shack down the coast than to live in splendor and respect while running one of the most prestigious businesses in the area?" His mother gaped at him.

"If it comes to that, then yes. It will seem like paradise compared to where I've been living for the past three years."

"You really have changed." She shook her head, pacing the room as if searching for something. Finally, she stopped and nodded to herself before staring him down. "Alright then, you've forced my hand. If you see her again, I'll ruin her family. You might not care about *your* family, but I bet she still cares about hers. I'll make sure no one buys any fish or vegetables or paintings from them and they are shunned as well. Is that what you want?"

He shook with fury. His mother was worse than the enemy he'd faced in war, worse than the monster Kathleen was married to. His mother was ruthless and cold and heartless and cruel, caring more about her precious reputation than about her own son. He would never forgive her. Joseph loved Kathleen with all his heart, but he couldn't bear to see her heartbroken when his mother destroyed everything dear to her. He ground his teeth, biting back what he wanted to say, and shook his head no in surrender.

"Good boy. You'll see this is best for everyone concerned, you included. When you get better, you'll thank me someday. I'll call Beverly first thing in the morning."

Joseph would never get better and would never thank her, but he would play the game a bit longer until he came up with a plan. She might have won this battle, but he would never be defeated. The war was far from over. Somehow someway he would find a way to be with his love.

PRESENT DAY: *Beacon Bay, Maine*

"Got it!" Logan said as he unearthed another treasure box buried beneath a bench at Lighthouse Lane Park. It was late July and a steamy hot day, the sun baking everything in sight. He sat on his bare heels and wiped the sweat from his forehead with the back of his hand, his white, dry-fit tank top and navy-blue basketball shorts soaked through.

"Hurry, shove the dirt back in before we get caught. This park belongs to the town, and we defaced its property." Emma helped him scoop the dirt back into the hole and pat it into place, giggling all the way.

Her hair was pulled into a tight knot at the back of her head with little pieces curling damply at her temples. She rubbed her dirty hands on the grass and rested them on her tanned legs below her short, snug, denim shorts. Her chest shook with her laughter, and Logan tried like hell not to let his eyes wander to the front of her buttercup yellow tank top that was growing wetter by the minute, revealing the thin lacy bra she wore beneath. Swallowing dryly, he looked away.

"My heart's pounding," she said out of breath as she stood up. "I have to admit this is exciting."

He couldn't help grinning at her and letting a small chuckle slip. She looked like Trevor on Christmas morning. Logan shook his head and helped her to her feet. They took the box and sat on the bench. "Exciting and safe," he made sure to point out. "I'd rather face the judge than the Coast Guard any day."

"Dr. Worrywart's back." She rolled her eyes. "Though I have to admit I've had my fill of rough seas and super-high trees and critters in the woods."

"Building a fire was cool, though." He stared at the island they'd been stranded on way off in the distance beyond the ocean. It hadn't been that far away, but it had seemed like they were the last two people on earth. No outside world, completely unplugged, just the two of them. Was it so wrong for him to long to go back?

"True." Her gaze met his, her sarcastic humor slipping to one of wistful sincerity. "Not everything that happened on that island was bad."

Logan immediately thought of lying on top of her with her legs wrapped tightly around him, holding him intimately to her as he caressed her breasts and kissed the breath out of her. Not everything was bad? That was the understatement of the year. It had been damned incredible, and so had she, even if they both had been dreaming.

She seemed to realize where his thoughts were headed because her face flushed a becoming shade of pink. "But now we're back, firmly grounded in reality where we should most definitely stay. Let's open the box, Doc. I'm dying to see what happens next."

So was he, but he was too chicken to find out if she felt the same way. Inhaling a deep breath, he said, "Do you want to do the honors?" He held the box out to her.

She bit her bottom lip, and he had to stifle another groan. "I say we both open it," she said, breathless with excitement.

"On the count of three," he said, and she placed her hands beside his as he began to count. "One, two—"

She yanked it open on a laugh. "Sorry, I am so impatient. I'm working on it, though, so bear with me."

He laughed out loud. "You, my dear Lois, are never predictable."

She shrugged. "I've been called worse. In my book, 'never predictable' is a compliment, McGiant."

"It was meant to be."

She snatched the box from him and glanced down at her lap as she opened it with a wide-eyed look of anticipation. She clapped her hands and let out a squeal. "Sorry." She slapped a hand over her mouth and said through her fingers in a muffled tone, "I'm not usually such a spaz."

"Really? Because from what I've seen, this seems like perfectly normal behavior for you."

She pushed him, and he fell back chuckling. "Funny. In my defense, there's another letter. Forgive me for being a teeny bit excited."

"Seriously?" He sat up straight, all kidding aside as excitement filled him. He held out his hand. "Let me see."

"No way." She hugged the letter to her chest and tossed the map at him. "You can decipher the code to our next destination, but I get dibs on reading the letter."

"Fair enough." He sat back to listen as he unfolded the map.

She read the letter Joseph had written to Kathleen, telling her he was coming home on leave at the end of the summer. He wasn't due to get out of the service for another year, but at least she would get to see him soon. Then Emma read the letter Kathleen wrote and never got to send about worrying where he was and if he was safe and how she was so looking forward to seeing him, even if only for a moment. There were other letters as well. Ones after he got home from him saying how incredible it was to see her in person for the first time and how much he loved her and how he would find a way for them to be together. Then one from her saying yes, she would meet him in the park and she understood the code.

"Wow," Emma said, her hands falling to her lap. "I can't believe the lengths they went through to be together. They must have really loved each other. I didn't think love like that existed." She sighed wistfully.

Logan knew firsthand that true love existed. He'd had it and feared he never would again. Love like that was rare and special. An anger like he'd never known welled up inside of him on Joseph's behalf. "I can't believe how terrible his family was to her. I mean, they literally forced them to go into hiding instead of celebrating the fact that he'd made it home alive and had found happiness. The man was a hero, and they treated him like dirt."

"They were terrible parents. So were hers. I know times were tough back then, but who treats their children that way?"

"At least they had parents," Logan said with a frown and fiddled with the map to hide his own emotions. There was a time he would have given anything for parents of any kind.

"True, but I'm beginning to wonder if 'some' were any better than none." Emma set her jaw in an angry line.

"Trust me they were," Logan grudgingly admitted. "Joseph's parents might have been wrong in their beliefs and the way they handled things, but they loved their son." Logan thought back on his dark days as a boy in the foster care system. He'd bounced around from home to home in and out of trouble. Probably why he was such a worrywart now. Amanda and Trevor were the only family he'd ever known, and now her family was his.

Emma looked out over the water; her features pinched. "Maybe I should call my mother." She sighed, sounding a little defeated and resigned and guilty.

"Maybe you should," he said gently, taking her hand in his and threading his fingers through hers, beginning to understand the lengths a man would go to for love. Feelings he hadn't felt in a long time took root in his heart no matter how hard he fought for them not to. His gaze met hers, wanting to be there for her and help her any way he could. He nodded reassuringly. "It's time."

~

LATER THAT DAY Emma walked along the same beach where she'd found the bottle, only today was much warmer with the summer half over. She stood for a long moment, staring out across the calm ocean, realizing once more it matched her mood. She felt calm now. Settled. Grounded, even. Logan had helped her to find her inner peace. Every time she was around him, she felt like everything was going to be okay.

Maybe it really was going to be okay.

Emma might never know what happened to Mark, but she had to find a way to let that go. If Kathleen could move on, then so could she. She had to stop blaming herself and thinking she was unlovable or wasn't good enough, no matter how hard that might be. She had to forgive her parents, forgive Mark, and forgive herself. Starting with the easiest of the three, she pulled out her phone and called her mother.

"Darling, I'm so glad you finally called. I've been worried sick," Chelsea Hendricks said through the line. "Please tell me you have come to your senses and are coming home. Stacy seemed to think you were going to stay because of some story you're working on, but that can't be right. You don't belong there."

"I'm not coming home, Mother," Emma responded, sitting on a big piece of driftwood next to the water's edge. "I don't belong in Boston either, that's for sure, but I do believe I've finally come to my senses. There was no need to worry. I had Stacy let you all know where I was going for the summer before I left. Beacon Bay is a small town, not some big scary city. I'm fine."

"Getting stranded on some remote island with a man you barely know doesn't sound fine to me." Her mother left *It sounds scandalous* unspoken, but Emma knew Chelsea Hendricks well enough to know what she was thinking. "I mean, you're an engaged woman, my dear." The censure in her mother's voice came through the line loud and clear.

Emma clenched her jaw and counted to ten, reminding herself that Logan was right. She had to forgive in order to forget and move on. She took a deep breath. "Actually, Mother, I'm not engaged. I haven't been since Mark walked out on me seven months ago."

"But you don't know why he did that or where he went."

"No, I don't, and that's his fault for not reaching out to me. If he was dead, we would have found out about it by now. And someone who gets kidnapped doesn't pack their belongings and clean out their bank account first."

"Does that mean you're not looking into his disappearance anymore? His parents will be distraught. And what will everyone think about us as your parents? Your father will never survive the scandal of it all. And what about poor Stacy? Now that she's single, she'll never find another husband if her family name is tainted."

"Stacy will be fine, just ask her. The last thing she needs or wants right now is another man. Frankly, I don't care what anyone thinks. This is the twenty-first century." Emma took a breath, counted to ten again, and spoke with a less harsh tone. "Mark's parents can hire their own private investigator if they are so concerned about their son. They should have done that in the first place instead of relying on me."

"But that's what you do. Find facts and get to the bottom of a story. Get to the truth. Don't you want to know the truth?"

"More than anything, but I have to think of myself for a change. This obsession with Mark is destroying me. It's not healthy. What I've learned this summer is that many people all around the world from both yesterday and today are faced with hardships far worse than mine. It's how you pick up the pieces and move forward with your life that matters. I have to let some things go and make peace with them in order to have any kind of peace for myself. That's why I called."

"I don't understand."

"I forgive you."

There was a pause on the line. "*You* forgive *me*?" her mother sputtered, her tone implying, *Shouldn't it be the other way around?*

"I'm the victim here, Mother. No one seems to get that." Emma rubbed her temple, closing her eyes for a moment. She had to stay focused and keep her anger in check. This wasn't about her mother; it was about herself and *for* her own well-being. "Yes, I forgive you and Father and Mark's parents." She opened her eyes, feeling better already just for saying the words out loud, but she was a realist. She threw a pebble at the water. "Forgiving Mark is going to take a bit longer."

"I don't understand. We've always had your best interest at heart. You know we love you, right?"

"In your own way, yes, I know you love me."

"Then what on earth do we need your forgiveness for?"

Emma wanted to say, *For making me doubt myself and making me think I wasn't good enough and making me think I was unlovable and sticking up for Mark over me,* but in the end she simply said, "For everything."

Her mother was stunned into silence for the first time in her life.

Emma said, "That's all I have to say for now. I'll be in touch soon. Give Father my love. Goodbye Mother." Emma hung up the phone and just like that a weight was lifted from her shoulders and a small part of her heart began to heal. Forgiving wasn't easy, but it was freeing.

One down, two to go.

13

PRESENT DAY: BEACON BAY, MAINE

Logan flipped the steaks he had seasoned and placed on the grill beside the roasted corn and buttered baked potatoes out back on his concrete patio. He had a small, fenced-in yard with a patio table, umbrella and chairs, but it was enough for Trevor and him. A little bit of room for his boy to run around, shaded by a large oak tree. His house was small. A two-bedroom single bath, but that too had worked for them. He knew he didn't want any more children or to get married again, so what would be the point in getting something bigger? Besides, it was right in town and close to the hospital.

Logan lifted his face to the evening breeze, inhaling the smells of fresh-cut grass and wildflowers. Someone's dog was barking a few houses down and the sounds of children laughing made him smile. He took a sip of the Cabernet he'd opened and thought about how proud his mother-in-law would be of him. He was actually doing something for himself. Taking a night off and treating himself to a home-cooked meal.

Logan enjoyed cooking and used to surprise Amanda with a meal whenever he got home from work first. She often said she was the luckiest woman alive. His smile lingered, and he realized it was getting easier to think about her and even talk about her these days. It was a Saturday night, and he hadn't volunteered to be on call this weekend. Shocking for him, but then again, he'd done a lot of surprising things this summer, and he owed it all to one person.

Emma Hendricks.

Emma had shown Logan how to live again. How to take chances and be in the moment, to think about something other than work or helping people. To think of himself for a change. He would be forever grateful to her for that, because it would make him a better father to his son, Trevor. He missed his son something fierce and couldn't wait to see him again in a couple of weeks.

Speaking of Emma, Logan hadn't seen her in almost a week. Ever since they'd found the map and letters buried beneath the bench at Lighthouse Lane Park, she'd been distant. He'd encouraged her to talk to her mother. She hadn't spoken to her all summer. He knew Emma was mad at her, but he also knew she didn't realize how lucky she was to have parents of *any* kind, let alone ones who cared about her.

Emma had become a good friend to him, and he didn't want to see her stubbornness get in the way of her happiness. She needed to forgive in order to let go and move on. That's all there was to it. She had thanked him for his advice and then had left, saying she'd be in touch when she was ready to set out on their next adventure.

He hadn't heard a word.

"Knock, knock," came a familiar voice from behind him.

He turned around in surprise. *Speak of the devil*, he thought and had to smile. He'd recognize that silky auburn hair and those amber eyes that haunted his dreams every night anywhere. Emma's face barely reached over the top of his fence. He walked across the lawn and let her in.

"You're just in time," he said, admittedly way too happy to see her.

"For what?" she asked as she walked into his yard, carrying a six pack of beer.

"Dinner." He held up his wine and smiled.

She'd probably assumed a guy like him drank beer, as he stood there in his charcoal gray dry-fit shorts and white tank-top undershirt. Same way he had assumed a woman like her only drank martinis and wine, all decked out in her short white mini-skirt with wedged sandals and chartreuse silk blouse. Yet he preferred wine and she preferred beer. Guess they'd both judged each other unfairly. Before he'd met her, he wouldn't have looked twice at her, sensing they were from two very different worlds. Now he felt like he couldn't exist in any world without her in it.

"You cook?" She blinked, staring at him all wide-eyed with wonder as if he were a foreign species the likes of which she'd never come across.

"You don't?" He raised a brow in mock horror but then winked. Damn he'd missed her. And she looked *way* too good.

"Never had to cook." She shrugged. "Grew up with nannies, housekeepers, and cooks because of my parents. Probably why I don't care for people in my house now."

This time he did stare at her with genuine surprise. "You didn't cook even after you lived on your own?"

"More hired help. Mark's idea, not mine. He's the dependent one. And no, I didn't move out until I met Mark." She held up her hand. "Don't judge."

Logan slapped a palm over his heart. "I would never think of it."

"Where would you like this?" she asked as she held out the beer.

"You can put it in the fridge. Straight through the sliding

glass doors to your right. I'm grilling steaks, so I'll stick with red wine if you don't mind, but help yourself to whatever."

"That would be beer for me."

She carried the beer inside and spent longer than she needed to, which meant she was either checking out his place or checking out her reflection in the bathroom off the kitchen. Moments later she emerged with her hair scooped up into a messy knot at the back of her head and a beer mug in hand and a longneck bottle of beer, indicating she had done a little of both.

"Hope you don't mind. I helped myself. Cute place by the way."

"Thanks." He flipped the steaks, turned the corn over, and poked the potatoes then lowered the lid. "It's small, but it's perfect for Trevor and me." He faced her and reached out for the bottle in her hand. She handed it to him a little too eagerly, indicating something was bothering her, just as he'd suspected. He popped the top and filled her mug, then handed it back to her, studying her curiously but not saying a word.

"Thank you." She eyed him discreetly, which gave him hope she might be checking him out as well. He still didn't know if he was ready for anything more than friendship with any woman, but it was nice to know he wasn't alone in recognizing *something* was happening between them. She took a big drink before speaking again. "Everything looks great, but I have to ask. Why'd you cook so much if you planned to dine alone? Or did I interrupt something?"

He let out a laugh at that. "No, no. There hasn't been *something* to interrupt in quite some time."

"That's what I thought," she blurted, and then flushed pink, probably over her mouth running away from her again. She took another big drink of her beer. He was starting to love her mouth, especially when she bit her full bottom lip. He tore his gaze away and had to stifle a groan. "I mean," she hastened to explain, "you pretty much said so yourself when you mentioned it had been six years since...well...you know."

"No, I don't know. Whatever do you mean? Please, enlighten me." He tried like hell not to grin, but it was difficult, so he took a drink of his wine.

She lightly punched him on the arm and gave him a sarcastic smirk. "Very funny."

"I like to think so." He laughed on a choke and then wiped his mouth with a napkin. "And by the way, I haven't heard from you all week. Seems to me *you're* the one with something to interrupt." He eyed her pointedly.

"Trust me, that's so not the case." She shook her head as she made a beeline for his kitchen and returned with plates and silverware and another beer—an obvious avoidance tactic.

He puckered his brow and stared at her, studying her for a moment before saying, "Okay, I'll bite. A pretty, young woman like you is here at a pathetic widower's place—who still cooks as if his wife were still alive—on a Saturday night, with alcohol in tow. What's up, Hendricks?"

"You think I'm pretty?" Emma asked, and then frowned immediately after. "And for the record, you're hardly pathetic." Her gaze met his, locked, and held. "More like lonely, as am I, Doc."

"Touché." They clinked his glass to her mug. "And for the record, yes, I think you're pretty. Beautiful, in fact, but I imagine you've heard that plenty of times." She flushed and looked like she sincerely wasn't used to receiving compliments, which floored him. There was so much more to her than he'd ever imagined. "Seriously though," he tried to steer the conversation back to safer waters, "I can tell something is eating at you, so spill it."

"I needed a friend, that's all."

He dished up dinner on their plates, shut off the grill, and carried the plates over to the patio table, trying to think of how to convince her to open up to him. Sitting down across from her, he finally replied, "Don't we all, Lois. But as your *friend*, I can't help you if you don't tell me what's wrong."

"Okay, so I admit it." She cut her steak, not meeting his eyes. "I've been avoiding you all week."

"Why?" He dug into his own food, enjoying the savory steak seasonings mixed with melted buttered corn and baked potatoes.

"Because I feel like I let you down," she said after she finished chewing. "This is delicious by the way."

"Thank you, and that's crazy, by the way." He took another sip of his wine and studied her. "You could never let me down."

She finally met his gaze. "You know the advice you gave me?"

He raised a brow. "Yeah?"

"Well, I took it to heart." She set down her fork and sat back, swirling her mug of beer and staring off as though thinking carefully about her words. "As hard as it was, I called my mother."

"And?"

Emma looked him in the eye. "And I forgave her, just like you said to do."

"And that's bad how?"

"It's not bad. I felt much better after forgiving her, even though she doesn't have a clue what I forgave her for, but I have learned that's her issue and not mine."

"Good girl."

"I know, right? I felt pretty pleased with myself after that." She smiled, but it didn't quite reach her eyes.

"But?" he prodded, knowing there was still something bothering her.

"But I am having a bit of trouble," she admitted.

"With what?" He refilled his glass and opened the other beer she'd brought out for her.

"It wasn't as hard to forgive myself for being such a gullible idiot in thinking Mark and I actually had a chance. I mean, he gave me all the signs. He asked me to marry him, for Pete's sake." Her tone raised an octave higher in her anger. "It wasn't my fault he left me to go off and do God knows what? I can rationally understand that."

"Then what's the problem?"

She downed three gulps of her beer before replying through her teeth, "Forgiving Mark. My blood boils just saying his name. He doesn't deserve forgiveness. How am I supposed to move on?"

"Ah, I do understand. He hurt you. How can you forgive someone who hurt you? But that's entirely the point. If you don't forgive him, then you won't move on. End of story. He wins."

"He's not going to win."

"Then don't let him." Logan stood up and went into the house, returning shortly with two shot glasses and a bottle of whiskey. "I figured this conversation requires something a bit stronger."

"Dr. Worrywart isn't so afraid after all, thank God." She took the shot glass from him and tossed it back. He poured her another and then sat down, recognizing need when he saw it because it was the same need he'd had since his wife died. He didn't give in to it on a daily basis to numb the pain because of his son, but once in a while, he allowed himself to wallow in self-pity.

Tonight was definitely one of those nights.

"Trust me, I've done plenty wrong in my life." He thought of what had really happened to his wife and how he had kept it from everyone. He'd told himself it was for their own good, but he wasn't fooling anyone. He'd done it for himself because he couldn't live with the world knowing her death was all his fault. He poured himself another shot and joined Emma in a party for two.

"Somehow I doubt that." She snorted, looking far more relaxed already. "What could you possibly have done that was so bad?"

This time she sipped her shot glass, which was probably a good idea. One of them needed to keep their wits about them because he was suddenly in the mood to get shit-faced drunk, which took him twice as long since he was double the size of her. He downed another shot, unable to speak. Emma eyed him curiously but didn't press the matter when he poured another. She had no clue what had really happened. No one did. Living alone with his lie had been eating him up inside for six long years. Forgiving Amanda had been easy. It wasn't her fault. It was his. Forgiving himself was the issue. And until he did, he and any other woman wouldn't stand a chance.

"Okay, fine, I admit it," Emma said, staring down into her shot glass. "I am having a hard time forgiving Mark for what he did to me. It's not fair. He doesn't deserve my forgiveness. He shouldn't get a free pass."

"Why not?" Frustration was bottling up inside of Logan. Emma's fiancé might have walked out on her with no explanation and hurt her feelings, but at least he was still alive. She had the chance to fix things with him if she wanted to, where Logan would never have that chance again with Amanda. Talk about things not being fair.

Emma blinked at him, totally shocked. "What do you mean, why not?"

"You don't know for certain what happened to Mark. What if he has a great excuse? I know you don't have closure, but you still have possibilities. Your outcome could be much bleaker, that's all I'm saying." Logan stared down into his empty shot glass and wanted more. He wanted to keep drinking until it numbed the pain if only for a little while.

"If and when Mark ever returns, no excuse on earth could make up for what he did," Emma ground out, obviously growing angry with him. "I don't care what his excuse is. It won't be nearly good enough to make up for what he put me through. Why are you taking his side? You sound like my parents."

"I'm not taking his side. I'm trying to be rational. Logical. You might try that yourself," Logan snapped back at her with a harsher tone than he'd intended. Another reason why he shouldn't keep drinking. He tossed back another shot anyway. "What if Mark was trying his best to deal with a situation he never expected and didn't ask for but was dealt with nonetheless?" Logan added, thinking of himself.

"What are you talking about? How can you have sympathy for him? He left me willingly. I don't care what the situation was, I would have moved heaven and earth before I ever left him. So would you. Your wife was taken from you when she would have given anything to stay. She didn't leave you willingly. She was taken from you, so you don't know what you're talking about, and you sure as hell don't know what I'm going through or how it feels." Emma surged to her feet. "Coming here was a mistake."

"You're damn right it was!" Logan launched from his chair and threw his shot glass across the yard until it hit the fence and smashed into a million tiny little jagged pieces. "Goddammit, you and I both know I'm not just your friend!" he bellowed, not holding anything back now. Goddamned alcohol! "But what you don't know is that I'm not free to be anything more."

Emma stared at him wide-eyed, like he was some sort of monster. He was, and she should be very afraid.

He thrust a finger in her direction, his whole body shaking with too many emotions screaming to break free. "Don't you dare tell me I don't know what I'm talking about." His voice broke, and he could no longer keep his emotions in check as the words he'd buried deep inside for so long finally broke free. "My wife left me, too. Goddammit, she left me too, okay? You're not fucking alone. I know exactly how you feel. And if I can forgive her, then you sure as hell can forgive him."

"I know she left you, and I'm so sorry." Emma's face transformed into one of pity as she dropped her hand from the gate and stared at him.

Logan had to tell her the rest, then she would understand, but getting the words out was so hard. He fisted his hands and grit his teeth but couldn't stop the pain from overcoming him. Tears withheld from six years of repressing them came surging to the surface and broke free on an agonized sob. He fell to his knees and his voice shook as he said the words that had haunted his soul for six long years, "My wife willingly left me, too."

His shoulders shook as he hung his head, trying to hold his emotions back. He finally caved and cried for all the feelings he had kept bottled up for so long now and for the words he hadn't spoken to another living soul on earth. It was freeing and liberating and somehow right with Emma. His eyes were squeezed shut and he hadn't thought she was still there until he felt her touch. She cradled his cheeks and pulled him into her embrace as she stood before him. He was on his knees with his face buried in her stomach as he snaked his arms around her lower back, holding her to him as if he would die if she walked away now.

Truth be told, he probably would.

She ran her hands through his hair and stroked his back over and over. "What happened?" she finally asked. "You need to say the words. Talk to me. Let it all out. I'm here, and I'm not going anywhere."

With his tears wetting the front of her expensive shirt, he spoke in a muffled voice. "Trevor was a big baby. The birth was difficult. Amanda hemorrhaged and had a lot of bleeding, but she survived. I thought we were in the clear, but I could tell she wasn't herself. About two weeks in she started to act a little differently. At first, I questioned her about it, but she was a damned good nurse. I was in the height of my career and determined to make it to the top, no matter the cost. I'd had to work so hard my entire life, I wanted to make sure she and Trevor were taken care of, but she couldn't handle him alone. I should have known that."

"It's okay. It's going to be okay," Emma kept saying over and over as she continued to touch every part of him she could reach, and for the first time, Logan had a glimmer of hope that maybe someday he might believe that.

"Amanda understood working so hard to get ahead in your career and understood me like no one else ever had," he continued with his story. "She was my biggest cheerleader. She knew all about post-partum depression, so when the signs hit, she hid them. She didn't want to upset me and she didn't want to stop me from achieving all of my dreams. When things became too unbearable for her, she didn't tell me because she knew I probably couldn't have handled it at that time. My angel was always thinking of me, and then I let her down in the biggest way imaginable. I'm a doctor, for God's sake. I should have known what was going on and gotten her help. I don't deserve to be happy, Emma. I don't." He squeezed her tighter and sobbed harder into her stomach.

Her hands continued to caress him, and she kept kissing him tenderly. "Logan, you're way too hard on yourself. You have to get this off your chest. You can't keep these kinds of feelings inside. I'm surprised you haven't had a breakdown long before now. I'm here for you. You can tell me anything. What happened?"

He shuddered and did the one thing he'd never thought he

would. He opened up. "I came home one day and found her in a pool of blood. She'd hemorrhaged again. It was awful. I felt horrible for not seeing the signs. The big baby, the hard labor, hemorrhaging in the hospital. I should have known she was at high risk for hemorrhaging again. You can hemorrhage for several weeks after having a baby."

"But that's not your fault. She died tragically. Everyone knows that. How is that her leaving you willingly?"

"That's what I thought for a long time. Her parents were grief-stricken as she was their only child, and poor Trevor was just a baby in need of his mama. It was all such a horrible tragedy. But then I found her note."

He felt Emma stiffen and her hands stilled before she spoke. "There was a note?"

"Oh yeah. Amanda made sure I wouldn't find it until a month later when I was packing up our things to take Trevor and move to Beacon Bay so he could experience what was left of his family. We had talked about it before, so she must have suspected that's what I would do. My wife's death was tragic, but it was no accident. She knew she was hemorrhaging, but she purposely didn't call for help. She didn't do a damn thing to stop it. Thank God the baby was in his crib. She was too deep into her post-partum depression and didn't have the will or the energy to go on living. She let herself bleed to death, but she couldn't leave without saying goodbye to me. She wrote me a suicide note and hid it in Trevor's keepsake box so I wouldn't find it until much later."

"Oh my God, I am so sorry." Emma dropped to her knees and wrapped her arms around his neck, pressing her body to his.

"It's so unfair. She got to say goodbye to me, but I never did to her, and I will never have the chance to now." He held Emma tightly pressed against him with his face buried in her neck.

"She willingly left me too, Emma. She fucking willingly left me too. Sometimes I hate her for what she did, but I can't because of Trevor. And her parents are Catholic. They needed to know their baby went to heaven. I couldn't tell them. I'm so alone."

"You're not alone. You're not alone. I'm right here." Emma leaned her head back and cradled his cheeks in her palms as she stared into his eyes. "It's going to be okay; do you hear me? I'm not going anywhere."

"I need you," he choked out, letting everything he was feeling show in his eyes. "So damn much," he added on a whisper.

"I know. I need you, too," she said with strong emotions shimmering in the tears welling up in her eyes mixed with something more he couldn't quite identify and didn't care to as she pressed her lips to his.

14

PRESENT DAY: BEACON BAY, MAINE

Emma didn't fully understand what had come over her. She knew she had to kiss Logan, right that minute, in the middle of his backyard beneath the stars that had emerged sparkling in the evening sky. Maybe it was the alcohol. Or maybe it was the full moon that lit up his yard with an unearthly glow.

Kissing him was certainly out of this world.

She forgot to think, forgot to breathe, just went on instinct and let herself feel. They'd both been through so much with their loves leaving them on purpose. She didn't know if she could ever forgive Mark for walking away from her any more than Logan could forgive himself for not helping Amanda in time. They were damaged, maybe beyond repair, but they needed each other right now. Beyond that, only time would tell.

She felt herself being lifted into Logan's strong arms. He never broke the kiss as he carried her through the sliding doors and into his bedroom. His tongue traced every inch of her mouth, sweeping inside to taste and touch her own, sending pulses of electricity throughout her body. She plunged her hands into his thick curly hair, raking her fingernails over his scalp gently, then sweeping down to stroke his neck and squeeze his broad muscular shoulders. She wanted—no she *needed*—to touch him, feel him. She felt like if they stopped, she would crumble and fall apart.

He pulled his mouth away from hers long enough to rumble in a deep voice, "Are you sure about this?"

"No," she responded with a breathy tone, "are you?"

He shook his head but tightened his hold on her as if he too was afraid to let go. "But I think I'll die if we stop."

"Good, that makes me feel better. So stop thinking and just feel." She cradled his face in her palms. "You need me and I need you. That's all that matters right now, don't you think? Or am I crazy?"

"You're not crazy." He rested his forehead against hers. "Please don't leave. Tell me you'll stay the night."

"Okay," she said without hesitation, knowing there was no turning back from what they were about to do, but she didn't care. She needed him way too much. Needed to comfort him. Needed to help herself.

Logan had said she was beautiful earlier and acted like she should know that. He had no idea she'd never felt pretty or wanted or good enough for anyone. Knowing he felt that way about her was a gift. Maybe it was time she showed him how she felt about him as well. Emma wrapped her arms around his neck and leaned back until they fell onto the bed with him on top of her. His lips tipped up a hair in amusement until she pushed him over and rolled on top of him. He sucked in a breath, his smile disappearing in an instant.

Straddling him, she sat up and her mini-skirt shoved up by her hips, leaving nothing but her lace panties and his silky shorts as a barrier between them. She ran her fingertips over his firm chest and down his flat stomach, the fine layer of hair tickling her hands through his tank top. She could feel him grow hard beneath her and sucked in her own breath over the sheer size of him. She pressed herself against him more firmly, and he grabbed her hips to still her.

"Easy, babe," he managed to get out between groans. "I'm gonna lose it if you're not careful."

She bit her bottom lip, then said, "I'm not worried. We've got all night."

She slowly pulled off her blouse and tossed it aside, loving the way he looked at her. For the first time in way too long, she actually *felt* beautiful. She reached for the front clasp of her bra, but he stilled her hands with his own. He brought each of them one at a time to his lips and kissed her palms then placed her hands at her sides. Spanning her waist with his wide palms, he slid his hands up slowly, stroking her belly with his thumbs along the way. When he reached the clasp of her bra, she was squirming with anticipation, which only seemed to make him moan harder.

He undid the clasp and peeled back the lace, his lips parting in awe as his eyes worshipped her. In one swift motion he surged to a sitting position, arched her back and took her breast in his mouth. She let out a cry of pure ecstasy as waves of sensations shot through her. If he was about to lose it, she was already halfway there. She wrapped her legs around him and he slid one hand down to cup her bottom and pull her tighter to him while supporting her back with his other hand.

"Too many clothes," he muttered after giving her other breast equal attention and quickly flipped her onto her back.

"Agreed," she breathed, barely able to talk.

Everything happened so fast and suddenly they were both naked as they kissed their way over each other's bodies, touching and tasting every inch of each other. And then he entered her, filling her so deeply and completely, tears leaked from the corners of her eyes. She didn't know how to describe it, but she felt more connected to him than she had ever felt to anyone, as if they were a part of each other like soul-mates, and it terrified her.

"What's wrong, babe, did I hurt you?" He stilled.

She shook her head hard. "No, no, don't stop. You're perfect," was all she dared to say.

He rolled them over, still joined together, and stroked her back. Kissing her tenderly, he ran his hands through her hair as if to show her rather than say what was on his mind, but she could feel how he felt, and that was somehow more special. They moved together as one in a beautiful dance that started slow and picked up in tempo until a powerful and beautiful climax hit them both simultaneously. They shouted each other's names and then collapsed together in a tangled sweaty heap on the mattress.

Neither one spoke, they just lay in each other's arms, listening to each other's heartbeats as their breathing slowed. Emma was terrified words would ruin the perfect world they had created if only for one night. She wasn't ready for reality and doubts to creep back in. Everything seemed so right between them and she actually began to hope maybe they could be more than friends, but a nagging feeling at the back of her mind told her something was very wrong.

LOGAN LOOKED up from the map he was reading at the marina and glanced at his phone. Still no text or call from Emma. He had been avoiding her for the past week, and now she was angry. Rightfully so. It had been stupid to avoid her, but he couldn't help himself, although she had probably misunderstood the reason why. It had nothing to do with her, and everything to do with him, but telling her that would have been like saying, "It's not you, it's me." Something no man or woman wanted to hear, especially after making love.

Making love to Emma had been incredible, and that was the problem. She had been there for him when he'd needed someone more than he ever had before. He'd spilled his secret and was having a hard time with her knowing him intimately. Not physical intimacy—he could handle that—but emotional intimacy was a whole other beast. Emma had crawled deep inside his heart and his soul, and it scared the hell out of him.

Not to mention, she'd told him she wasn't on the pill anymore when they were on the island. He was a doctor, for Pete's sake. He should have known better than to get carried away and have unprotected sex. It had only been a week, so it was probably too soon to tell, and he had no idea how to ask her if she'd gotten her period without sounding like an ass. Avoidance had been the best option on so many levels until he screwed his head on straight.

Logan didn't want to hurt Emma, but he knew that was exactly what was going to happen. He'd lived with his guilt and pain for too long to change now. He couldn't forgive himself, no matter how hard he tried, not even for Emma. But he owed her for helping him and he'd made a promise to her and to his son to finish this quest.

Logan glanced at the ever-darkening sky. Gray clouds had rolled in and the wind started to pick up. If they didn't act soon, the brewing storm would be upon them. He sighed deeply and sent her a text once more, asking yet again if she planned on meeting him at the marina today. He had sent her a text yesterday saying everything was fine and he hadn't fallen off the face of the earth—as she'd put it—which had amused him as usual. He would miss her terribly when she left. He'd said he had been swamped at work, but tomorrow he could meet her at the marina. Well, tomorrow was today, and she had yet to respond. Payback, he guessed.

The last map they'd found had shown the rendezvous spot for Joseph and Kathleen was at the marina. Maybe this would be it, and Logan and Emma could finish their adventure and set each other free. He needed to soon because the more time he spent with her, the harder it was going to be to let her go.

"Hey," he heard from behind him.

His heart jumped into his throat at the sound of her voice. He turned around to face her. She wore spandex workout pants and a tank top as if she'd come from a run, her hair still a bit damp at the temples. She'd never looked better. He frowned and cleared his throat. "You're here. I'm glad."

She checked her watch and counted her pulse before answering. "I was busy this week, too. You aren't the only one with a life."

"Emma, I—"

"Can we not go there? It's cool. We both knew that night was about need, and nothing more. I don't want that any more than you do, so you can relax, Doc."

Guilt plagued him over her words. Guilt and something more. Disappointment maybe? He admitted he couldn't handle how he felt about her, but the thought that she didn't feel anything at all about him was a bit unsettling. He didn't exactly know how to handle that either. "I didn't want you to think—"

"I didn't think anything. Look, I wasn't expecting flowers but what I *did* expect was for you to answer your phone like an adult and not ignore me. We have a quest to finish, remember?"

"I was going to say I didn't want you to think making love with you wasn't good, or anything. It was—"

"It was hot, Doc, and of course it was good." She shrugged. "You were with me."

He knew that was her defense mechanism. To be sarcastic

and act like she didn't give a damn to protect herself from getting hurt, but he suspected she gave too much of a damn and was just as scared as he was. "It was more than good, Lois. It was incredible," he finished softly, adding, "even if we weren't very smart about it," in hopes that she would get his drift.

"I am pretty amazing." A little smile tilted her lips as a slight blush tinted her cheeks in obvious pleasure she couldn't quite hide. "And you can relax, Doc. I might be passionate, but I'm not stupid. I had just finished my period the day before we were together, so there's no McBaby in this oven."

"I'm sorry," he said sincerely.

"Good. Apology accepted." She nodded once and brushed off her hands, looking as if nothing had ever happened between them.

He raised a brow. "Just like that?"

She lifted one shoulder. "Just like that, McGiant. You'll find I'm not like most women." She huffed.

No, she was not. He fought to keep his lips from twitching.

"Now that we've moved past that, let's get to work." She snatched the map from his hands and studied it. "Your thoughts?" she finally asked and looked up at him.

He pointed to the corner of the marina where a gazebo stood. "X marks the spot is right there. I'm thinking that gazebo wasn't there when Joseph and Kathleen buried their treasure decades ago."

"You're kidding. What are we going to do?"

He scratched his head and looked around. "I don't think there's much we can do. This might be the end of the road for us."

Emma was already shaking her head. "No way. It can't be." She marched over to the gazebo and walked around it. Scanning the area, she said, "No one's around, so I say we dig until we find something."

"Are you crazy? We can't rip up the floorboards. That's destroying property that belongs to the town."

"Dr. Worrywart's back." She rolled her eyes. "We don't have to rip anything up. We're going to crawl beneath it."

He could feel his face pale. "I don't exactly like confined spaces."

"Yeah, well, I don't like critters, but I still hiked through the woods and camped out on a deserted island for you." She poked him in the chest. "You owe me, Doc. Call it your punishment for blowing me off all week."

"Fine, but when we wind up in jail, you're taking the blame and bailing us out," he grumbled. "I have a son to put through college and a reputation to uphold."

"Deal." She held out her hand.

He shook it and then headed over to the gazebo with resignation and a little bit of excitement that he'd never admit to her. Walking around the wooden building as well, he stopped at one section. "Look here, the lattice is loose in this spot. I'll have to tell Manny. He takes care of security at the marina. Since it needs to be fixed anyway, I guess there's no harm in helping him remove part of it."

"And you say *I'm* a piece of work." Emma scoffed.

"Funny." Dropping to his knees, Logan gently pulled at the lattice until it gave way, careful not to damage anything else. "This should be big enough for the two of us."

"You want me to go with you?" she squeaked.

"I'm not doing this alone. And if memory serves me right, you blew me off the week before I ignored you. I say this makes us even."

"Did I mention I don't like spiders any more than I like critters?"

"Now who's the chicken?" He grabbed her hand and pulled

her with him as she groaned every step of the way. "Don't worry, I'll protect you."

Ten minutes later, they were fully submerged beneath the gazebo. Rays of what was left of the sunlight streamed through the slats of the lattice, casting distorted diamond shapes all over the ground. Once their eyes adjusted to the dim light, Emma's head kept swiveling as she searched for bugs while Logan fought to remain calm in the tight space.

"Let's get this over with before we both have panic attacks and are rendered useless," he said. He pulled out a garden shovel which was small enough to fit in the large pocket of his cargo shorts. In the past he hadn't brought one and they'd needed it, but then on their next adventure he'd brought a big one and they didn't. This time he'd apparently brought the perfect size.

"For once, you got it right," she said with a grin.

"Maybe it's a sign this will be easy."

She laughed. "When has anything ever been easy for us?"

He pinned her with a look.

Thirty minutes later, after digging up just about every spec of dirt they could find, they finally hit something.

"Of course, it's the last spot we chose to dig." Emma huffed. Thunder rumbled outside, and the first spatters of raindrops pelted the gazebo.

"Just in time by the sound of it." Logan dug deep enough until he was able to pull out a wooden box like the others that had become such treasures to them both. "Let's go," he said, more than ready to get out from beneath the gazebo.

Emma started to shimmy backwards when they spotted a flashlight outside.

"Wait," Logan whispered, grabbing her arm.

"Why?" she whispered back, but Logan pressed his finger to

her lips. They froze as the person with the flashlight walked around whistling an old Irish jig.

Manny.

When everything grew quiet and the light vanished, Logan let out a sigh of relief. They shimmied the rest of the way out from beneath the gazebo and stood up.

"Aha! Caught ya," said a voice full of gravel as the flashlight switched on to shine in their eyes.

Logan jumped and shoved the box at Emma behind him, then shielded his eyes with his hand. "Do you mind, Manny?"

"Doc?" The flashlight lowered and an old man with balding stark white hair and crooked, yellow teeth stared back at them with wide watery gray eyes. "What in the world are you doing beneath the gazebo in this kind of weather, and who's that with you?"

"This is Ms. Emma Hendricks. She's visiting our small town, and I was showing her around when the storm rolled in." Logan held up the broken lattice. "I couldn't leave without retrieving your broken lattice. I saw it beneath the gazebo and knew you would want to have it fixed."

Manny rubbed his whiskers and eyed them suspiciously. "It takes two of you to do that job?"

"Trust me, Manny. He needs all the help he can get. I had to hold his hand because of the tight spaces and all. He's kind of a big chicken, but his heart's in the right place." Emma patted Logan's shoulder.

Manny's eyes twinkled as he looked between the two of them, and then he threw back his head and let out a cackling laugh. "That's our Doc. Always trying to help everyone. I see how it is. He's lucky to have you as his sidekick." The old man winked.

"Why, yes he is. Thank you for noticing, Manny. It's nice to be appreciated by someone." Emma grinned.

"Much obliged, ma'am. I hope you enjoy your stay." He bowed his head at her, and then turned to Logan. "Thanks for letting me know, Doc. I'll be sure to let the town council know. Anyway, you best be getting on home now. It's gonna be a doozy of a storm."

"Thanks, Manny," Logan called after the old-timer security guard as he walked away whistling another jig. "Chicken?" He looked at Emma.

"I had to say something. He was getting suspicious. Come on. You heard the man. It's gonna be a doozy, and I'm getting wet."

"Where are we going?" Logan asked.

"My place. I need a shower." She glanced over her shoulder as she started walking away. "Get your mind out of the gutter, McGiant. The other night was a one-time deal. All we're going to do is open this box and explore our treasure." Her words said one thing, but her body moved in a way that said so much more.

"Whatever you say," he responded as he followed closely behind, helpless to do otherwise. Because—stupid or not—if there was even a chance he could explore the treasure of her once more, then he was all in...

Consequences be damned.

15

AUGUST 1943: BEACON BAY, MAINE

Kathleen ventured into town on a hot and steamy August day. She still avoided Beacon Bay's downtown area as much as possible, but she wanted to buy a few things to make a strawberry pie—Joseph's favorite. He'd sent a coded map for her to meet him at the marina by his boat. His family's business was right down the shore from the marina, and he kept his own personal boat in the last slot in the harbor. It was a bit away from the other boats, and no one would think to look for them down below in the cuddy cabin.

She hated sneaking around. It made their love feel cheap and wrong when it was the most beautiful thing she'd ever experienced. So, they'd lived their fairytale in secret. It was hard to keep up the charade when she loved him so much. He told her time and again that he loved her too, and she believed him. She understood why he had to go along with his mother's plan, acting like he was going to marry Beverly. If he didn't, then his mother would ruin Kathleen's parents. As much as they had wronged her and broken her heart, she couldn't do that to them. They did love her; they just weren't as strong as she was.

Kathleen had forgiven them. How could she not? She truly

believed everything happened for a reason. Had she not been shunned by the town, she wouldn't have been thrown out of their house and sent to live in the cottage. And had she not lived in the cottage, she never would have met Joseph. He was the love of her life. Her soul-mate. She knew their time would come, she just had to be patient, no matter how difficult that might be.

With a feeling of anticipation, she decided not to let anything get her down. Their rendezvous were to be cherished, not tainted with negative thoughts. They still wrote love letters to one another even though he was home, and she still loved reading every word he wrote. As she walked into a store, she was thinking about what she would write to him after she got home and baked his pie.

Voices from the back made her look up. She froze, the smile on her face fading fast as her lips parted in shocked surprise. Pain sliced through her at the sight of Joseph standing beside Beverly with his hand on the small of her back. His head was bent toward hers as if to hear her better. Her face was flushed as she lifted her chin and said something for his ears only. His lips tipped up at the corners in a small smile of amusement. Joseph's gaze suddenly met Kathleen's and his expression froze in a look of surprise followed by panic. He blinked, but then quickly masked any recognition.

Not quickly enough, apparently.

"What's the matter, darling?" his mother asked as she joined them. "You look as if you've seen a ghost." She glanced in the direction he had been staring, and her gaze hardened as it settled on Kathleen. Hilary sniffed sharply. "I think we're through here. Let's go someplace classier, shall we?"

Beverly's brow puckered in confusion, and she turned to see what all the fuss was about. She didn't know Joseph's proposal was a sham to buy them time. She didn't know he wanted to be with Kathleen instead. And she most certainly didn't know his mother was blackmailing him into going along with her plan. Therefore, Beverly didn't see Kathleen as a threat. She simply saw her as everyone else in town did—a piece of trash not worth anything and meant to be discarded.

Beverly looked down her nose at Kathleen. "Oh, yes, I see," she responded to Hilary, obviously thinking she was referring to the scandal. "I must say I agree, don't you sweetheart? This place is beneath us. Let's go somewhere with a lot more to offer." She looked back up at Joseph expectantly.

His gaze remained a mask and he refused to look at either his mother or Kathleen. He held his eyes on his fiancé and said, "Whatever you want, my love."

The trio turned away to walk out of the store, and Hilary shot a gloating satisfied look over her shoulder at Kathleen as she closed the door firmly behind her.

Kathleen's hand fluttered to her chest to hold her broken heart together. She'd known Joseph had to play along with the charade, but to witness it firsthand was torture. And for him to shun her like the rest of the town, when he alone had been her savior, was simply unbearable. She couldn't do this anymore. She turned around and ran out of the store without another thought to making him a pie.

Out on the street, she ran into William. Kathleen bounced off his broad chest, and he caught her before she could fall. "Are you okay? What's wrong, did someone hurt you?" he asked, looking genuinely concerned. Ironic since he was the only person who had ever hurt her, physically anyway. But the emotional hurt Joseph had just inflicted upon her had been far more painful.

She shook her head and backed away from him. It was all too much. Turning around, she fled as fast as her legs would carry her. Each stride and each tear chipped away the strength she had left. Let them look and wonder, she thought as several people stopped to stare. She didn't care about any of it anymore.

The only letter she would be writing to Joseph would be one of farewell.

❧

JOSEPH PACED the wooden dock at the marina, waiting for Kathleen to show up. He felt so bad about what happened at the store. He would have given anything to have it be Kathleen by his side instead of Beverly. Anything to spare her the pain he'd seen flash across her face. He prayed she wasn't too angry with him, and he was willing to take his punishment if she was. Whatever wrath she would bestow he would gladly accept because she was his destiny, and a life without her was not an option. If only his family were more understanding, things could be so different.

His mother had spies among the staff. So far, he had been able to be discreet. He kept sneaking about, telling her he was meeting up with his old friends for cards or a night on the town like he used to, when he was really sneaking off to be with Kathleen. For the most part his friends had covered for him, though they didn't know where he was going or understand why he was so different.

Joseph didn't care about meaningless things such as a night on town like he had partaken in regularly several years ago. After all he'd witnessed overseas, it seemed silly to get drunk and chase after easy women. He needed more in his life. He needed someone who made him feel like he mattered. Like he was special and could do anything. Like there was a reason he had been spared.

He needed Kathleen Connor.

And now he was petrified he'd lost her for good. He had

panicked when he'd seen her in the store. Beverly knew about the scandal surrounding Kathleen, but she didn't have a clue about anything else. And given that Beverly was just as shallow as he'd suspected, of course she'd wanted nothing to do with Kathleen. Well Joseph had had enough. He'd made a mistake. Yes, he wanted to protect Kathleen's family, but he'd hurt her in the process, and that was unacceptable. The look in her eyes had ripped a hole in his heart.

It was obvious she wasn't going to show up. His heart ached and his soul felt empty. This wasn't the punishment he'd had in mind. Yelling, anger, even tears he could handle. But the thought of spending another night without her was devastating. What if he never saw her again? He couldn't lose her. Not now, not ever. It would be risky, but he knew what he had to do. And he didn't give a damn what anyone else thought about it. For once in his life, he was going to do something for himself. And for Kathleen. They deserved to be happy.

To hell with everyone else.

KATHLEEN'S STOMACH churned with anxiety. She couldn't stop crying. It had been a long shot to think she and Joseph had ever stood a chance, but she'd fallen into the trap of believing fairy tales existed. A fresh wave of tears hit her as she remembered the scene vividly in her mind. Joseph smiling down lovingly at Beverly and agreeing with everything she had said and calling her "my love" all while ignoring Kathleen. *My love* was his term of endearment for her, not any other woman. Now it felt like those were mere words and not something special between the two of them.

It had been worse than if he had died.

Immediately, she knew she didn't mean that. He was the love

of her life. If he was forced to or even wanted to move on and be with Beverly, Kathleen knew she would be happy for him if that would finally make him content in life. She would be grateful for the time she'd had with him and the letters he had written her, holding them near and dear to her heart for the rest of her days. She owed him everything because without him she would never have made it.

That didn't mean she was a martyr.

Kathleen was serious when she'd said she couldn't do this anymore. She pulled out a pen and a pad of paper and walked out onto her deck in the light of the full moon, then sat in her rocking chair facing the ocean as she thought about the goodbye letter she would write to Joseph. It would be impossible to say goodbye, but she knew in her soul she must. She sat down in her rocking chair and began to write.

DEAR JOSEPH,

I don't know where to start. This has to be the hardest thing I've ever done. You mean the world to me, but today opened my eyes to the real truth. You have been upfront with me from the beginning. I knew exactly what you were doing in playing along with your mother's wishes and why you were doing it. You wanted to protect my family from further hurt. I love you for that, but I can't carry on this way.

Seeing you willingly shun me in public was too much to bear. I don't think we will ever find a way out of the situation we are in; therefore, I am letting you go. I'm setting you free. Lord knows, my darling, I don't want to. But it's something I have to do. I can see by the worry lines surrounding your eyes this whole charade is taking a toll on you as well. I don't blame you. It's something you have to do, as a result, you have hurt me deeply. You are the only person who has supported me, remaining by my side and not followed the entire town

in turning their backs on me. To see you shun me firsthand was
simply too much to take.

I don't know how I am going to live with never seeing you again
or holding you in my arms or telling you how much I love you...

KATHLEEN COULDN'T GO ON. Her tears rolled down her cheeks
and dripped onto the paper, smudging the ink. Her heart was
breaking as if someone had plunged a dagger deep through its
core. How was she to go on without him? She felt dead inside,
but she picked up her pen and reached for the paper once more
anyway.

"Don't," a familiar voice strummed from behind her, emit-
ting the most beautiful achingly sad musical notes imaginable.
He gently placed his hand over hers and pulled it away from the
paper. "Please don't write anymore," his voice dropped to a
strained whisper. He cleared his throat and continued. "I can't
bear the thought of you leaving, Kathleen. I'm so sorry. I was
being stupid, and it was heartless and cruel. You must know it
didn't mean a thing. Please forgive me. Say you'll stay with me
always."

Kathleen tipped her head up to see Joseph standing over her.
She sucked in a breath. He had tears rolling down his cheeks as
well, and his eyes were swimming with the same anguish she
felt. "What are you doing here? It's too dangerous." She didn't
have the heart to answer him yet as confusion warred with her
head.

"I don't care." He knelt down beside her and cupped her
cheek in his hand. "Don't you see you're my everything? I was
going along with my mother's farce of an engagement to protect
you until I could figure out the perfect time for us to run away
together. But instead, I hurt you. I will never forgive myself for
that. I don't care about any of that now. I only care about you,

and I will surely die if you make me live without you. You are the only one who gives a damn about me and cares about what makes me happy. *You* make me happy, my love. Only you."

Kathleen knew she could no more live without him than live without air. She didn't say a word—couldn't even if she tried—she just leaned in and pressed her lips to his. As always, a kaleidoscope of colors flashed through her mind's eye, followed by a symphony of feelings from a slow throbbing burn of the bass to a rounding acceleration of the treble topped off with a climactic clash of the symbols.

And that was just from Joseph's kiss.

She wanted more. No, she *needed* more. Right or wrong, she needed to make love to him, right here, right now. She stood and took his hands in hers and tugged until he followed her to the bedroom. Once they were there, she lit a candle and watched the fire in his eyes match the steadily burning flame as they flickered and caressed her body with their heated gaze. That gave her courage. This wasn't the first time they had made love, but there was something different about it, something more intense and permanent.

She slowly undid her dress and let it fall to the floor. Next, she undid her undergarments and let them follow as well. Standing in all her naked glory before him, she let the love and desire she felt shine boldly in her eyes as the flames from the candles swayed in the evening breeze floating through her bedroom window, casting a romantic and cozy glow.

"You're so beautiful," he said in awe. "You have no idea how incredible you are, do you?"

She shook her head slightly, not wanting him to stop making love to her with his words.

He quickly shed his own clothing and limped forward, uttering words of appreciation and love. Starting with her forehead, he slowly kissed his way down her entire body, lingering on her breasts and then dropping lower to her naval. When she sucked in a breath, he gently pushed her until she fell on her back on the bed. And then he did something he had never done before. Kneeling on the floor before her, he spread her knees wide and lowered his head. She hitched her chin and let out a cry of ecstasy as he kissed her intimately. Parting her folds with his fingers, he stroked her a couple of times and then thrust his tongue deep.

Kathleen had never been loved so intimately. Her mother had always stressed for her not to expect much, that lovemaking was meant to bear children, and anything else was inappropriate. But if this was wrong, Kathleen would gladly welcome damnation. It was almost as if Joseph wanted to make sure she knew she was special. There was no other woman for him.

Proper or not, he wanted all of her, and she willingly gave herself to him. She screamed out his name as she came undone upon a tidal wave of feelings, and then he slid up her body, whispering words of encouragement as he entered her gently and they became one. He'd always fulfilled her like no other man could, but this time she reached the peak of pleasure multiple times. Another first. Its beauty brought her to tears.

He matched her pace and found release as well, his face contorting with intense pleasure and pain until he collapsed on top of her at last. He lay sprawled between her welcoming thighs with his cheek resting on her breast, his breath fanning her nipple, and it was the most natural thing in the world to hold him to her. She never wanted to let him go. He was hers, and she had been a fool to think they could live without one another.

~

A KNOCK SOUNDED at the door in the wee hours of the morning.

"Kathleen, I said open up. I know you're in there!" came a voice that would forever induce chills within her.

William!

She'd meant to rest her eyes for only a moment and have Joseph steal away at some point during the night, but they'd slept so soundly in each other's arms. Kathleen gently shook Joseph awake. They were still naked and entwined, a part of him she treasured still halfway inside of her. As much as she hated for him to be torn apart from her, she knew he must leave now.

She had known the evening before was risky. William watched her like a hawk. He had seen her upset at the store earlier that day and naturally wouldn't let the matter drop. She should have known he would check up on her. If he caught her in bed with another man, he would kill Joseph for sure and not give a second thought to the town discovering his secret.

Kathleen gently shook Joseph awake.

"Hmmm?" he mumbled, still in a deep fog and then took her nipple in his mouth, the part of him she so loved stirring to life once more inside of her and stealing her breath.

Fighting back the moan of pleasure, she pushed his head away from her breast until his tongue left her.

He muttered, "What's wrong, my love?" as he started to move his hips, thrusting deeper inside of her, still half out of it and not really hearing her.

"Oh, God, you have to stop," she managed to get out while gripping his buttocks and holding him to her. She couldn't help herself. He felt so incredible she never wanted their time together to end.

"Why?" he picked up the pace, then bent his head and sucked harder as he reached his hand between them and touched her intimately while making love to her.

"Oh, God, don't stop," she panted, "but wait, you have to," she choked, "William is outside."

"No please, not yet," Joseph grunted and thrust furiously into her until they both screamed out their release. Only then did he finally come back to reality and say, "Wait, what?"

But it was too late.

William broke down the door and charged through the cottage to her open bedroom door, standing before them like a crazed grizzly bear, his eyes wide in shock. The covers had been tossed off the bed, and Joseph was fully engorged and thrust deep inside of Kathleen still, where she admittedly never wanted him to leave, consequences be damned. But reality hit them both like an ice bucket as William roared. Joseph pulled out of her and rolled off the bed, naked and still aroused with his hands balled tightly into fists in a ready position. She knew he would die defending her if need be.

Meanwhile, Kathleen reached for the blankets and pulled them up tight to wrap them securely around her, terrified of what her husband would do. Standing up to a bully was the only way to defeat them. "William, what are you doing? You need to leave now," she demanded forcefully. "This is my house, not yours, and you're not welcome here."

"You're my wife," he ground out, his balled fists twice the size of Joseph's as he took a step forward.

"We are legally separated; you just refuse to acknowledge that or give me a divorce." She hopped off the bed with the blankets still tightly wrapped around her like armor and stepped between the men.

"But he's engaged." William thrust a meaty finger in Joseph's direction. "Why would you reduce yourself to playing the whore for him?"

"Watch yourself, sir." Joseph pulled on his pants and stood up straight as best he could, given his bum leg. "Kathleen's a lady and the love of my life. I was never truly engaged to Beverly. That was all for show. Kathleen's the one I want to marry."

"She's my wife and always will be," William growled, "you'll never have her."

"Watch me," Joseph growled back, and the two men stepped around Kathleen and lunged at each other, landing blows as they rolled on the floor.

Kathleen screamed. She ran to her closet as the men threw fists and punches furiously, each striving to gain the upper hand. Joseph was a better fighter, but it was clear William was the stronger of the two. Someone would surely die if she didn't do something and quick. Without hesitation, she reached into the closet and pulled out the only useful thing her father had ever given to her.

A gun.

Loading it with ammunition, she cocked the shotgun and that brought the men to attention. "Let him go," she said to William with a calm, deadly tone.

William eyed her a moment as if he didn't know for sure exactly what she would do. She leveled the gun, and finally his common sense took over, pushing his stubborn pride and damaged ego aside. "Fine," he said in a low deadly voice as he dropped his fists and rolled to his feet, "but this is far from over."

After he left, Kathleen closed the door and wedged a chair beneath the knob. She faced Joseph and her bravado crumbled as she let out a rash of tears that had been begging to fall. "What have we done?" she muttered between sobs and the gun fell from her hands.

Joseph rushed forward to take her in his arms. "We've just moved up what was inevitable, my love."

"Wh-What's that?"

"Our running away together," he said firmly as he pulled back to look her in the eyes. "It's not safe anymore. I've seen that look before in the eyes of the enemy. He will kill us both given the first opportunity. I want you to stay with me tonight on my boat and then, when William is at work tomorrow, you can return home to pack your things. I will leave word in your mailbox about where to meet me. I love you, Kathleen. And I want to spend the rest of my life with you, even if that means we run away together and leave town to start over completely on our own with nothing. Are you with me?"

She searched his eyes, but really there was no question. "Always," she said, and had never meant anything more.

16

PRESENT DAY: BEACON BAY, MAINE

"I thought you said we weren't going to do this again," Logan mumbled into Emma's ear. She was bent over her bed, stark naked with him standing behind her deeply imbedded within her, his chest resting against her back. She felt safe and protected and delicious, but his words triggered the common sense part of her brain.

"Thanks for reminding me. Last week was safe. This week not so much," she managed to mutter and tried to move, but he slid his hand beneath her belly and down the front of her until he cupped her intimately while they were still joined as he continued to stroke her insides with the giant part of him she suddenly couldn't get enough of. "Oh, I ... Oh, God," she blurted, followed by a cry of ecstasy.

"Shhhh, babe, it's okay." He kissed her neck. "Easy now, I've got you. Last time was my turn, this time it's yours. I'll pull out in time, I promise. Let yourself go, sweetheart. Let yourself feel everything."

Emma stopped thinking and let go. Her skin prickled and nerves danced in delight as waves of sensations hummed through her veins. God, he felt so damned good. Warm muscles, firm skin, thick... She moaned her pleasure as he picked up the pace, holding her hips as he thrust deep and hard inside of her until she saw stars and screamed his name. He ground his teeth but held back his own pleasure as promised.

Finally, Logan stood up but stayed inside of her from behind as he stroked her back until she quieted and the quivers of supreme pleasure finally left her. She pushed against him until he pulled out of her and then she slowly turned around. His eyes were glazed, still so full of desire as he hadn't reached his release because he'd thought of her first. He tended to do that a lot.

While Emma appreciated it, she sat on the bed before him and had the strongest urge to please him. She wanted him dripping with passion and out of his mind. Before he could make a move or figure out her intention, she slid her hands over his hips and around him to cup his buttocks and pull him to her. Oral sex had never been her thing, but with him, she was quivering with anticipation, wanting to give back. He was such a caring thoughtful person, always the one to give but never the one to receive. Nothing filled her with more joy than to be the person to pleasure him.

"Babe, you don't have to—"

"Shhh, I know. I want to." Her gaze met his seconds before she wet her lips and took him deep inside her mouth to suck hard, over and over and over. She stroked him with her fingers and tongue and lips, working a magical spell of intense desire over him and becoming more aroused than she ever thought possible in doing so. She felt unbelievably powerful in making such a virile strong man weak and vulnerable.

He was at her mercy, and she thrived on it.

His hands raked through her hair until his legs shook, and he couldn't take it anymore. Throwing back his head, he moaned, letting out a guttural sound, and then he grabbed her beneath the arms and lifted her all in one motion, straight off the floor and onto his engorged shaft. She wrapped her legs and arms around him and held on tight as he kissed the breath out of her, spinning her around to press her against her bedroom wall and make love hard.

She was a good match for him. She didn't need or want careful and gentle. She wanted out of control and explosive. He needed to know not all women were fragile, and it was okay to be himself. He wasn't going to hurt her, but she might hurt him if he stopped. His shoulders were so wide, his chest massive, his hands huge...she felt petite and feminine and utterly cherished. He worshipped her body as if she were a goddess, and soon she found another release in unison with him.

As promised, Logan pulled out seconds before his release and shouted her name. She fell against him in a quivering heap, exhausted but more satisfied than she had ever thought possible. Just when she thought he would put her down, he carried her with him to the shower. Turning the water on, he kissed her sensually until it was hot,then they slowly washed each other off and made love yet again in a lazy delicious way.

A half hour later, he wore only boxers and she wore a skimpy silk robe with nothing beneath. "You hungry?" she asked.

"Starving," he said, his gaze still heated making her blush as it slowly traced over every inch of her, and she realized he was still just as hungry for her.

She wasn't supposed to let things get this far again. Not because of a possible pregnancy—babies didn't scare her—but because of how he'd reacted after they'd made love the last time. She certainly didn't need for him to make her feel like the most desirable woman on earth one minute and then like she was a bottom feeder the next, not worthy of a single phone call. But he was so damned sexy.

He had the most amazing body, gorgeous thick curly hair, and a sexy as hell constant five o'clock shadow. It wasn't fair. She was powerless against him. But what concerned her the most was the intense feelings he brought out in her that had nothing to do with sex. She wanted to make him happy and pleasure him and comfort him, putting his needs before her own, and that scared the hell out of her.

Only, unlike him, she wasn't running.

Deciding not to dwell on what might happen, she said, "I have fresh caught fish, fixings for a big salad, and white wine chilling in the fridge."

"I didn't take you for the fishing type."

"You'd be correct. That would require getting down and dirty."

His eyes grew hooded. "Now *that* I've seen firsthand."

"What can I say, I have skills," she thrust a finger at him, "but not when it comes to fishing, silly man. Don't you know I have connections? I'm a journalist. I have my sources. It doesn't matter where I go, I usually find a way to get what I want."

"I'll bet you do." He smiled tenderly.

She cleared her throat. No matter how much of a smartass she was, he always found a way to turn the conversation into a sweet and sincere one. If she wasn't careful, she was going to lose her heart and that wouldn't be good for either of them. "Okay, then, let's get started." She decided to focus on the lighter topic of their evening meal.

They cooked dinner together, with her making the salad and him grilling the fish out on the patio. She carried the salad and wine out to join him so they could stare out at the ocean that felt more and more like coming home as they ate in silence, both fully aware the sex had ended and feelings were brimming beneath the surface. When they were finished, they opened their treasure box and read the letters eagerly. Anything to avoid a conversation that might get too heavy. They both sat quietly for a moment, reflecting on the new knowledge they had discovered.

"That's it?" Emma finally asked, her mind refusing to accept the facts.

"I'm afraid so," Logan answered in a low voice that sounded both sad yet somehow relieved. "There's no map." He shrugged.

"But that can't be it. We don't know what happened yet. We don't know all the facts," Emma said almost desperately. "Did William come back the next day and catch them? Is that why Joseph went missing and why Kathleen vanished? Did William kill them both and then hide their bodies like he had his first love? Or did they escape together and start over, never to be heard from again? I have to know what happened. The town records are too vague, and there are no more letters. This can't be it. Their love was too beautiful. It can't end this way." She shook her head and fought to hold back her tears. It was silly crying over a story from the past, yet she couldn't help herself. She felt too connected to it, as if it affected her own future and happiness.

After a long pause, Logan spoke. "Sometimes things end whether we want them to or not." He frowned down into his glass of wine, and Emma could tell he was remembering his wife. She could feel him pulling away from her already.

"Wait, what about the map I found in the water? I think that might be the final map we're missing."

"It doesn't matter."

"Why?"

"Because that map's corner was ripped off. We don't know where their final meeting spot was supposed to take place, which means we have no way of finding out anything more about them." Logan's eyes met hers. "You have to face facts, Emma. Their story's over. We'll never know what really happened to them." He swallowed hard, his Adam's apple bobbing once. "It's over."

She sucked in a sharp breath. "What if they didn't want it to be over?" she bravely blurted, suddenly not talking about Joseph and Kathleen.

Logan stared at her for a long moment, looking as if he wanted to say something more, but then he didn't. He stared out over the ocean, far away from her, as he said, "Maybe they didn't have a choice. Just like we don't have a choice that our adventure is over as well."

This time she was the one to pause. Staring in shock and disbelief, she finally managed to ask in a small quiet voice, "Just like that?" Emma fought the tears battling to flood her eyes, but it was getting increasingly difficult as reality slapped her in the face.

Logan steeled his features and finally responded, "Unfortunately, yes. Just like that." He stood and picked up their dirty dishes. "Speaking of over, the summer is almost over. All good things must come to an end." He tried to laugh, but it sounded forced. "I think I'll leave in the morning to join my in-laws and Trevor for a week before he has to go back to school. I have the time, and we're overstaffed." He stared at his dishes for a moment before meeting her gaze with guilt and pity warring within it. "Thank you, Emma."

"For what?" she could barely talk, but she'd be damned if she'd break down in front of him.

"For one hell of an adventure. If it wasn't for you, I would still be stuck in a rut, but now I think I'm going to be okay for the first time." Sincerity rang through in his tone, and she couldn't blame him for her misguided hopes and foolish schoolgirl dreams. He'd never made any promises to her and had let her know right from the start exactly who he was.

"No worries," she flicked her wrist in his direction as if it was no big deal, and she finished with, "what are friends for, right?" She'd never been a coward and had always been one to speak her mind and tell it like it is, but once again, she wanted Logan to be happy. If he couldn't handle her or a relationship or whatever the hell was between them, then she had to let him go and set him free. That's what being in love was all about: making the other person happy. She could relate to everything Kathleen must have felt.

He hesitated a beat, giving Emma a fraction of hope, but then he said, "Right. Want me to do the dishes?"

She swallowed the lump in her throat, feeling the crushing weight of his rejection. "Nah, I'll throw them in the dishwasher. I'm going to finish my wine out here while I watch the sun go down. You can let yourself out. Say hi to Trevor for me, and remember, if you get the story wrong, I'll be sure to fill him in."

Logan chuckled softly. "I'm sure you will." And then he walked away, out of her life, gone for good.

She held in the sobs until she heard him dress and the front door close with such finality, she knew that was the end for them. Whatever was between them was over, and she was once more alone. He was leaving her like Mark had.

Guess she really wasn't good enough or lovable after all.

"Screw it!" Emma said to herself in the rear-view mirror of her Mercedes as she drove down Coastal Ridge road away from her beach house. She'd never been one to wallow in self-pity, and she sure as hell wasn't about to start now.

She'd been all packed and ready to go home, wanting to leave before Logan returned from his week away because facing him would be too hard, but she couldn't leave yet. She owed it to Kathleen Connor to set the record straight. That meant Emma couldn't go anywhere until she discovered the rest of Kathleen's story.

Emma had to admit with the distraction of Logan gone, she could finally think more clearly. She'd thought hard, but couldn't come up with anything other than Kathleen's cottage. It was a long shot, but that was where Emma had found the original wooden box. Maybe Kathleen's nephew had missed something. It was worth the time to at least look, except her nephew had left town and Emma didn't want to wait. She was desperate and determined and Dr. Worrywart wasn't here to stop her.

Pulling into the driveway of the cottage at 137 Coastal Ridge Road, Emma cut the engine to her car and looked around. The lot was empty. Perfect. The property was for sale now so technically anyone could come by at any moment, but Emma was willing to take that risk. She threw caution to the wind and tried the front door. Locked. She tried a few windows, but those were locked as well. She even walked out back onto the deck and tried the back door, but that was locked up tight, too. Except that lock didn't look like it had been replaced with a sturdier one like the front one had.

Emma chewed her bottom lip. She could work with this. She remembered one of her informants she was particularly fond of. He'd been hot as hell, but even she had scruples. She'd drawn the line at dating shady people, but that didn't mean he hadn't come in handy. He'd shown her how to pick a lock to perfection. Pulling a bobby pin from her hair, she crouched down on her knees and got to work. It didn't take long before the lock clicked. Stuffing the pin back in her hair, she stood and opened the door.

Emma left the door open to better hear if anyone pulled up. She'd been to the cottage before but had never stepped foot inside. The air felt charged as if Kathleen were still there.

Emma didn't believe in ghosts, but she did believe in fate and that everything happened for a reason. She was somehow meant to be on this journey and to finish this quest. She'd felt drawn to Kathleen's story right from the start, the same way that something had pulled her back to the cottage.

Emma felt at peace as she walked around the kitchen and living room. The cottage was small but quaint, consisting of only one big room that housed the kitchen and living room, with a small bedroom and bathroom in the back. The furniture looked as if it were ancient, the knickknacks antiques, like no one had bothered to replace anything. Emma entered the bedroom, then turned around and noticed it faced the front door.

If you left the door open, the bed was in plain view of whoever walked into the cabin. All Emma could think about was this was where Kathleen had stood when William came barging into her cabin and fought with Joseph. Emma shuddered, feeling the fear Kathleen must have felt. Emma shivered, thinking Kathleen must have been one brave woman.

Needing some air, Emma headed to the window and opened it, taking a deep breath. After a moment, she closed the window and started to walk out of the room when the floorboards creaked beneath her sandaled feet. She paused and looked down. It looked perfectly normal if you weren't paying attention, but she always paid attention to the small details. It was her job, enabling her to notice things the average person didn't.

Kneeling down, she inspected the board closer. The wood was weathered and old. Some of the nails had rusted and come loose from many boards, but these looked as if they had been pried out and carefully returned. It didn't take much work to lift the nails back out with the same bobby pin she had used to break in with. Once she had the nails out, the board groaned with protest but finally came loose. After lifting it away, Emma smiled with satisfaction.

Another box.

Gently rescuing her treasure from its burial spot, Emma

leaned against the wall and slowly opened the box with anticipation. She exhaled a huge sigh of relief when she saw another
letter. It wasn't over. Not by a long shot. She thought of how
excited Logan would be, but then just as quickly thought of how
easily he'd given up on her...on them. Their quest might not be
over, but *they* surely were. Emma stubbornly raised her chin and
opened the letter without him. He didn't deserve to see how
their adventure ended.

Except nothing could have prepared her for what was to
come.

17

AUGUST, 1943: BEACON BAY, MAINE

Joseph checked one last time to make sure he hadn't forgotten anything. He'd sent word to Kathleen to meet him at their favorite lighthouse on the far corner of Beacon Bay. You could see the same lighthouse from her cottage, as well as the marina. He'd spent many a night on his boat, staring at that lighthouse and finding solace in the fact that she was looking at the same thing. They'd made a pact to stop and look at it at 10 p.m. every evening, no matter where they were or who they were with or what they were doing. Joseph hadn't missed a single night, and it made him feel close to Kathleen always.

Excitement filled him with the thought that now they would finally be together. He would meet her at the lighthouse and his boat would be waiting with enough supplies to take them away from Beacon Bay forever. They could pick anywhere they wanted to live and start over. He'd avoided William, not willing to risk another confrontation, and his mother as well, not wanting to explain how he'd gotten the black eye and fat lip.

It wasn't that he was afraid of William. He'd been through far worse. It was more about his desire to do real harm to William for what he had done to Kathleen. The last thing she needed was more trouble, so Joseph would take the high road and walk away. The important thing was spending the rest of his life with the woman he loved. Once they were settled someplace, he would write to his mother and let her know he was okay, but not before then. She would only try to stop him.

Sneaking out of his parents' house before they could ask questions, he slipped away to the marina. He glanced at the sky and frowned. Storm clouds were rolling in, and a strange feeling of doom swept over him. As a boat crafter, an avid sailor, and a soldier of the Navy who'd lived through the hell of war, he'd long ago learned to heed the warning sirens going off in his head. Not this time. Joseph and Kathleen couldn't wait, not with William knowing they were lovers. He'd seen the look in the man's eye. William wouldn't stop harassing them until he got his revenge. They needed to leave tonight no matter what the weather.

Joseph slipped onto his boat and stored his belongings. When everything was secure, he untied the vessel and glanced fondly at the shore where he and Kathleen had buried their love letters. He would miss Beacon Bay and even his family. It was home and always would be, but his happiness was more important, and he would do anything to put a smile back on his beloved's angelic face.

Pushing away from the shore, he pulled out of the harbor without looking back. The wind had picked up and the waves were growing bigger by the hour, but he knew how to handle a boat. His palms grew sweaty and his heart started beating faster, but not from fear. He was so excited to start this next journey in life. They'd waited so long to be together. *Freely* be together with no more sneaking around.

It was finally their time.

He rounded the bend and pulled into a spot further down the shoreline where the lighthouse sat. Kathleen would be able to walk or get a ride to the lighthouse just as soon as she could. In the meantime, he would make preparations to meet her. He docked his boat on the backside of the lighthouse, facing the open ocean, where no one from the bay could see it.

This lighthouse was the oldest one used in their small bay, yet held the most charm. The newer lighthouses were pristine white with red or blue accents, attached to the lighthouse keeper's house. This lighthouse consisted of an old stone tower with a glassed-in lantern room at the top, containing the lamp and lens meant to be used as a navigational aid to sailors. It was the lighthouse keeper's job to make sure the lantern never went out so ships wouldn't lose their way, becoming lost at sea.

Joseph had always found lighthouses fascinating, listening intently to his father's stories when he was little. Ancient lighthouses consisted of fires set in high places for sailors to see and had evolved with the invention of vaporized oil burners followed by the use of gas as an illuminant, but the world was changing rapidly. Joseph often felt like he couldn't keep up. He had grown up and gone off to war, only to come back and see modern technology taking over in a furious way. He could only imagine what the future had in store for so many things.

This lighthouse was still used but it hadn't been maintained like it should have been. The house in the back had been rundown, and the lighthouse keeper no longer stayed there. He didn't need to as long as he kept watch from his home down the shore and kept checking on the lighthouse periodically, which made it a perfectly safe place for Joseph to meet Kathleen without being disturbed.

Besides, it held such a special meaning for them both. It had been their beacon of hope for a long time now, doing its job of guiding them safely home into each other's arms where they belonged. Scanning the area, there was no one in sight. Joseph made his way up the rocky cliff, choosing to venture inside the lighthouse just in case the heavens opened up and poured down upon them. The ever-darkening sky threatened to do just that as Joseph walked into a tower structure supporting the lantern room where the light operated. He wandered the entire area, looking around with reverence every step of the way.

A set of stone stairs spiraled up to the lantern room, the glassed-in area at the top of a lighthouse tower containing the lamp and lens. The metal cupola roof had a lightning rod and grounding system that provided a safe conduit for any lightning strikes. This safe haven had been the perfect place for he and Kathleen to watch the impressive summer storms across the ocean. But tonight, he needed the seas to cooperate. Their escape was nerve-racking enough. He prayed Mother Nature was on their side.

Joseph stepped outside onto the open platform and stared out at the raging sea as he waited for Kathleen to join him. The wind whipped furiously now and the rain started to fall, splattering against the glass and soaking his clothes. He turned away to go back inside when he suddenly realized his love was trekking along the shore by herself in this retched weather. This might not have been his best idea having her meet him here. He started to make his way down the stairs to meet her when thunder boomed outside, shaking the lighthouse, followed quickly by a symphony of lightning that lit up the room seconds before hitting the lighthouse tower.

Joseph fell to the floor, hitting it hard and sending intense pain radiating up from his bad leg. He rolled onto his back to catch his breath and squeezed his eyes shut. He grit his teeth, knowing his leg was broken. He'd been so stupid and careless, risking everything to satisfy some romantic fantasy of making love to Kathleen in their lighthouse before sailing away to start their new life together. The pain hadn't subsided but a noise sounded that had his eyes whipping open in horror. It couldn't be. Not now. Not after everything they'd gone through to get here, was his last thought before the unthinkable happened.

KATHLEEN HURRIED as fast as she could through the pelting rain. It was coming down in sheets now. She'd woken up in the cabin of Joseph's boat after making the most beautiful love all night long. Joseph's family and William had nearly destroyed what was between them, but Kathleen refused to let that happen. Joseph loved her and they were meant to be together, whether William granted her a divorce or not and even if his family never accepted her. She realized she could no longer worry about any of them, not even her own family. She had always put everyone else first, and this time she refused to.

She'd waited until she knew William was at work, just like Joseph had told her to, and then she'd slipped away from his boat and made her way back to her cottage. Gathering only her essential belongings, she left everything else behind and set out in the direction of her favorite lighthouse. The beacon of hope that had kept them connected for so long now. The special place that was going to launch their new life together, and she could hardly wait.

The rain came down in sheets now as she painstakingly made her way down the shore and around the bend until she reached the lighthouse. She breathed a sigh of relief when she saw Joseph's boat. He'd made it. She was concerned when she saw the big waves and angry clouds. Deciding they could store her things in his boat later, she ducked into the lighthouse to get out of the rain. Setting her things down, she called out his name.

"Joseph? It's Kathleen. I'm here. Where are you?"

"Up here," came a faraway weak-sounding voice, but it was the most beautiful sound she'd ever heard.

She dropped her belongings and raced up the winding staircase to meet the love of her life. Running into the watch room, Kathleen came to an abrupt halt. Sheer horror and fear like she'd never known paralyzed her. When she was able to move, her shaking hand fluttered to her face and she covered her trembling lips. Fighting for air, she shook her head no. This was so unfair. This couldn't happen to them. She wouldn't let it.

"Sweetheart, don't do this to yourself," Joseph said, and reached out a hand to her, looking so weak.

Kathleen realized she needed to be strong for him. She took a deep breath and wiped away her tears, still in a daze of shock. Suddenly she found herself acting on instinct, as if out of her body and watching the scene unfold below her. Quickly walking over to him, she felt a surge of adrenalin like nothing she'd ever felt before. She tugged with all of her might and lifted a large beam that had splintered away from the wall and fallen on top of her beloved. His bad leg was bent at an odd angle, which would normally cause her stomach to revolt, but she stared at it oddly. It was clearly broken.

The heavy beam had trapped him beneath its weight across his mid-section, probably crushing his insides. Looking at it now, she was shocked she'd been able to move it at all. She'd read about people finding super-human strength when it came to life-or-death situations. Even the thought of death had her tears welling up all over again.

"Maybe if I go get help, we can save you."

"It won't matter," he said, wiping a trickle of blood away from the corner of his mouth. "I've already lost too much blood."

"It's all my fault," her voice wobbled, as reality finally started to set in. "If I had hurried, I would have been here sooner." She dropped to her knees and lifted his head onto her lap.

"Shhh, there is nothing you could have done, darling. The beam caused internal bleeding the second it hit. Through sheer will and lots of praying, I did the only thing I cared to do," he said with tears in his beautiful blue eyes. "I held on until I could see you one more time. I needed to be able to say goodbye." His voice hitched.

She lost her battle and wept unabashedly. "Y-You can't leave me, Joseph. P-Please don't leave me. We've been through so much. I can't lose you now." She kept stroking his hair over and over, and touching every inch of his face.

He reached up weakly and caressed her cheek, running his thumb beneath her eye and wiping away her tears. "You won't lose me. I will always be with you. We're one, you and me. Linked together forever with far more than just our physical bodies. You have my heart and soul, and I yours."

"This is so unfair."

"I know, sweetheart, but I feel like I've lived a thousand lives since I met you. I honestly don't think I would have survived if not for you. Your letters kept me going through the war, and then your loving arms became my world since I've been home. You're the only one who understands me, who loves all of me— even the broken parts—without censure. You're the only one who has succeeded in keeping the nightmares away. Know this, that wherever I go, I am taking you with me, and maybe finally I will be at peace." He went into a coughing fit, and his eyes rolled back in his head as he fought to hold on and catch his breath.

She nodded. "It's okay, it's okay, it's okay my darling," she kept repeating over and over through her soft sobs. He was in pain and it broke her heart to see him suffering. "You can go now. I'm here. I'll be okay. You rest now. I'll watch over you."

His eyes sprang open one last time, and he rasped, "No. You must leave. Everyone will blame you for my death. They are looking for a way to ruin you forever, and if they don't, then William will. I will never be at peace unless I know you're safe. I know it will be hard, but dig deep and drag me out to my boat. The water is my home. It always has been."

A coughing fit seized him, and she thought she'd lost him. After several minutes, he managed to finish. "I've dreamed of being sent off with a burial at sea like sailors from long ago. I should have died in the war anyway. Everyone will think I drowned in the storm. Then I want you to leave and never come back. Vanish without a trace. Change your name and start over someplace new like we planned. I will find you and be with you in spirit. Always. Promise me."

She nodded, a fresh wave of tears rolling down her cheeks. "I promise." Then she bent over and pressed her lips to his one last time. When she sat back up, Joseph stared at her with lifeless, vacant eyes. His chest lay still, and no more sounds gurgled from his throat.

He was gone.

An hour later, after sobbing hysterically and saying her goodbyes, Kathleen knew what she had to do. She'd made Joseph a promise, and she wouldn't let him down. It took some doing, but she managed to lift him from beneath his arms and slowly drag him toward the winding staircase. Gravity was her friend as she gently slid his lifeless body down the stairs one agonizing step at a time. She couldn't think about the fact that he was no longer with her. She had to latch onto his last words — he would be with her in spirit always.

Once she reached the base of the lighthouse, she opened the door. The storm raged outside, matching the storm thundering through her. Without a thought to her own well-being, she dragged him down the cliffside, the drenching rain soaking right through her clothes and chilling her very core with its pelting drops piercing her skin like needles. She welcomed the pain, hoping it would ease the ache she felt on the inside. She managed to lift him over the side of his boat, and the thud as he landed on the deck made her stomach turn.

Oh, God, she couldn't do this.

She fell to her knees, sobbing uncontrollably. "No!" She pounded the ground. "No, damn you! How much more am I supposed to take?" She stared up at the heavens. "Haven't I suffered enough?" Her shoulders shook and she felt as if she had nothing left to give. What was she supposed to do without him? Where would she go? How would she make it on her own? Maybe she should join him on his boat and leave this world in a blaze of glory with him by her side. Life would be so much easier that way, and they could still be together.

As soon as she had that thought, she felt a strong presence engulf her in warmth, and a calm peaceful feeling settled over her. *Joseph.* As promised, she knew he was with her and would be by her side always. He would be so upset if she didn't carry out his wishes. She knew that with every fiber of her being, and that alone kept her going. She was meant to carry on in this world like she'd promised him. He had given her the strength to make it on her own, and she wouldn't let him down now.

Climbing over the boat, she made him as comfortable as possible on the upper deck and kissed his lips that had already cooled. Searching his cabin below, she found some matches and an idea came to her. She would keep Joseph up top and set the fire down below in the cabin. Then turn the boat on and put it in drive, facing the open ocean. That way it would carry him out to sea until the fire burning below engulfed the entire boat and it sank. By then, he would be far enough out, and in the raging storm, no one would see him. They would assume he set sail on his own and got lost at sea in the tempest.

His mother might assume Kathleen was lost at sea with him, but no one else would know and Kathleen doubted Hilary would want the scandal spreading, so she would never breathe a word. Neither would William. He would rather the town think Kathleen ran away from him, leaving him the poor broken-hearted victim or they might speculate over her vanishing without a trace like his first love had. Kathleen didn't care what anyone thought. She was done with all of that.

It was time she started living for herself.

Striking the match, she set Joseph's bed on fire and then climbed out of the cuddy cabin to close the door and start the boat. The engine roared to life, but the storm was so loud, no one could possibly have heard. Kissing Joseph's lips one last time as a single tear fell from her eye to caress his cheek, she said goodbye. "Until Tomorrow, my love."

Then she put the boat in gear, and it strained against the rope holding it to the dock. She managed to climb off the boat and untie the rope seconds before it would have brought the whole dock down. The boat took off out to sea, a low light flickering from inside as the fire burned brighter. Kathleen watched for as long as she could, until the boat grew smaller and smaller, and then it finally disappeared into the middle of the raging storm.

She hugged her arms close as a boom of thunder sounded and lightning streaked across the sky. It was done, and there was no turning back now. Stepping inside the lighthouse, she gathered her meager belongings and left Beacon Bay without looking over her shoulder even once. There was nothing left for her there, and there was only one thing left for her to do.

Fulfill the rest of her promise.

18

PRESENT DAY: BEACON BAY, MAINE

"It's good to be home, don't you think?" Logan asked Trevor as they unloaded his son's things from his mother-in-law's van into the driveway of his house. It was a beautiful, sunny day with a cool ocean breeze. A sign of good things to come, he hoped. He needed something to change, and quickly, because he'd been a downer—as his son had put it—for long enough.

Logan hadn't seen or spoken to Emma in two weeks, and it was killing him. There had been nothing left to keep her here since their adventure had stalled at a dead end and he had chickened out on telling her how he really felt. It should be safe to venture around town since Emma would be long gone by now. He frowned. No matter how hard he had tried, he couldn't get her out of his mind. And the disappointment he felt over the thought of not seeing her again was suffocating him. If avoiding her was supposed to keep his heart from breaking, then why the hell did it hurt so damn much?

"I always have more fun at camp than here." Trevor stuck out his lower lip in a major pout.

"I promise I won't work all the time until you're back to school. We'll do something fun, okay buddy?"

Suddenly Trevor brightened and started hopping up and down. "Can I go on the rest of your adventure with that nice lady?"

Logan's heart did a funny little flip. "I told you that adventure only led to a dead end. It's over now."

"I want to talk to Miss Emma." Trevor narrowed his shrewd little eyes. "She said she would tell me the whole truth if you were fibbing."

"Who says I'm fibbing?" Logan tried to keep a straight face.

"You're not telling all those fact things like she said. I can tell."

Logan shook his head in wonder. His son was way too smart for his own good. "I told you everything there was to tell about the adventure. The rest of the facts are boring grown-up stuff."

Trevor crossed his arms stubbornly. "I still want to talk to Miss Emma."

"She's long gone by now. Sorry, buddy." Logan crossed his arms, squaring off with his six-year-old.

"No, she's not," his mother-in-law said, coming in on the last part of the conversation but obviously having heard enough. She eyed both of them and rolled her eyes. "And you wonder where he gets it from?" Rebecca shook her head.

Logan uncrossed his arms but then jolted as her words sank in, and a zing of electricity he couldn't deny snaked through his stomach. "Wait...Emma's not gone?" He swallowed hard, his throat suddenly dry. "How do you know?"

"You may take the fastest most direct way home, but I always take the scenic route along the lake. When you get to be my age, you learn to slow down and appreciate the world spinning by you before it's too late." She winked. "I saw Ms. Hendrick's car still parked at her beach house."

"See, Daddy? I was right. Yay! Yay! Yay! We're going to see

Miss Emma." Trevor raced off as fast as his little legs would carry him. As if seeing Emma would be that easy.

Meanwhile, all sorts of things ran through Logan's mind as he stood frozen in shock with no clue what to do. Why was Emma still in Beacon Bay if their adventure was over? Did she discover something new? Or was she waiting for him to come back? Or maybe she'd stuck around long enough to give him a piece of her mind, which would be just like her. He couldn't stop the tender smile from tipping up the corners of his lips.

"Don't you think you've punished yourself long enough?" Rebecca said, her eyes so like her daughter's, shining bright with compassion and understanding.

"What do you mean?" Logan played dumb, but his mother-in-law was no fool.

"Trevor's not the only one to notice you haven't told us the whole story about a lot of things. You've kept so much inside for all these years. Emma Hendricks is the first person since Amanda who has made you smile and open up in ways I was afraid you never would again. She's good for you. You've changed, my boy." Rebecca reached out and squeezed his hand. "For the better. Don't be afraid to be happy again, Logan. It's what Amanda would have wanted." Rebecca wandered off to take the last of Trevor's things from out of her car and leave him with his thoughts.

Could it really be that simple? Logan had to admit he had changed since Emma had come into his life. Did he deserve to be happy? Was it actually possible to move on? He glanced over at his son waiting patiently in his truck, and he knew of only one way to find out. He stowed Trevor's things in his house and locked the door, then said goodbye to his mother-in-law and climbed inside the cab of his truck.

Trevor stared up at Logan wide-eyed and brimming with hope. "Are we really going to see Miss Emma, Daddy?"

He had vowed to be as honest with his son as he could from here on out. This time was no exception. "I'm not sure, Buddy. Maybe, but there's someplace I need to go first."

"Where's that?" Trevor asked, albeit sounding a bit disappointed yet curious.

"To see Mommy."

LOGAN PULLED into the cemetery at the top of a cliff with a beautiful lookout over Beacon Bay. The sun was high in the sky now, the ocean breeze just the right amount, and the seagulls soaring over the docked boats in the harbor below. If you looked to the right, you could see the lighthouse across from the park, and if you looked far enough out, you could see the island where he and Emma had been stranded.

Just the thought of Emma touched him somewhere deep inside. Yes, his stomach still turned over with anxiety, but the overwhelming excitement she filled him with overpowered that. She challenged him and kept him on his toes and took care of him just as much as he took care of her. She brought joy and fun into his life and made him remember life was about more than paying the bills, putting food on the table, and protecting his loved ones. His son deserved that.

He deserved that.

"You ready?" Logan asked Trevor.

Trevor nodded and grabbed the flowers on the seat between them, hopping out of the truck and skipping to his mother's grave. Trevor was never sad because he'd never really known what he was missing. Amanda had died when he was just a baby, and Rebecca had stepped in without missing a beat to take her place. They had all tried to make sure Trevor knew who his mother was, and he did. He just never actually knew *her*.

That was why visiting her grave had never bothered Trevor. It was just another adventure. But for Logan, it was always sad and painful. Knowing she had willingly left them both had been hard to accept, let alone keep quiet. There were times he had wanted to shout to the world she wasn't the woman they thought she was. She had stolen Trevor's right to have a mother in his life, and Logan's future to grow old with the woman he loved. But just as quickly, he remembered the woman he had fallen in love with wasn't the same woman who had let her life willingly slip away.

And for that, he blamed himself.

If he had only been in tune with the world around him instead of just thinking about himself and getting ahead in his career, he would have picked up on the signs and might have been able to save her. He slowly climbed out of his truck and made his way over to join his son, who was gleefully skipping around her tombstone.

"Do you want to plant the flowers?" he asked his son.

"Nah, you can. I already talked to Mommy. Can I go look over the wall and watch the boats in the harbor, Daddy?"

"Yes, but you know the rule."

"No climbing. The wall's there to protect me from falling in the ocean."

"Exactly."

Trevor ran off, and Logan watched until he was sure his son stopped where he was supposed to. With a tender look on his face, Logan focused on Amanda's grave and planted the wildflowers Trevor had picked out.

"You would be so proud of our boy. He's so much like you it makes my heart ache sometimes." A lump formed in Logan's throat like it always did, but it somehow wasn't as bad this time. He cleared his throat and managed to speak. "He's getting so big I think he might grow to be taller than I am. Can you imagine?"

His smile dimmed. "No, I don't suppose you can. I forgave you a long time ago for leaving me because I know it was as much my fault as it was yours. Actually, it was *all* my fault, and I'm so damned sorry."

He looked up and checked on his son before speaking again. His voice hitched. "I was fine. I had accepted my punishment and resigned myself to living my life alone and taking care of our son, but then *she* came along." He shook his head. "Her name is Emma Hendricks, and she drives me crazy. She is stubborn and irresponsible and careless...and spontaneous and impulsive and fun. I didn't want to fall in love with her."

His eyes welled up, but he fought back the tears. "I feel like I'm betraying you just by saying the words out loud. To be honest I hadn't even admitted that to myself before now. But I can't deny my feelings any longer, even though I don't deserve to have them. I tried to end our relationship, to walk away, but she won't let me. I don't know what to do, Mandy." He stroked his fingertips over her tombstone but couldn't allow himself to fall apart. His shoulders shook with his effort to hold his emotions back.

"Sweetheart, please tell me what to do?" he asked when he could speak again, knowing he was asking the impossible. He sat back and listened but only felt a gust of wind, carrying with it the sounds of birds chirping overhead and the rustle of leaves and acorns from squirrels scampering across the grass and up the trees.

Logan sighed. Feeling like he didn't have any more answers than when he'd arrived, he stood up and let out a whistle. "You ready, Trevor?"

Trevor's head popped up from leaning over the wall, and he ran back to join Logan as they walked to the truck. "Why are your eyes red and puffy, Daddy?"

"Allergies."

"Oh, yuck. I hate allergies. You should take the stuff Nanna gives me."

"Maybe I will." Logan started his truck and headed for home, no closer to an answer now than when he'd first driven back into town and discovered Emma was still there.

"Wait, where are we going?" Trevor's neck swiveled like a bobble head. "This isn't the way to Miss Emma's?"

"No, buddy, it isn't. I don't think this is a good time."

Trevor nailed him with a serious look. "Well, I do."

Logan's brow buckled. "Why?"

"Because Mommy said so."

The truck jerked as Logan hit the brakes, and he managed to pull over to the side of the road. "What did you say?"

"Mommy said it was okay." Trevor shrugged and looked up at him with innocent curiosity. "Didn't you hear her?"

Logan sat there, dumbfounded for a long moment. "No, son," he finally got out. "No, I didn't." Logan swallowed hard. "Did you?" He stared at Trevor in awe and held his breath while he waited.

Trevor nodded his head vigorously. "She talked to me like she always does. Doesn't she talk to you too?"

Logan slowly shook his head. "How long has she been talking to you?"

"Since I was born, silly." Trevor stared at him as if he didn't have a clue. "That's what mommies do."

So many emotions swamped Logan, it was hard to process them all at once, let alone think straight. "You're lucky," he finally managed.

"I know." Trevor played with his toy car, making vroom vroom sounds as if he hadn't said anything earth-shattering at all.

Logan stared at his son and couldn't contain the warmth welling up inside of him. Trevor had a mother after all, and she'd been with him for all these years. Maybe not physically, but she'd found a way to be there for him after all.

"She wants you to be happy, Daddy." Trevor stopped playing with his car and looked up at Logan as if he should know that and was frustrated he didn't get it. "She told me so. She's been trying to tell you, too. Maybe you need to listen better."

"Maybe I do." Logan's voice wobbled.

Trevor frowned. "Why are your eyes all watery looking? Allergies again?"

Logan nodded, the lump in his throat too big to speak over. He wiped his eyes with a tissue and blew his nose. "Better," he finally said.

"Good. *Now* can we go see Miss Emma?" Trevor whined.

Logan chuckled. "Yes, Buddy, I do believe we can."

"CAN I GIVE HER THE FLOWERS?" Trevor asked, squirming in his seat in the driveway of Emma's beach house.

"In a minute. I think I need to talk to her first if that's okay." Emma's Mercedes was in the driveway, indicating she was home, but a BMW was parked next to it. Her sister had probably come to help her move back home to Boston. If he was going to get up the nerve to makes things right, he needed to act quickly.

"Like when Nanna Becca is mad at Grandpa Barry after he does something naughty, he makes me go to my room until he says he's sorry and she forgives him?" Trevor asked, and Logan nodded. Trevor paused a beat and then added, "Then when he's out of the doghouse, he gets me from my room and we go for ice cream."

Logan shook his head. The kid was good. "Ice cream it is. But first, sit tight, okay?"

Trevor nodded with a devilish smile on his face. He knew exactly how to get whatever he wanted, and Logan admitted he was a big softie and a total pushover when it came to his son. Climbing out of his truck, Logan made his way to the front of Emma's beach house. His hands were sweating as he tried to think of what to say. Sorry would be a good start—sorry for leaving, sorry for not telling her how he really felt, sorry for being terrified and almost letting her slip away.

He was about to knock, but her windows were open. He heard voices inside that made him frown. The more he listened, the more his stomach rolled and acid hit the back of his throat. He didn't have to look to know what he would see, but he stepped to the side of the door and looked through the window anyway.

Mark.

Logically, Logan had known that Mark returning someday was a definite possibility. Emotionally, he had prayed like hell it would never happen. He had a feeling he wouldn't like what he heard, but unable to stop himself, he strained to listen to what they were saying anyway. Oh, yeah. He was right. It wasn't good, but damned if he didn't stay glued to his spot to hear every word.

"It's been eight months, Mark. Eight months!" Emma faced Mark, standing ramrod straight with her arms crossed over her chest, looking gorgeous. She had on a mint-green sundress that complimented her auburn hair and suntan perfectly.

Logan could just imagine her snappy amber eyes blazing sparks of yellow fire as she stared Mark down. Logan's smile turned sad because he knew he was helpless to stop the scene from unfolding before him. Mark had been her fiancé, a man she'd loved enough to say yes to marry. Logan didn't stand a chance against that. And after losing Mandy, he would never get in the way of their happiness if there was even a chance they could reconnect and salvage what they once had. He wanted Emma to be happy, and if that was with someone other than him, then he would set her free and wish her the best, even if it broke his heart.

"Darling, you have to let me explain." Mark gently touched Emma's shoulders, and she didn't pull away.

Logan's shoulders drooped. The man was taller than her—but not too tall—in great shape—but not too big—and had perfectly styled pale blond hair. He looked like a model, definitely not an unkempt giant like himself. A much better fit for a woman like Emma, but still, Logan remained rooted to his spot with a glimmer of hope still simmering in his heart. Mandy had given her blessing.

That had to mean something.

"What could you possibly have to say that would excuse what you did to me?" Emma hissed, still boiling with rage. She'd never looked more magnificent.

"I had no choice," Mark pleaded. "I had to leave without saying a word to you. And I wasn't able to reach out to you, either. How could you think I would walk away from you willingly? I love you, Emma. I wouldn't have asked you to marry me if I didn't."

Some of the anger faded away from her face, the lines softening a hair, but Logan noticed. His hope was dwindling fast. "You have a funny way of showing your love," she said with far less heat. "And everyone has a choice."

Mark dropped his hands from her shoulders and scrubbed them through his hair in an obviously uncharacteristic gesture. "Not if I wanted to keep you safe." The frustration in his tone was evident.

Emma looked surprised and then curious. "What are you talking about?"

"I was working with the FBI. My accountant conducted some shady deals with company money I knew nothing about, I swear. The FBI got wind of it and questioned me. Apparently, these men are pros at white collar crimes, and the FBI has been after them for years, but they are always too late. Hence the need for super-secret security. We hatched a plan that involved me dropping everything and going undercover to help them finally catch the men, but also involved me not saying a word to anyone and leaving immediately, or the whole operation would be at risk."

"Then why return now?"

"We finally brought the ringleader down and my company is safe, I am free at last to return home to everything that's important to me. These last eight months have been just as hard on me, sweetheart. I felt horrible for my poor family, and I've missed you terribly, but I couldn't let everything my father had worked so hard to build be taken away from him. You of all people should understand, right?" He caressed her cheek. "I can prove everything if you'll give me another chance."

Emma frowned and Logan could see the first flicker of doubt ignite within her. She was a journalist who was all about discovering the facts, and she had always put her career above everything else. It was only a matter of time before she forgave him. She slowly nodded. "Yes, I do understand. I mean it's a crazy story, but everyone knows truth is stranger than fiction."

"I'm so glad to hear you say that. It gives me hope."

"Funny, a good friend of mine once told me not to give up hope. That you just might come walking back into my life one day with a good explanation for why you disappeared without a trace and no word. I didn't believe it was possible at the time." She shook her head in wonder. "But I get it. I really do get why you left, and for the record, I would have done the same thing."

"Then you forgive me? Please say you'll forgive me, my darling. I couldn't bear it if you didn't."

"Yes, I forgive you. How could I not?" she said with such sincerity, Logan knew she meant every word...which meant the end for them. His heart squeezed painfully in his chest as he closed his eyes and accepted the truth, no matter how much his heart was breaking.

He was too late.

19

PRESENT DAY: BEACON BAY, MAINE

E mma looked toward her front door. For some reason she'd had the strangest feeling someone was watching her, but she didn't see anything. Shrugging at her overactive imagination, she stared at Mark, still a little in shock over his story. Logan was right. Her fiancé had come back and with one hell of a good explanation. He hadn't been a coward, he'd been noble. She had been more than good enough for him, and he loved her. The problem was, it didn't matter anymore. She didn't love him. She'd lost her heart completely to an insufferable giant who had no clue what a catch he actually was.

No matter how hard she tried, she couldn't get Dr. Logan Mayfield out of her mind.

Emma had been so angry with him for running away scared, especially after everything they'd shared together. They'd grown so close over the summer, starting out as friends and helping each other overcome their own personal hardships along the way, and then turning into so much more. Making love to him had changed her forever. She'd known immediately that no one else would ever compare or be good enough for her. He'd ruined her for anyone else, and she had thought he'd felt the same way.

Until he'd left her.

She knew he didn't feel free to be with her because he still hadn't forgiven himself for his wife's death, so he didn't think he deserved to be happy. Honestly, she was all talk. Up until this moment, she hadn't felt free to move on with him either. If she were being candid, she would admit that once her anger had worn off, she'd been a little relieved Logan had left. He had saved her from freaking out on him and leaving him, which would have killed her knowing she'd caused him more pain after all he'd been through.

It wasn't until Mark had shown up at her beach house a few moments ago that Emma had realized just how much in love with Logan Mayfield she really was. Head over heels crazy in love. She didn't want to lose what they had, and the only way to move forward was to set her stubborn pride aside and forgive Mark.

Now that she had, she felt free.

"I'm so happy you forgive me," Mark said. "I love you and can't wait to marry you." He leaned in to kiss her.

Emma leaned back, away from Mark, and turned her head so his lips brushed her cheek. He raised his brows in question. There was only one man whose lips she wanted to kiss and body she wanted to melt into until they became one. And it wasn't Mark. She realized now, if none of this had ever happened, she would have settled and thought she was happy. Kind of like her sister had. She never thought in a million years she would say this, but Mark had done her a favor by running out on her.

Taking a deep breath, she ripped the proverbial Band-Aid off, hoping for less pain. "I'm sorry, Mark. Yes, I forgive you, but that doesn't mean I love you."

He blinked. "What does that mean?"

"I can't marry you."

He looked floored, and then confused, and then resigned. "You're still angry. You need time."

"No, I don't." She smiled sympathetically. "Don't you see, I'm actually not angry? And if you search your heart, I think you will also see you're not either. We were never meant for each other, Mark. Not really. We allowed our parents to fix us up because it was easy and convenient and less work. But love isn't easy or convenient and it's a lot of work. It's messy and scary but so worth it when you find the right person.

"You need to find someone who will make you happy. Truly happy. And someone who appreciates you for the wonderful man you are. That's not me. I'm an impulsive-break-the-rules-could-give-a-hoot-about-conforming-to-society kind of girl. While you are a steadfast-play-by-the-rules-bask-in-the-glow-of-society kind of guy. There's nothing wrong with either of us, we're just not a good match for each other."

"You've met someone, haven't you?" he asked almost accusingly.

"Actually yes," she said, not about to shy away from the truth now. Not after all he had put her through. That was who she was, and he knew it, for better or worse. "But that's not the point. You know I'm right."

He surprised her by asking in a sincere tone, "Does he make you happy?"

Her whole body melted—she couldn't help it. "Yes," she said on a breathy whisper. "He makes me care about something other than the next big story, which I honestly never thought would happen." She reached out and squeezed his hand. "I really am sorry, Mark."

"Don't be." His face looked pained, yet it softened with understanding. "I'm sure I will thank you one day for this. It's hard right now, but I do understand. I took a chance by leaving, and knowing your personality, I honestly worried you would never speak to me again. I really do want you to be happy, and one day maybe we can be friends. You'll understand if it's too soon right now."

"Of course." She nodded, smiling past the lump in her throat, hating the thought of hurting him. "You're a great guy, Mark. I hope someday you will find someone who makes you happy." Suddenly her sister's face swam before her eyes, and Emma knew instinctively that they might be the perfect match. Their personalities and morals and values and everything were perfect for each other. It was too soon to bring it up now, but they were both terrific people.

Someday it might be worth a shot.

"Well, then, I'll take that as my cue to leave." He started walking toward her front door, turning around at the last second. "Don't worry about your family or mine. I'll handle everything." His gaze caressed her from head to toe for one last time before he said, "Be happy, Em," and then he walked out of her life for good.

THE NEXT MORNING Logan dropped his pouting son off at his mother-in-law's as he got ready to head into work. The hospital actually had the shift covered; he just couldn't take his son's crestfallen face anymore. Trevor was so disappointed in Logan for not letting him give the flowers to Emma. He didn't understand it wasn't a good time. Emma had been busy with her company and might not want to see them right then, so Logan had left.

Trevor had said Logan was afraid, and that "Mommy" had said Emma *did* want to see him. Logan liked to believe his wife had given him her blessing to move on, but he wasn't sure about believing she'd honestly spoken to Trevor. It was a comforting thought she might be connected to her son still, but spooky to actually think she might be actually communicating with him.

"So that's it?" Rebecca asked, crossing her arms and staring him down from the doorway of her house.

"What do you mean?" Logan shifted his weight from one foot to the other. The woman was no bigger than her daughter but damned intimidating nonetheless. "The hospital needs me. I don't have a choice."

"Bullshit."

He blinked, taken back. Rebecca never swore. "Excuse me?" He couldn't have heard her right.

"That's right," she said. "You heard me, Logan Mayfield, aka *head* doctor. You have more choices than most. I might not officially be your mother-in-law anymore or even your mother, but you will always be like a son to me. I'm the closest thing to a mother you will ever have, and I love you more than most love their biological children. I have been patient and I've stood by and given you space, but I have had enough. I will not stand by any longer. I refuse to watch you wallow in self-pity anymore. You're too good for that."

"Rebecca...Mom...please. You don't understand," he tried to explain.

She held up her hand. "I know I don't fully know what *really* happened to my daughter, but I've never pressed the issue. I've sensed something was off for a long time now, but I guess I wasn't ready to hear it then. I might not even be ready now, which is so unfair to you, I know, but that's life. Your shoulders have always been so broad, but it was wrong of me to make you bear that alone. Someday you will tell me, but right now that's beside the point."

"It's okay," Logan said, realizing she was right as he took her hands in his. She'd been more like a mother to him than anyone he'd ever met. He should have known she would sense something was off all these years. He would do anything for her and Barry, and he had with no regrets.

"No, it's not alright." She touched his cheek. "What I *do* know is you were not and will never be responsible for Amanda's death, so quit trying to be a martyr by bearing that weight alone. It's crushing you, which is such a shame because you have so much to give. I want to see you happy and thriving and moving on. I want more grandchildren, dammit." She nodded once, hard, and Logan couldn't help but smile. "And Trevor deserves a sibling," she went on with conviction.

That made Logan pause and frown. He hadn't even thought about his son. He'd only thought of himself and that he couldn't handle anything bad happening to anyone else, and he'd thought of Emma and not wanting to risk anything happening to her because of him. He'd never once thought of Trevor. Hell, adoption had always been a possibility as well. When had Logan made everything about him? Maybe it was time he started getting out of his own head and looking at the people around him. What did *they* want? Maybe it was time he asked.

"Stop wasting your life by grieving and start living, Logan." Rebecca stared deeply into his eyes, hers brimming with tears. "You only get one ride, my son. Don't waste it. I saw the way Emma Hendricks looked at you, and I definitely saw the way you looked at her. She changed you this summer, for the better. Don't you dare let that slip away." She squeezed his hands. "Do you hear me? I don't know what happened when you went over to her house, but a woman like that doesn't come along very often. Don't go to work, Logan..." She stared him down to make sure he was listening to her as she finished with, "Go to her!"

Logan pulled the only mother he'd ever known into his warm embrace and he hugged her tight. "I love you, Mom," he whispered into her ear.

"I know, son." She patted his back while hugging him just as tight, letting him know she was there for him no matter what. "Now go get her and find your happy ending, whatever that may be."

He kissed her cheek and headed to his truck without another word, but he wasn't going to work. He was going to find the woman who had stolen his heart and convince her to make him the happiest man on earth and marry him. He was through with being noble and doing the right thing. It was time Logan Mayfield remembered who he once was.

It was time to fight.

LOGAN SEARCHED Emma's beach house, but she wasn't there. The BMW was gone, as well as her car. Panic set in. Maybe he should have gone after her sooner. What if she'd left town with Mark? Amanda hadn't willingly left Logan, she was sick. He now understood there was nothing he could have done to stop it. He'd finally forgiven himself and was ready to move on. But with Emma, he could damn well try to stop her and change his fate.

Logan didn't want a future without her, and if there was even a remote chance she felt the same way about him, then she was worth the fight. He frowned, pausing as he turned the knob. Except Emma had left her door unlocked, almost as if on purpose. People who left town didn't do that. If she didn't leave town, then what was she trying to tell him? He stepped inside and looked around.

It didn't take long for him to find out.

Logan picked up the letter he had missed when he'd first entered her beach house. His heart constricted when he recognized her handwriting in a letter just like the ones Kathleen and Joseph had written to each other. Good or bad, he knew his fate rested in the contents of this piece of paper. Slowly unfolding the letter, he read her words.

MY DEAREST LOGAN,

I have been through so much lately. You'll never guess who showed up. Mark. And just like you said, he had a great excuse. I forgave him, and it felt wonderful. The funny thing is, it didn't matter how good his excuse was. I don't love Mark. I'm not sure I ever did. I think I was settling because he looked good on paper, and it was easy. But after spending this summer with you, I realized what true love really is. Yes, you heard me right. I love you, Dr. McGiant. Even though you are one big worrywart.

LOGAN'S HEART did a funny little flip. He fought the moisture in his eyes, overcome with emotion at her words, but stood there grinning like an idiot. Damn he loved this woman. He really was a chicken. He should have listened to his instincts and trusted in what they had said by sticking around and confronting her instead of running away again. His son was right. He needed to learn to listen better. If Emma took him back, Logan would never run away again. He would spend the rest of his life proving to her she was beautiful and worthy and way too good for him. Looking down, he continued to read her letter.

I HAVE to admit I was so mad at you when you left me after all we had been through and shared. You can't tell me making love wasn't life-changing. I didn't know lovemaking could be like that. For the first time in my life, I didn't care about what I wanted, I just wanted to make you happy and to please you. You've ruined me for any other man, so if you don't feel the same way about me, my life will totally suck. Just sayin'.

LOGAN LAUGHED OUT LOUD. That was his girl, telling him exactly what was what and not sugar coating anything, consequences be damned. He wanted to know how she felt at all times and when he was being an ass and when he was doing something right. He needed that. He needed her, and he couldn't wait to tell her. But first he had to find her. He kept reading.

HAHA, *seriously no pressure. Because once again, this is all about you, not me. Honestly, I just want you to be happy. You deserve that. And I admit I too was scared at first. If you hadn't called things off with me, I probably would have with you. You unsettle me, Doc, and I don't like to be unsettled. I am all about the facts and things that are logical. The way I feel about you is totally illogical and completely unsettling and doesn't make any sense to me at all.*

Who cares!

I have finally, for the first time in my life, thrown caution to the wind. I took a chance that if you wanted to be with me, you would show up here eventually. In fact, you're going to think I'm crazy, but I could have sworn I felt your presence. I took it as a sign, so I left you this letter telling you how I felt and hoping you would see it in time. If you don't show up at the rendezvous spot, then I guess I'll have my answer. It will kill me, but I will be okay as long as I know you're happy.

Okay, I've waited long enough. I am so excited to tell you that I figured out the rest of our adventure, all by myself I might add. I'll explain the letter if I see you again. In the meantime, if you feel the same way about me and want to see where this crazy adventure takes us, follow the map I left you. It's the final rendezvous spot for Kathleen and Joseph. I hope I see you soon. If not, you were worth the risk and I sincerely hope you will be happy. I love you with all my heart!

Until Tomorrow,

Emma Hendricks

LOGAN STUDIED the map Emma had drawn and his jaw fell open. Of course. It was perfect. The lighthouse! Of course that was the final meeting place, and his Emma was there now. She loved him and was waiting for him. His heart beat faster at the thought that he'd been so wrong. She hadn't gone back to Mark, she'd chosen him. If Logan had stuck around long enough, he would have heard her tell him no, that she didn't want to get back together with him no matter how good his excuse was. She had found the perfect man for her. Logan couldn't believe that man was him.

Emma loved him as much as he loved her.

Through with berating himself and second guessing every move, he decided to throw caution to the wind as well. His heart filled with joy and excitement as he glanced at his watch. He couldn't let her down. She'd written the note, made her preparations, and left this morning on the final leg of their adventure. According to her letter, she would be waiting for him all day. But come sundown, if he didn't show up, she would have her answer.

Come hell or high water, he would be there.

Logan brought her letter and map with him—tucking them into his pocket to be read and treasured for years to come, the first of many from them both he hoped—as he left her beach house. There was something to be said about taking the time to tell the people you loved how much they meant to you, and something even more special about going old-school and writing it down in your own hand.

It didn't take Logan long to get to the lighthouse, and finally he arrived at the address. It was old and rarely used, but charming nonetheless. He could see how Joseph and Kathleen had been drawn to it. Throwing his truck into park, Logan stepped out and took a moment to look around the area. It was a beautiful sunny day. Perfect.

He couldn't help but wonder what the day had been like so very long ago when Joseph and Kathleen had met for the final time. Had they found their happy ending after all? Had William caught up with them? The town records had been so vague, stating he had disappeared and she had vanished. Logan had been childish to let their story end there. He should have stuck around and fought harder to find out what happened. He'd let Emma down, but starting today, he would make it up to her for the rest of their lives if she would let him.

Not wanting to waste any more time, he walked forward and opened the door to the lighthouse. Racing up the stairs, he made his way into the watch room and a feeling of déjà vu swept over him. Something had gone horribly wrong in this room. He could feel it. Blinking to adjust his eyes to the dim light, he focused on the sight before him and sucked in a sharp breath.

"No," he whispered hoarsely. This couldn't happen to them. Not now. Not after all they'd been through. He wouldn't let it.

20

E mma moaned. This had to rank in the top ten of the dumbest things she'd ever done. The lighthouse might be charming, but there was a reason it had been locked. It was a historical landmark, so it couldn't be torn down, but the inside was unsafe and they didn't give tours anymore. Logan had been smart in worrying about them entering the cottage on the deserted island. She should have known better than to enter the ancient lighthouse at the edge of Beacon Bay, especially since she knew what had really happened to Joseph.

Decades later, the building was in far worse shape. Emma had left the note for Logan, impulsively venturing out on her own, thinking she had everything under control as usual. She needed McGiant. He was good for her. He made her pause and take a breath, which usually led to rethinking her plan of action, or at the very least being a bit more careful. Without him, she was a hot mess.

If he didn't show, she would be in real trouble this time.

She'd been so stupid. Anyone with half a brain could see the place was old and the walls weren't stable, but that hadn't stopped her. She'd run in there, raced up the stairs full throttle, and crashed into a table. She had wanted to relive what had happened to Kathleen and Joseph, but not literally, yet she'd wound up in the same predicament. The beam on the wall had trembled from the impact and then caved, falling on top of her.

She just lay there in disbelief, thinking this was the new millennium. This wasn't supposed to happen, yet it *had* happened, and she was helpless to do anything but hope and pray Logan would find her letter and show up to rescue her in time.

Emma understood what Joseph must have been going through all those years ago. You make a great plan, wait anxiously for the love of your life to show up, and then have a stupid, tragic accident happen that could take it all away and change the outcome of your future. It sucked. It left you helpless and vulnerable and completely at the mercy of another human being. Emma hated not being in control of anything, but a part of her realized she would never be truly happy until she surrendered to her fate.

Emma closed her eyes and took a deep breath. She spread her arms out wide and let go. As soon as she gave up control, she heard a sound.

"Emma?" came a voice from across the room. At first, she thought she'd only imagined it, but then it came again. The most beautiful voice she'd ever heard said, "Emma Hendricks, are you in here or not? If you are, I need you to answer me now."

Logan.

She started laughing and crying at the same time. "Yes, oh God yes! I'm here, Logan. I'm in the corner."

Emma was pretty sure her leg was broken, and she was terrified she might have internal injuries as well. It was uncanny how similar Logan and her story had been to Joseph and Kathleen's, except in this case their roles had been reversed and she knew better. The difference was, she didn't give a hoot what people thought of her. Both she and Kathleen were strong, independent women, but Emma was free to speak her mind and do what she wanted, where Kathleen had been persecuted for that very trait.

And now here Emma was, just like Joseph, getting injured while waiting for her love. Except when the beam fell on Emma, she had a moment where she was frozen in fear but then some force urged her to roll away at the last second. She prayed she'd moved enough and that she wouldn't die like Joseph had. The beam had still fallen on her, but she felt more bruised than crushed. She liked to think Kathleen had saved her. Kathleen hadn't been able to save Joseph, so maybe this was her way of atoning for that. Not to mention, Emma felt more compelled than ever to write Kathleen's story and set the record straight now. Emma had to be okay. She had too much to live for.

Logan rushed to her side, his face looking pale and panicked. "Are you okay? What happened?" Suddenly he morphed into doctor mode, his face calming into a serene mask as he checked her pupils and pulse, then ran his hands over her, searching her limbs for breaks and feeling her stomach for lumps or pain. He was hiding his worry for her sake, but she couldn't help thinking the worst.

She stilled his hands with hers until he looked at her. "Am I going to die, Doc?"

His eyes met hers and he hesitated before replying, "I'm going to go outside and call for help."

"Don't leave me," she said, her voice sounding shaky to her own ears. He hadn't said no she wasn't going to die because he wouldn't lie to her. While she appreciated his honesty, it only made her more afraid.

His features were tight, but he relaxed them and said firmly, "I'll be right back. I promise."

She let go of his hand, knowing he wouldn't break a promise to her, either. He quickly left the room, and she could feel her energy draining. She had no idea how long she had been there now or how much blood she had lost from the gash on her leg. What if this was the last time she got to speak with Logan? She needed to tell him how she felt. Joseph and Kathleen's story had taught her that much.

Logan came back into the room moments later and knelt by her side, covering her with a blanket he'd brought with him. "Stay with me, Emma. Keep talking until the ambulance gets here." He checked her pulse again.

She opened her eyes and placed her hand over his as she added softly, "You came."

"Of course, I came." His gaze traced her features.

"Then you got my note?" She had to know.

This time his voice turned soft. "Yeah, Lois. I got your note."

"You gonna be my Superman?" She winced in pain.

A flash of desperation transformed his face. "If you'll have me." He stroked her hair with his free hand. "I am so sorry for being an ass."

"It's okay." She shrugged, trying not to let him know the agony she felt.

"I thought I was doing the right thing by leaving," he admitted, staring down at their hands and looking ashamed.

"I know." She tightened her grip. "And it's okay."

His forehead wrinkled. "No, it's not okay. I thought it would be easier not seeing you, and that I would protect myself from getting hurt. But I came back missing you terribly and hurting something fierce anyway. I thought you'd left. When you hadn't, I thought I'd been given another chance even though I didn't deserve it." He looked her in the eyes. "But when I went to your house yesterday—"

"I knew someone was there," she said weakly. "I *felt* you."

He continued to stroke her hair tenderly. "I should have

stayed and confronted you. Instead, I thought I was setting you free and giving you what you wanted. Mark."

She shook her head a little. "I didn't want Mark. I don't think I ever did."

"No?" Logan's voice sounded raspy.

"No, Doc. I want you."

"But Mark's so perfect." Logan frowned. "He has a great job. He has a great background. He—"

"Isn't you." It took a lot of effort to lift her hand, and she tried to hide her pain as she stroked his jaw, brushing his lips with her fingertips. "I don't love him, McGiant. I love *you*."

Logan covered her hand with his own and turned his face into her palm to kiss it. "Well, that's good because I love you, too. That's why you need to fight to stay with me."

Tears pooled in Emma's eyes. "Do you really love me? I know I'm not Amanda, but—"

"No, you're not, but that's also okay. Amanda was my past. You are my future. I can't imagine my life without you."

"But what if I—"

"Don't say it." He cut her off. "You make me happy. When I'm with you, I feel alive. With you I have fun, which is something I never thought I would have again." His voice hitched, and he cleared it. "I can't believe that would be taken from me twice."

"It won't happen," she said, trying to reassure him now. "I promised Trevor one heck of a story." She glanced around and a weak laugh escaped from her lips. "I'd say this will do."

"I say we take time to have more adventures until we grow old. What do you say, sweetheart?"

Emma blinked, her throat clogging with emotion at the implication his words incited. "What do you mean?"

"Marry me, Emma Hendricks. I know we've only known each other for a little while, but I feel like I've known you forever. After the adventure we've been on, don't you think we owe it to ourselves and to Kathleen and Joseph not to waste any more time?"

"But..." she couldn't finish her thought as the room around her began to spin. She vaguely heard the sirens of the ambulance grow louder.

"No buts, just fight." Logan gripped her hand and didn't let go as he added urgently, "I'm gonna make sure you marry me, Lois."

"I'm going to hold you to that, Doc," was the last thing Emma remembered whispering before she slipped into unconsciousness.

∼

8 MONTHS AGO: *Boston, Massachusetts*

Katy Ford lay in her bed at her quaint home on the waters of the Boston coast, surrounded by her daughter Josephine Ruth Ford-McDonald, her daughter's husband, her children, her grandchildren and her great grandchildren. Katy was ninety-eight years old and had lived a long full life, just as Joseph would have wanted. She smiled when thinking of Joseph Henry Rutherford III, and thought about who she had once been back in those days.

Kathleen Connor.

A married woman, abused by her husband, forsaken by her family, and shunned by the town. She'd had nothing left to live for, all because she'd stood up for herself. But then she'd met Joseph and her life had changed. He'd become her reason for being, and he'd saved her from a life of pain. If it hadn't been for him and the hope he had given her and the lessons he had taught her, she never would have had the will to go on and become something more. And become something more, she had...

World famous poet, Katy Ford.

On top of all of that, he had given her a precious piece of him. A daughter she'd named Josephine Ruth Ford after him. Kathleen had changed her name and started over in Boston with their baby girl, leaving her family and his to wonder whatever became of them. But Kathleen had put the past behind her, living for the moment and in the future, where her daughter had given her a family. The only one she needed. Kathleen had been happy. She'd never remarried, content with her memories of Joseph and her grandbabies. People connected with her poems and her writing had taken her on many adventures.

Joseph would have been so proud.

When Kathleen was diagnosed with congestive heart failure, she'd known she didn't have long at her age. She was too old and frankly, her heart was tired. It was ready to be rejoined with the love of her life. She'd waited a long time for this, having always known one day they would be reunited again. She'd stopped dwelling on the past a long time ago, but had always known in her soul, when the time was right, the truth would come out. She didn't know how or when, but she knew it would.

She could feel it.

And with that, she was free to be at peace with her love. "It'll be okay, sweetheart," she said to Josephine. "I'm going to be with Daddy, and everything will be all right. You'll see."

Her daughter had been a college professor of women's studies, publishing many of her own pieces on women's rights and feminism, now happily retired having led a fulfilling life of her own as a strong independent woman. Kathleen had never been prouder. Her work was done here now, and it was time to go off on her next adventure.

Kathleen remembered back to the night she'd lost her love. After she'd set fire to Joseph's boat and given him a burial at sea, she'd placed the final map into a glass bottle and sealed it with a kiss, tossing it out to sea with an, "Until Tomorrow, my love," vowing one day she would be reunited with him.

Joseph had given her so many gifts. He came into her life when she needed someone the most, making her believe she had value and it was okay to speak her mind and long for something more. And she had given him happiness in a time when he was so lonely and wounded. He'd never really gotten over the war or his nightmares, but for a while, he had been happy with her. And now he was at peace. She would be forever grateful for every second they had shared together and would never regret a moment of her time with him.

Now that it was time for her to join him, she blew a kiss to her daughter as she said, "I love you, my darling Josi Girl," and then she closed her eyes, whispering to the man of her dreams, "I'm coming, my love."

And then she was gone.

~

"WE'RE TOO LATE," Emma said in the present, while standing with the help of crutches on the deck of Kathleen's cottage by the sea. Emma and Logan had thought about buying the old place, but it had already sold to someone else according to the sign in the yard.

"That's okay, babe," Logan said from behind her as he slipped his arms around her waist and slid his hand over her tummy. "This place wouldn't have been big enough for Trevor, you and myself, now that we're expecting our little surprise."

She placed her hand over his, feeling thankful to be alive and for her second chance at happiness. "Are you sure you're okay with this?"

"I'm more than okay with being a father again. I love you." He kissed her neck. "I was dead before you came into my life.

You've saved me in so many ways. Knowing we are having a baby together is a blessing. I was actually shocked I didn't feel afraid like I thought I would. In fact, I think you're more afraid than I am. I'm so ready for this: you, the baby, our life together. I want it all."

She leaned her head back against him. "I'm so happy to hear you say that, and yeah, I'm scared to death." He chuckled as she continued. "I didn't even know I wanted children until we were on the island. But as much as I love the idea of being a mother, I never would have done anything to make you unhappy."

"I know, and I love you for it." He leaned down and kissed the side of her neck. "And I love this baby. It's going to be okay, Emma. It's going to be *more* than okay. You've changed me for the better, and I owe you everything. Seeing you this happy fills me with joy."

Suddenly her phone buzzed from inside her pocket. She pulled the phone out and read the text. Looking up at him in surprise, she said, "I won an award. Can you believe it?"

"That doesn't surprise me. Your story on Kathleen Connor and Joseph Rutherford was award-worthy. You told the truth and set the record straight all while being sensitive to both sides. Your compassion for the multiple parties involved was clearly evident, as was your way with words. You have a real talent. You should be proud. I know I am."

"Thanks. Still, I feel like something's missing. We know what happened with Joseph. I just wish there was a way we could find out what happened to Kathleen. We know she left, but it's like she vanished. I hope she found the peace and happiness she deserved."

"She did," came an unfamiliar voice from the side of the house. A woman Emma didn't recognize walked around the cottage and onto the deck. She looked familiar, but Emma couldn't place her.

"I'm sorry, who are you?" Emma asked, eying her curiously.

Logan stepped around beside Emma in an equal show of support, but she knew he was ready to protect her at a moment's notice. As independent as she was, she secretly loved his chivalry.

"I'm the one who should be sorry. Forgive my manners." The woman held out her hand. "I'm Josephine Ruth Ford, aka daughter of the famous poet Katy Ford."

Emma's mouth fell open.

Logan looked at her with wide eyes when the woman's words registered.

Emma closed her mouth and shook herself out of her stupor. "Sorry, that's my favorite poet. I'm Emma Hendricks and this is my fiancé Dr. Logan Mayfield."

Josephine shook both their hands. "I know exactly who you are. You're the woman who wrote a story about my mother."

Emma frowned. "I've written lots of stories, but none about Katy Ford the poet. Trust me, that one I would remember."

"Ah, but Katy Ford wasn't always a poet." Josephine carefully said, "She was formerly known as Kathleen Connor."

Emma gasped, her stomach jumping into her throat. She stood there for a moment in silence, and then a slow smile spread across her face. Kathleen had gotten her happy ending after all. Emma took a minute to process everything she'd heard before replying, "So Kathleen Connor changed her name to Katy Ford when she left?"

"Yes. My mother knew my father's parents would have never allowed her to keep me if they had known about my existence. If she'd lost me, it would have killed her, and Joseph Rutherford would not have wanted that. So she changed her name to Katy Ford and me to Josephine Ruth Ford and never looked back. She never remarried or had any other children, but she most definitely became the something more my father would have wanted."

"I'll say," Emma said, still in shock.

"She talked about my father but never told me the whole story. You don't know the gift you've given me. You've cleared my mother's name and reputation, and given me a piece of her past I never thought I would have. I am the one who bought this cottage. It helps ease the acceptance of her passing."

"I hope you don't mind, but can I ask what happened to her?"

"My mother lived a long full life. She was ninety-eight. Nine months ago, she was diagnosed with congestive heart failure. She knew she didn't have long to live, but she held on until suddenly she was at peace. She said something like, 'It's done. I can go now.' I didn't understand at the time, but now I'm beginning to think I do now. She was waiting for you to write her story."

Emma sat in shock over Josephine's words. Suddenly everything made perfect sense. "Nine months ago, my life was completely turned upside down," she confessed. "I felt so lost and alone, I didn't know what I was going to do. But then I discovered this poetry by Katy Ford. I could relate to her voice in so many ways. She wrote about the coast of Maine a lot, so I followed my instincts and decided to spend my summer in Beacon Bay. That's where I found the bottle with the map in it, and that's what started my quest. I became obsessed with Kathleen Connor, feeling a connection to her I couldn't explain. In telling her story, I found the greatest treasure of all." Emma took Logan's hand in hers. "Love."

"That sounds just like my mother." Josephine smiled. "She was the most compassionate, caring woman I've ever known. So proud and brave and independent. Very much like you, I must say."

"I always thought we were a lot alike, and she helped me more than you'll ever know. I was only repaying the favor. I don't know how she managed to live in a time that didn't value her independent spirit. I'm so happy she was happy. She deserved that. She truly was an amazing woman."

"She was. And now because of you, the whole world knows it."

EPILOGUE

ONE YEAR LATER: BEACON BAY, MAINE

"You okay, Dr. Worrywart?" Emma asked while standing behind the wheel of Logan's new boat. Her crutches were long gone, but she was left with a permanent limp. Strangely, she didn't mind because it made her think of Joseph and reminded her every day of how lucky she was to be alive.

The boat was a gift from Logan's father-in-law he couldn't turn down—most likely so he wouldn't risk the Mandy Marie again. Logan's son Trevor was delighted because he instinctively knew it would be his someday. That was probably why he'd named it the Trevinator.

"Very funny, Mrs. Worrywart," Logan said dryly while standing behind her with his arms waiting and ready should she slip up and need his assistance. "I still don't like the water, but at least I compromised and agreed to start our honeymoon with a quick trip to our island."

"And I appreciate that," she said with a soft tone. "You know how important it is for me to thank Kathleen."

"I know." He hugged her, adding in a tender voice, "It's also where we fell in love."

Her voice turned serious as she looked up at him with everything she felt in her heart. "Have I told you how lucky I am to have you in my life?"

His expression softened and he wrapped his arms around her tight as if he never wanted to let go. "I love you."

"I love you, too. And I promise, as soon as we throw our bottle into the sea by the island, we can fly away to our honeymoon in Hawaii and never look back."

"Deal. Now let me ask you. Are *you* okay with leaving little Katy for a whole week?" He eyed her knowingly, and she knew he would turn the boat around in an instant if she wanted him to. He always put her first, even though she knew how much he was looking forward to a week on a gorgeous *modern* island with all the amenities.

Emma could feel her face pale when his words sank in. "I know little Katy will be in great hands with them. Besides big brother Trevor is on duty. It's all good, right?" Emma swallowed hard and repeated, "Right?"

"She'll be fine." Logan cupped her cheek. "I promise."

Emma took a deep breath, suddenly realizing why her husband worried so much. Being responsible for someone else's life was a heavy burden. One she welcomed with more love than she ever thought possible, but feared nonetheless. She couldn't imagine raising a baby alone like Kathleen had. Focusing on the task at hand, she put her worries and fears aside and decided to enjoy the first of many adventures with her new husband.

They pulled up as close as they could to the island and threw the anchor. This time it stuck. Finally, something was going to go right for Emma, but she was still worried she would never be able to do enough to show her gratitude to Kathleen. Emma had been so lost, and Kathleen had grounded her, the connection between them powerful and strong. She'd shown Emma that it was okay to be herself and had taught her not to settle. To go after her dreams and fight for what she wanted. But mostly Kathleen had taught Emma that everything was going to be all right.

"Okay, this is it. Did you put the map in there?" she asked Logan.

"Yes, honey." His voice was filled with patience.

"A blank map with no code?" she clarified just to be sure.

"Yes, Emma. Whoever finds this bottle will be free to create their own journey by following a map to anywhere. The point is the journey itself, right?"

"Exactly. And what about the letter?" She needed to make sure everything went right for Kathleen. Emma owed her that much. She owed her everything.

"I've got the letter, too, sweetheart. Don't worry so much. It's all here. She knows you're thankful, Emma. You've done enough." He cupped her cheeks in his hands and made her look him in the eye. "It's okay to let go now."

Emma squeezed her eyes shut and took a deep breath, then nodded. "I'm trying." Emma kissed the bottle and so did Logan, then she tossed it as far as she could, saying, "Until tomorrow."

No sooner had that happened than a rare double rainbow appeared across the horizon, looking like lovers embracing in an ethereal glow. Kathleen had found her Joseph. It was a sign. Tomorrow was today, and life couldn't be better, so don't waste it. A gust of wind picked up, carrying the scent of pine. Emma breathed deeply and a feeling of being blessed filled her. She shared a knowing smile filled with the promise of happiness and a world of possibilities with her new husband as they wrapped their arms around each other.

Thank you was a whisper on the wind.

Kathleen had given her blessing for Emma to embrace life and seek out her next grand adventure. And Emma vowed never to let herself down again, and to carry Kathleen's message forward with her own daughter.

Staring up at the rainbow, Emma whispered back, "You're welcome," finally feeling free to let go and live the life she was meant to live.

ACKNOWLEDGMENTS

Thanks as always to my family and friends for supporting me no matter what, and accepting the life of an author can be crazy. It's not just what we do, it's who we are.

ABOUT THE AUTHOR

Kari Lee Townsend is a National Bestselling Author of mysteries & a tween superhero series. She also writes romance and women's fiction as Kari Lee Harmon. With a background in English education, she's now a full-time writer, wife to her own superhero, mom of 3 sons, 1 darling diva, 1 daughter-in-law & 2 lovable fur babies. These days you'll find her walking her dogs or hard at work on her next story, living a blessed life.

ALSO BY THE AUTHOR

WRITING AS KARI LEE TOWNSEND

A SUNNY MEADOWS MYSTERY

Tempest in the Tea Leaves

Corpse in the Crystal Ball

Trouble in the Tarot

Shenanigans in the Shadows

Perish in the Palm

Hazard in the Horoscope

OTHER MYSTERIES

Peril for Your Thoughts

Kicking the Habit

DIGITAL DIVA SERIES

Talk to the Hand

Rise of the Phenoteens

WRITING AS KARI LEE HARMON

Destiny Wears Spurs

Spurred by Fate

Project Produce

Love Lessons

COMFORT CLUB SERIES

Sleeping in the Middle